The Antiquarian

a novel by David Edgar Grinnell

Nicholas Ainsworth

To Iulia Hasdeu
(1869-1888)

Preface

It is my wish to affirm the origin of *The Antiquarian* to any curious reader who may find this knowledge engaging. Such an engagement made me embrace my most prized genre to write and study in English literature, which is the gothic. A mentor of mine once said, "Gothic is such oft-trodden ground that it is difficult to say something new." As an academic, it is difficult to say something new, but the idea of this story came to me during extensive research in history and not gothic romanticism. It was October of 2015 when I took a history course in western civilization as an undergraduate freshman at Cleveland State University. One of the core topics discussed was the European witch craze of the 14th to 17th centuries. A unique historical combination of accusations against people, especially women, where witchcraft became a phenomenon. The phenomenon of witchcraft provided me with a hunch that if witches are of mass hysterias during these centuries, what about other creatures of the night?

Much like Nicholas Ainsworth with his feverous academic pursuits on deviant burials, I too, fell into such a trance. The project I worked on was entitled "The Rise & Fall of Monstrous Hysteria: 1500s-1800s." All the research conducted are a mixture of primary sources and secondary sources used to learn about deviant burials and mass hysterias of werewolves, witches, and vampires. The various stories behind these hysterias include specific historical figures such as Gilles de Laval, a famous and powerful nobleman. He was accused of child abduction by offering the missing children to the devil. The hype of the accusation made the Bishop of Nantes take a personal interest and the Duke of Brittany ordered an investigation, "'They spoke of a fierce red glare irradiated the chamber at times, and of sharp cries ringing out of it, through the hushed woods, to be answered only by the howl of a wolf as it rose from its lair'" (Beresford 139). Gilles was given a public trial and one of Gilles 'servants confessed: "'It gave him great pleasure to hack off a child's head... Sometimes he had all their limbs chopped off... I remember having brought three little girls... He bade me cut their throats whist he looked on.'" (Beresford 141). Gilles had no choice. He confessed, was hanged, and burned. Gilles 'death and trial leaves a lasting impression for the next on-hundred years known as The Werewolf Witch Trials.

Acquiring such knowledge about the various trials and executions on The Werewolf Witch Trials, pressed me to inquire about vampires. Surely, if there are hysterias about werewolves and witches, why not vampires. It was during this semester that I was fortunate to attend a special lecture by a guest professor and archeologist who lectured about deviant burials on vampires. In this lecture, I learned about the hysteria of vampires where many dug up graves of those whom people believed were vampires. The head would be separated from the bodies of alleged vampires. Sometimes, stones were placed inside the mouth and all of this was to prevent a "vampire" from returning from the grave. After the lecture, I spent the rest of the day researching vampire hysterias. Various events and historical figures gave life to the vampire myth and hysteria. One of the events was The Black Death because of the reactions between the people and the church. Victims of the plague were discolored with black and blue faces. Victims were drenched in their own blood frantically clawing a way out of their coffins, and people did not understand the plague and they began to blame the undead. The church took this adaptation of the effect. One adaptation worth mentioning is the idea that the dead should be buried on grounds the church owned so the dead would not return from the grave as vampires.

On the contrary, The Black Death is not the only cause for vampire hysteria. Many historical figures also gave life to vampirism. Of course, there is Vlad the Impaler. A hero in Romania for liberating his lands from the Ottoman Empire and a ruthless tyrant. Vlad's family name Dracul became the inspiration for Bram Stoker's antagonist Dracula, however, Vlad the Impaler is not the influence to base this novel's story. It wasn't until I stumbled upon Countess Elizabeth Bathory who was known as "The Blood Countess." Many know her for bathing in the blood of her victims and drinking it. Anna Darvulia, known as a witch may have been Elizabeth's lover who influenced her with these vampiric activities. Bathory believed taking the blood of young virgin women would give her eternal youth, but eventually, her servants became careless of disposing the bodies over time. Bathory was placed under arrest in her own castle. She was never brought to trial and was kept in confinement where she was sealed away in her chamber.

At that moment in time, I was fascinated with the idea of a female vampire when I didn't know about Joseph Sheridan Le Fanu's *Carmilla*. I wasn't even an English literature student but had the strong desire to write a story based on all this research I found. So, I started naturally looking up haunted places. Out of everything, I stumbled upon the Iulia Hasdeu Castle in Romania. I became obsessed with Iulia's life, her castle, and all the strange matters associated with it. I was moved and saddened by how young and tragic her death was. I never wrote a horror story before, but I was enthralled by Iulia. The first genre I became familiar with was historical fiction from World War II. It's the time period besides my grandmother's influence that made me want to write stories. I fell in love with historical fiction and a rule of thumb for any writer is to write what you know. So, I had my setting, and time period figured out especially when I learned that Iulia's castle was abandoned in its ruin throughout the World War II time frame. It was the perfect match for a classic gothic horror story.

The Antiquarian was a short story which I called "The Diary of Nicholas Ainsworth." As a short story, it had entries fifty-six, fifty-seven, and sections of entry seventy-four which included the ending. I remember when I first finished it inside the Michael Schwartz Library at Cleveland State. I stayed until closing and didn't realize it was dark, but I knew I had a special story. For years, I held onto it. When I became a student of English literature, I took the story to the writing center and the tutor who read it was drawn in. I recall specifically what he, Logan, wrote on the paper draft I gave him. It read, "Antiquarian Horror." Logan explained to me simply that Antiquarian Horror as a genre focuses on academic aesthetics and history. It features ghosts, curses, mysterious and malignant objects. Such a genre relies on suspense or "pleasing terrors" rather than shock. Lovecraftian horror stems from antiquarian horror because such writing invokes beings beyond the scope of humanity's understanding, however, Logan also introduced me to M.R. James.

M.R. James' Antiquarian Ghost Stories really laid the foundation and pushed my imagination for this story. As a tool, it helped develop Ainsworth as a character and his background. James 'method of storytelling is known as Jamesian where elements of a characterful setting in an English village, seaside town or country estate; an ancient town; or a venerable abbey or university is included. All of these settings are present in Ainsworth's life such as growing up in Yorkshire, his university, and especially when he travels to Romania. Nicholas as a protagonist also follows segments of the Jamesian. He is rather a naive, gentleman-scholar and becomes often reserved in nature, however, I do stray from these patterns as well. Ainsworth reminds me of myself and others as academics who lose themselves in knowledge and the passion for it. So, I bestowed a lot of my negative qualities such as how I obsess with academics and how it has affected past romantic and non-romantic relationships. With these negative traits, there are also positive traits with how vulnerable he is with characters such as Sasha. Lastly, one of the most essential elements to the Jamesian is the discovery of an old book or other antiquarian object that somehow unlocks, calls down the wrath, or at least attracts the unwelcome attention of a supernatural menace, usually from beyond the grave. This third element is deeply rooted in the novel when Ainsworth makes it to Romania and such plots allow room for ambiguity.

I believe the horror ambiguity of this novel plays an essential part of why and how this story works so well and why many who have read it, were drawn to it. For example, I brought this story to a fiction writing workshop as a short story where the entire class debated on what kind of entity Iulia Hasdeu was. Many did not know whether she was a ghost or a vampire. There is evidence to support both, but as a characteristic for antiquarian horror, mystery plays such a role. Iulia is also the most historically accurate based character in this work. Every detail on what Iulia tells, or Nicholas finds is mostly true in some form such as the exchange of letters between Iulia and her father Bogdan Hasdeu. I decided to expand this work into a novel because many felt the short story format also limited the story. There were details I left in the beginning that were worth expanding such as Nicholas 'background. Thus, I took the advice, challenge, and developed this work. May readers find such sensations in this creation I bid forth.

David Edgar Grinnell

20 August 1936
Entry One

’ve never recorded anything in my life. I shall write in this diary for academic, research, and personal use only. It is only fitting to start now since receiving my admission’s letter to attend the University of London. As a British gentleman, I am eager to begin my scholarly ambitions as an inspirational archaeologist. Since I was a young boy growing up in Yorkshire, I’ve always had a curious mind and I would go exploring the countryside. While growing up I became fascinated by Yorkshire’s rich Roman and Viking heritage and explored the many Norman castles, medieval abbeys, and even the national parks.

After my primary education, my father passed away from tuberculosis and my mother sent me to live with my wealthy Uncle Henry. Uncle Henry is my mother’s oldest brother, but he and my father never got along due to their social class differences. My father was always offended by my uncle's appearance as he always dressed in fine fancy coats and ties and when he came to visit us in Yorkshire during the holidays, he would arrive in his fine Crossley 19.6 modelled car. Living with Uncle Henry in London is enjoyable, however, during my time here, thoughts of my father and mother remain in my mind.

My mother is a grieving widow... She met my father at what is now my uncle's residence. My mother and uncle hosted a party at the residence to support our military. My father was a soldier. He was drafted in the royal army during the outbreak of the Great War. According to my mother, father was never the same after returning home. He was fighting in the trenches and was returned home after being wounded in action. I imagine the horrid conditions of the trenches triggered his later illness. Father never talked about the war; his hands were always shaking as if he was always tormented by a looming spirit. I am fifteen and just like any young man away from his parents for the first time, I feel homesick. I am an only child. Solitude kept me company while growing up in Yorkshire. Though I was not completely alone, I had a friend named Irene. She was pretty with black hair, soft-hued skin, and brown eyes. She wore a dark bluish grey dress with lace designs upon her chest. Not only was she my friend, but we became much closer than that. We'd go explore ruins such as Whitby Abbey.

Whitby Abbey with its gaunt, imposing remains, is what I believe to be the most romantic ruin. It is set high on a cliff above the Yorkshire seaside town of Whitby. It was founded in 657 by Saint Hilda. Whitby Abbey over the years was a bustling settlement, a kings 'burial place, the setting for a historic meeting between Celtic and Roman clerics, the home of saints including the poet Caedmon, and inspiration for Bram Stoker, author of *Dracula.* I've never been too keen on superstitions, poets, or Victorian authors such as Stoker. That bit of information was given to me by Irene. She loved all the Romantic poets and, in her solitude, would spend time reading Stoker's novel, while I, was more fascinated by the over two-thousand years of history of the site.

I miss her... We spent so much time together around the Whitby Abbey grounds. Any enthusiasm or discovery I shared with her; she'd giggle at me with her hand pressed against her lips. She would be sitting, leaning against one of the fallen pillars with her book, and say, "Oh, Nicksie... You're so cute!" She bit her lip at me, "What did you discover?" I'd sit next to her, she'd put her book down, and listen to me rant and rave about everything. She cared; and when those deep brown eyes met mine, it was difficult for me to finish speaking. It was like I was in a trance; mesmerised by her gentleness. She gave me a kiss upon my cheek. I didn't see it coming because I was too focused on her eyes. The next day, I broke Irene's heart. I met her at the abbey and told her my mother was sending me to live with my Uncle Henry. The clouds were dark and grey, and a roll of thunder echoed as she stood there comprehending what I told her. We felt raindrops dancing upon our heads. Irene's breath shallowed; every breath drained her. My eyes strained against the sight of her. It tore my heart; watching her. Irene's soft skin turned sallow. She was like a ghost or a corpse and darted away. The rain picked up as sheets of water soaked me to the bone. From the distance, my sight lost her amongst the downpour. I haven't seen her again since...

Irene is always on my mind. Ugh, he's bloody at it again! Though Uncle Henry can never have any children, he loves me, his only nephew, as his own. Sometimes, Uncle Henry has many birds come to his residence. He is sort of a pig when it comes to women, but yet at the same time, he is a gentleman to them. I don't know how though... I mean, my uncle can never stay with one bird. I shall write at another time when my brain is not bothered by the rambunctiousness from these thin walls.

5

Yours Truly,
Nicholas Ainsworth

21 August 1936
Entry Two

Finally, some time in silence and solitude this evening. I love my uncle dearly but he's such a ponce. It was early in the morning when I heard the woman he was with last night; scream at the top of her lungs at him. It wasn't the "velvet climax" either, but an indignant quarrel. My uncle mumbled something under his breath as I was getting dressed in my room. His room is next door to mine and that's when I heard his bird yell: "You're a daft bimbo! I'm Anna, not Pauline!" Then, a loud smack ruptured. "Cor, blimey that hurt!" Anna's feet thundered and shook my dresser, "We're done!" she roared and slammed my uncle's bedroom door shut. In a few moments, I heard his door creak open. The door from downstairs slammed and I tiptoed to check on my uncle. Wooden debris scattered from the door and a fissure had spread upon it. My uncle and I stared at each other as he chuckled, "Well, wasn't she just like a banshee?"

My uncle has brown hair swept up to the side with a brown moustache. He smudged his lips together while studying my appearance, "You need new clothes," he said rising from his bed. His room had sombre red wallpaper with black eloquent designs. The wallpaper only covered half of the walls as the rest of it was met by a dark wood finish. His floor was hardwood and a giant rug covered the centre of his room. It matched the wallpaper. My uncle ravaged through his closet while in his white muscle shirt and underpants. He spoke to me as his hangers clicked inside his closet, "Nicky, it's time to get you a suit. Now, I know you're not used to nice things, but every gentleman needs a suit." I pressed my lips into a thin line, "Uncle, are you sure that is necessary?" He stopped and turned his head in my direction. His eyes squinted at me in disgust, "Don't be daft boy! Of course, it is necessary! My boy needs to become a gentleman especially when he's been accepted into the University of London." I scratched the back of my neck with my head down, "Yes, but it's not like I've been accepted into Oxford or something..." My uncle snagged a light-grey dress shirt. He pushed his arms through the sleeves, "It doesn't matter Nicky. A suit makes a man. In this world, people will judge you on how you present yourself. This is especially true when dealing with people like me who are higher in class. Believe me, there will be professors at the university who will judge you on your appearance." As my uncle had said this, he buttoned up his shirt. "Nicky, can you grab my tie rack hanger?" He pointed to its direction upon the wall. I mooched over, grabbed it, and brought it to him. He studied the rack, "I want what's best for you. Don't do what your mother did." I bit my lip and clenched my teeth, "What do you mean, uncle?" Uncle Henry wrapped a black, silver, and white tie around his collar, "I am in no way speaking ill of your father, he served our country, and I respect him for it, but your mother traded her wealth for love." My knuckles popped from balling my hand into a fist, "Now, Nicky... Calm down. I'm trying to teach you a valuable lesson. Be careful who you fall in love with." My uncle tied a full Windsor knot, "What do you know about love?" I laughed under my breath. Uncle Henry pulled up the tie, adjusted it, and tucked the tail of his tie as he rose an eyebrow at me. "It may come at you as a surprise, but I wasn't always like the way I am. People are never the way they were before to shape who they are today." Those words struck me.

As I reflected upon my uncle's insight, he said, "Nicky, have you ever been with a woman before?" Irene flashed within my head. Those eyes and her standing before me. I mumbled under my breath, "Not officially, but there was a girl who had cared for me deeply..." My uncle nodded his head at me, "Well, there you go... Whomever this girl was, she will never be the way she was before." After my uncle's words, the last memory of seeing Irene creeped into my mind.

It pains me that I hurt her. I wonder if Irene will be as carefree as she was to me with other men. I would imagine not because of how she reacted to my rejection. It's like every breath she took from my words, they drained her of life and moulded her into a corpse. White as a pale ghost... Geez, here I am writing about superstitious rubbish. I've been listening to Irene's romantic intuition for far too long. I will be an archaeologist in the next four years. I cannot believe in ghostly rubbish. I do appreciate the suit my uncle bought. It's a blazer suit jacket with dark grey trousers, a red dress shirt, and a darker shaded red tie. I shall wear it on my first day at university. The first day of classes will start soon!

Yours Truly,
Nicholas Ainsworth

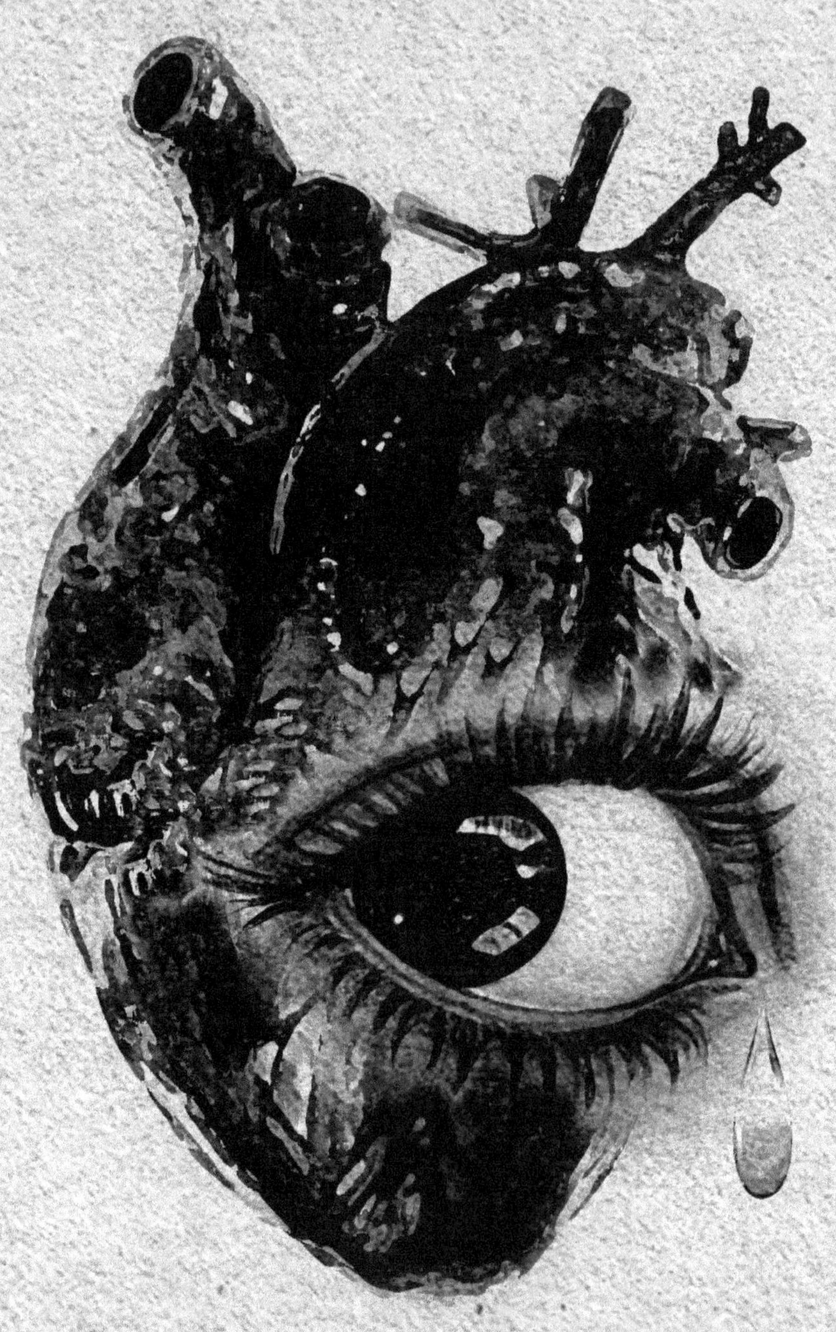

26 August 1936
Entry Three

The University of London is fascinating! I didn't know that the university was the first in the UK to award degrees to women, which it did in 1878.

I like some of my professors and some not so much, but there is one who I believe will stand out from the rest. His name is Dr Ralph Gilders. He's roughly a middle-aged man with a short white beard. He lectured in one of the bigger lecture halls. He's one of the many associate professors in archaeology and wore a fine fancy suit. In fact, many students wore suits too. I'm glad I followed my uncle's advice on getting a suit of my own. The entire week before classes, my uncle lectured me on how to be a gentleman. He gave me a bloody etiquette guide recently published called *Modern Manners* by Frederic J. Haskin. The cover features a cartoon drawing of a gentleman and a lady sitting across from each other at a dinner table. There are so many things to memorise such as invitations, introductions, cards, calls, engagements, weddings, christenings, funerals, at the table, on the street, at the theatre, at the movies, restaurant or hotel, travel, telephone, and even how to dress. For example, "Is it regarded as effeminate for men to wear wrist watches?" The guide's answer: "If such an idea ever existed, the World War dissipated it. The wristwatch was found convenient and practical. Since the War, its popularity has increased rather than diminished." What an explanatory answer to a simple yes or no question... My uncle is paying for my education though and so I must abide by his rules.

Besides the headache on the etiquette of a gentleman, Dr Gilders talked much about himself. He said he is part of The Prehistoric Society. A learned society which is devoted to the study of the human past from the earliest times until the emergence of written history. He ranted on about his group of colleagues V. Gordon Childe, Stuart Piggott, and Grahame Clark. It sounds fascinating! The society organises regular conferences, lectures, and other events that make grants for archaeological research. Dr Gilders spent some time with Childe in traveling to conferences. For instance, last year, he visited the Soviet

Union, spending twelve days in Leningrad and Moscow. Childe was impressed with the socialist state, and he was particularly interested in the social role of Soviet archaeology. Dr Gilders on the other hand, is unsure. He denounces European fascism, and he is outraged by the Nazi co-option of prehistoric archaeology to glorify their own conceptions of an Aryan racial heritage. Of course, why wouldn't he? I decided to visit him at his office to individually introduce myself to him.

Dr Gilders' office smelled like old books mixed with herbal tea. He was sipping on a cup of tea and munching on some crumpets. He swiped his hands to rid of the crumbs and reached for one of the many books upon his shelf. I caught a glimpse of the book but didn't get to observe what it was as I knocked. "Ah, yes come-in!"

"Greetings professor. I am delighted to meet you."

"How do you do? I am very glad to meet you."

"I am well, thank you. I'm Nicholas Ainsworth." Dr Gilders nodded his head and pointed out a chair across from his desk.

"I am much obliged." I sat down as the cushion squealed and sunk me in. I readjusted my posture in the chair, "Mr Ainsworth, do you care for a cup of tea?"

"No, thank you. That is quite a book you have there."

Dr Gilders' eyes gravitated to the book that was in his hand, "This, why yes... The Hebrew Bible. What can I do for you, Mr Ainsworth?"

"I wish to express my interest in working with you as I was intrigued with your involvement with The Prehistoric Society."

Dr Gilders smirked and his eyes gleamed, "Ah, an ambitious goal for a potential archaeologist." He sipped his tea again while extending his pinkie, "Very well." He placed his cup upon his saucer, "I'll give you the opportunity if you prove yourself in your studies. I'll keep a close eye on you, your performance, and how well you master the material. If you prove yourself worthy; we'll fund a field expedition abroad at a location of your choosing." I bolted from the chair as it squealed from sticking to my trousers. I shot my hand out, "I won't let you down sir!" He shook my hand, "Very good Mr Ainsworth. I look forward to it!"

What a goal and opportunity to work towards. I shall completely devote myself to my work and studies! I just wish I knew where it was, I would like to go, and what subject to explore in archaeology. An expedition to Egypt sounds too cliché. Maybe my studies will direct me in the right direction. Something to stand out amongst other archaeologists.

Yours Truly,
Nicholas Ainsworth

28 August 1936
Entry Four

ollege life and academics are challenging to adapt, but all is going well. Yesterday before Dr Gilders began his lecture; a new student wandered into the hall. She had fair auburn hair, fine blue eyes, and dark eyebrows that nearly met. She handed Dr Gilders a card, he grasped it, and read its context. His lips sunk in his mouth, he nodded his head, and glanced up at her with his arm extended. Voices muttered and mumbled under their breaths about this mysterious girl. She was short and inclined, but as she ambled toward my direction, her features were regular and finely cut. She sat in the row below me where there weren't that many students seated. Dr Gilders resumed his lecture.

I've been studying ahead in my academics for Dr Gilders' class, but this girl's beauty distracted me from the actual lecture. I squirmed in my seat, my eyeballs shifted between her and Dr Gilders. Some moments, my ears tuned out the lectured words. This never happened to me before. It reminded me of how I was mesmerised by Irene's brown eyes. I frolicked the pen in my hands playing with it. It did not help. As I glanced back at her, she caught me staring, but I turned my gaze away from her. I tapped my pen silently against the long table to rid myself of the senses of her staring back at me. I couldn't resist; I gazed back down at her, but she fixed her attention to her notebook and scribbled upon it.

When the lecture finally ended and class was dismissed, I was relieved because I wouldn't see the mysterious girl. I feel guilty just writing about it. How can a heart be tormented by two women? One who is a complete stranger and the other a childhood friend who probably loathes me? I still believe I won't ever see Irene again, but yet she haunts me. Her figure when I told her I was leaving. That sadness and sorrow. Lately, I've been pushing more into my academics to distract my mind from her. It helps, but in my passion for study, it is sometimes not enough. I remember Irene and I used to gaze upon the stars. The Yorkshire Dales and North York Moors are home to some of the darkest skies in the country, with large areas of unpolluted night sky where it's possible to see thousands of stars, the Milky Way, meteors and even the Northern Lights. Here in London, I don't get to see that anymore. I miss it and I miss her. Irene is my first love and I was hers. When we gazed upon the stars, she rested her head gracefully upon my chest. She had an exquisite loveliness, a rich heady fragrance that combines the green freshness of lilies, the valley with a spicy bite of gingerbread, and the voluptuousness of a white rose. Her natural scent was like a wild bluebell with hints of sharp floral notes. My heart aches as the scent still looms over me in a delicate twirl. Sometimes, my chest still feels the weight of her gentle head upon me. It hurts, that I cannot find the emotions or words to describe it. I feel guilty for destroying what was once good and pure. The memory of places, feeling the shadowy impressions of a person who stood in the exact place I hope to visit once more, but Irene's experience leaves only vaguely discernible echoes that I will strain to hear.

Nicholas Ainsworth

31 August 1936
Entry Five

Iam utterly disturbed... It is a reason for my brief absence from writing anything but writing about it may help me comprehend everything. I have developed the routine of spending many hours at the university's library devouring books of study. One day though, the library was quite crowded and there weren't many spots available to study in solitude. On the fourth floor, there was one table available to sit, but it was also occupied by the mysterious girl. She had books and papers scattered all around her, she scribbled restlessly in her notebook as if possessed by a vivacious desire. I mooched over, pulled a chair from across from her, and uneasily sat in it. She didn't seem to notice me at first until I placed my books upon the table. As I opened one of my books, I felt her gaze upon me. The tension was uncomfortable, I glanced at her open notebook, and saw what she drew upon a loose-leaf paper inside. It was a human skull with a giant stone lodged inside its mouth. There were illegible writings scattered all around the drawing. It was written in a language I did not recognise or understand because of her messy handwriting. She slammed her journal shut, stared at me, and gripped her notebook tightly.

"My apologies... I did not mean to intrude. Curiosity gets the best of me. I've seen you at Dr Gilders' lectures; do you have inspirations to become an archaeologist too?" My voice croaked because of her gaze, but she bit her lip as if she wanted to say something. She unloosened her grip on her notebook and placed it back on the table in front of her. "That was a peculiar skull I saw you draw, it is quite good, and I imagine you hope to study human remains of the past?"

"Yes... Yes, I do."

Her accent struck me. She is not from any English-speaking country.

"Where... I mean, how do you do? I am very glad to meet you."

She chuckled under her breath as she batted her eyes, "I am okay. I imagine it's your first time following a gentleman's code?" I smudged my lips, the words she spoke were slow, but good.

"Yes. Yes, it is..."

She laughed, "Well, do not worry so much. I appreciate your kind attempt. No ideal gentleman has spoken to me and so, I am flattered. I am Sasha."

"Nicholas Ainsworth... I have never heard of your name before." I fiddled with my pen.

"I imagine not... It's not a very common name in this country." I tapped the end of my pen against the table, "What country are you from if I may ask?" She broke her gaze and glared down at her notebook, "I..."

Silence.

"You're afraid?" I asked her.

She nodded her head, "If I say... You'll walk away and won't talk to me."

"As a gentleman's word of honour; I shall not."

Sasha stared into my eyes. Her blue eyes radiated with a tender glow. Those eyes gleamed in mystery, pain, gloom, and sorrow.

Finally, she spoke and whispered, "Россия."

I dropped my pen as her voice rang in my skull. The pen rolled off the table and fell onto the floor. My chair squeaked as I reached down and heard her gathering all her books and papers together. She was about to leave until I uttered, "No, please stay..."

"You think I'm monstrous because I am Russian."

"No..."

"That face of yours speaks more..."

"Sasha, I assure you those are not my thoughts."

She sank back into her chair, bit her lips, and shut her eyes. She clasped her hands against her face and wallowed into a short but silent sob. She rubbed her fingers underneath her eyelids, "You don't know what it was like over there..."

I pulled my chair to the side of the table and was closer to her, "Му родители..."

"Your what?"

Her lips sank into her mouth, her eyes glared up to the ceiling and back at me, "Parents... My parents..."

"What happened?"

After I said those words, her eyes conveyed a tender gaze at me, she inhaled a sharp breath and told me her story:

"I was five years-old when the Russian Revolution was still going on... It was near the end of the civil war between the Red and White armies. My father fought against the Bolsheviks. While my father battled during our civil war, he entrusted my uncle to keep my mother, sisters, and I safe under his protection. Violence and harrowing screams rang throughout the night. Gunfire echoed and death always stayed close. We were in hiding from the Cheka. One night my uncle had awakened us and ordered us to put on our clothes. As much as we could wear because we were under the assumption that my family would be moved to a safer location. The impending chaos reigned outside our hiding place. My uncle told us to go into the basement and wait for a truck to come escort us. A few minutes later, a squad of the Cheka barged in and my uncle read aloud the order given to him by the Ural Executive Committee:

'Tikhonova Maria Vasilievna, in knowing that your husband is continuing his attack on Soviet Russia, the Ural Executive Committee has decided to execute you and your children.'

My mother, facing us, turned and said, 'What, Dmitriy?' My uncle quickly repeated the order and the squad raised their weapons. My mother tried to bless herself but failed amid the terror. Uncle Dmitriy raised his colt gun at my mother's torso and fired, she fell, and was pierced with at least three bullets in her upper chest and died. As this was happening, I fled to the back of the basement. There were some stored crates against the wall that was tall enough for me to climb. My eyes caught glimpses of my uncle shooting at my sister Varya with a bullet wound to the head. He then shot at Anya, who ran for the double doors. By this time, I climbed through the broken basement window. The remaining squad fired chaotically and over each other's shoulders until the room was so filled with smoke and dust that no one could see anything at all in the darkness. I heard my uncle shout commands but I cannot recall them because of the noise.

There were dogs barking from our hiding quarters and the sound of gunshots roared despite the caterwaul sounds from the trucks 'engines. I heard my uncle shriek at the men to stop firing and kill me. I heard wallows of pain and suffering from within those basement walls, 'Bayonets! 'commanded my uncle. I imagined my sisters being stabbed knowing it was their moans and whimpers inside. Tears streamed my cheeks as I ran faster. My heart pounded, my breathing wild, and I had no recollection of where I was running. I was possessed by a frenzy..."

Sasha stopped. She shrouded her mouth to control and muffle her crying. "I'm sorry... I must go..." She darted with her books and papers as a few of them fluttered upon the floor. I stood as she slammed a door. Her feet echoed down upon the stairs. They became faint as I grabbed a few sheets of her papers. In my hand was the drawing of the skull I saw earlier. I studied the writing and realised it was all written in Russian.

I am utterly disturbed... Her story. I believe my father would know of Sasha's suffering because of the fighting he did in the trenches. The claustrophobia. This drawing though, it intrigues me. I must ask her about it. If I see her again; I will return this drawing.

Yours Truly,
Nicholas Ainsworth

1 September 1936
Entry Six

Sasha wasn't in class, but I did find her outside on the College Green field. She leaned against one of the trees and was reading. As I approached, I observed she was reading a book called, *The Vampyre*. The title was engraved with gold letterings with a black hardcover, "John Polidori?" I said seeing the author name glitter from the sun. She glared at me, "Yes... How are you Nicholas?"

"I am well. I've been looking for you."

There was a pause.

"Oh, may I sit down?"

"Of course."

I licked my dried lips, the breezed swayed my hair, and my eyes wandered over, "I deeply appreciate you sharing your past with me. Even though, I am a stranger; you confided in me."

"You gave me your word and you honoured it…"

"These are yours…" I presented the papers she left behind.

Sasha placed her book down, her face moulded into disbelief: "You saved them?"

"Yes, they looked important. I thought they were research notes."

She snatched the papers, "Yes, they are… My future dreams lie in these papers."

"What does it mean? What's the skull with the stone lodged in its mouth?" She picked up the book she once held, "See this book?" I rolled my eyes, "Yes, bloody vampires… So, what? What does this have to do about your academics?" Sasha pointed her index finger upward and she read from the book, "This is from the introduction of this volume: 'For many years vampirism was a serious subject of research. Medical authorities in the 1670s wrote Latin treatises about 'grave eating 'where the undead were dug up to find they had been eating their own shrouds and even feasting on their own limbs and bowels, according to research…'"

"Ok, rubbish!"

"It is but wait!"

I groaned; Sasha continued, "Sightings of vampires were reported in journals and gazettes in Poland and Russia in the 1690s. In Eastern Europe, for instance, where Bram Stoker drew inspiration for Dracula there have been numerous discoveries of corpses that have been 'staked.' Bulgaria has had multiple cases of seven-hundred-year-old skeletons with ploughshares, the hefty blade of a plough thrusted through them into the ground. Polish excavations unearthed skeletons with sickles placed around their waists or necks. Other techniques such as 'stoning 'have been found all over the world, from four-thousand-year-old Bronze Age burials pinned down with huge rocks, to graves from Ancient Greece weighted down with amphora fragments, to medieval English skeletons buried under grinding stones."

As Sasha read this to me, laughter built up inside me. I tried so hard to contain it, but after she finished reading, a wave of hot air exploded out from my mouth and cheeks, "I'm sorry for laughing Sasha, but I still call it rubbish. For instance, these claims of vampires are lacked by adequate scientific evidence. It cannot be excluded that a brick slid accidentally into the mouth." I laughed even more until my eyes caught her crossing her arms at me. Her eyebrows crinkled into a loathing gaze,

"I'm not trying to prove if vampires exist or not because they are just folkloric tales. My mother told me such tales to pass the time while in hiding because they were entertaining, but what I am interested in is to actually get to the bottom of these strange practices and resist misdirection."

I shook my head and sighed, "I worry that such literature biases could be influencing archaeology itself..." Sasha's eyes gleamed and glittered like a spark of inspiration, "Exactly, which is why as inspired archaeologists we must develop new systematic approaches by collating deviant burials into datasets."

Flights of fancy consumed my brain. Her words triggered a desire for knowledge and discovery. It all rushed like a fluttering dream, "Are you proposing we establish a comprehensive analysis to disprove these public fascinations?"

"Yes! Historically, archaeology hasn't paid much attention to deviant burials. I want to prove that these deviant burials weren't just some fringe practice, but to declare they are widespread across cultures. These so called 'discoveries 'of vampires are fuelled by abundant fictional coverage, but often I find it frustrating as an archaeologist, because many of the stories are based on unpublished findings that have yet to be thoroughly scrutinised."

I grinned, "Then let's start scrutinising and gather evidence!"

Sasha clenched both of her hands into fists and squeezed them vibrantly. She bolted towards me and hugged me, "Yes, a partner in crime!" I jolted from her embrace and thought about Irene, her drenched ghastly appearance flashed before me. It was like her sallow corpse stalked me and watched Sasha's arms wrap around me. The dark grim skies at Whitby Abbey ravaged inside my head; she's there with her soaked hair dangling upon her face.

"I'm sorry… Too much?"

Sasha's voice disrupted my trance. "What?"

"I didn't mean it as an advance towards you…"

"It's not you Sasha, I promise." My hands quivered, Sasha's touch lingered upon my shoulders. They were warm, but my body tingled against the imagination of Irene's embracement.

"Okay, but your eyes…," She said.

"Yes?"

The sun's rays glisten Sasha's blue eyes, "They're haunted," she said.

"As are yours…" My heart palpitated a burning ember throughout the chambers of my heart.

"Yes, but I am here… Away from danger and in the safest place to be." She smiled at me as her smile made me smile.

Ugh, I am a daft sod! My heart wretched by two women! No wonder Uncle Henry can't stick with one bird, but I'm not like him; he's a prat! I shouldn't write ill of my uncle, but I don't believe it gentlemanly of him poncing about with different women. One thing is certain though… I can't engage toward any advancement with Sasha because my heart grieves for Irene. It's not fair to Sasha. I still feel Sasha's touch as it revives my soul and reanimates my being with life. The blood in my veins flows warmly and vivaciously from her tender affection. I wonder what she thinks of me as… a friend, colleague, or… No… No, I can't fill my head with such nonsense.

Yours Truly,
Nicholas Ainsworth

The Antiquarian

37

2 September 1936
Entry Seven

My teeth; I am gnashing them in an uncontrollable manner. My wristwatch reads: 05:00... The sun shall rise soon. I saw Irene. She was here at least in a dream perhaps... I am unsure. The ticking from my watch is driving me mad. It's like it's keeping in time with me dancing with her. Yes — I was dancing with her at the abbey. At least that's what the shadowy place felt like. Whitby Abbey; my watch ticking in time with our waltz. A hypnotic lullaby with the beatings of my heart. As we waltzed and twirled, she rested her chin upon my shoulder. Her warm breath tickled the side of my neck, her lips barely touched my bare skin, and chilled me ever so tenderly. I gripped the back of her dress. Overwhelming passion possessed me. I held her safe and warm as our figures touched gracefully together. My lips rested against her neck; they felt the delicate radiance of her beating pulse. It was once something my heart knew as it yearned for what I once remembered; her kiss.

Even after this dream, my neck tingles where Irene's breath tickled it. It makes me mourn with the idea I may never see her again. Why would she want to see me? I broke her heart. Nothing is almost as powerful as a first love. Someone you love so much and learning how to live without them is one of the hardest things in life.

Yours Truly,
Nicholas Ainsworth

9 September 1936
Entry Eight

So many exciting things are going on! Sasha and I are becoming closer. We've begun researching a most comprehensive analysis of deviant burials. She and I have tracked down obscure references from the musty basements of university libraries, eventually compiling practically a well range of burials from Anglo-Saxon Britain: a growing one-thousand burials so far. Sasha has been recording the data into a vast spreadsheet, which allows us to organise the information into categories. One of the categories I recommended was, "position of decapitated heads" which I wager these heads are commonly missing.

While on our research endeavours, I learned Sasha has a fear of basements as it was difficult to get her to stay focused. Her hands trembled just like father's. She was deciphering the old wrinkled and dried papers stored in the University of London's archives. Papers fluttered away from the pile she was observing in her hands because of the shaking. I picked up a few of the papers, placed them back in the pile, and as I was taking the pile of papers from her, my hands touched hers. An innocent touch which both of our eyes jolted from. "My apologies... I'm only trying to help," my voice quivered. She smiled at me, her blue eyes sparkled from the overhead light, and her auburn hair fell between her eyes. She breathlessly giggled, "I know... I appreciate it. You're helping me get through this..."

"Oh?"

My hands grasped the papers for her to study and read.

"Yes, I don't think I could be down here without your support." Her eyes shifted between me and the papers. She spoke, "Sorry, I don't mean to stare at you... it's just..."

"Just?"

"Looking at you while multitasking between deciphering these papers helps me. It distracts me from knowing I am in a..." She stopped as she trembled again as if abandoned in a storm.

"It's quite alright... You don't have to say it. Just keep your eyes on me while transcribing these sheets." Sasha bent down to pick up her notebook and scribbled upon it, "We'll be here for a while..." She bit her lips while copying the written text in her notebook.

"I am at your service my lady."

She laughed, "Alright, Mr Peng... We'll put that hypothesis to the test, won't we?"

"Indeed."

Sasha smiled at me again, "Confidence, I like that."

The time passed... My knees ached and my feet tingled numb. I stamped my feet against the concrete. The air in the basement was hot and thick as sweat trickled my forehead, "Ugh, this infernal copying is driving me barking mad!" I chuckled out loud at Sasha's words. She pursed her lips forward and groaned hot air out of her mouth. Her breath flipped her hair from her face. "I would have never thought I'd hear an expression like that from you, 'barking mad.'" Sasha held her pen and notebook in one hand while she stretched out her arms. The bones in her elbows popped and she twisted her wrists as they crackled. "I guess I've been in London too long..." she halted from speaking as her eyes squinted.

"What?" I asked.

She brushed the top of her fingers against the side of my left temple, "You're sweaty..."

"Ugh, it's so stuffy in here I could drink dog's soup..."

"What?" She laughed and snorted under her breath.

"Dog's soup means water."

Sasha shrouded her mouth from snorting, "You Brits are hilarious... I'm sorry to laugh that way."

I clicked my tongue against the roof of my mouth, "It's all hunky-dory."

She smiled again. Sasha tried to hide it by shaking her head, "There you go again..."

"What?"

"Being cute..."

"I'm just being my natural-self."

Sasha sighed heavily, "What is it?" I asked.

"I just."

"Yes, speak up."

She suspired her breath, "I just hope as I spend my time here, I will never lose my Russian accent. The British accent is contagious."

"You sound good to me. Keep your Russian accent and don't Briticise it. Your Russian accent is beautiful." Her chest deflated from my words, "That's so sweet of you to say. My mother pushed me to learn English because my father believed it would become a universal language. You remind me of him a bit."

My eyebrows drifted apart, "In what way or manner?"

"Mother said he had a drive for education. He'd always tell her, 'knowledge is power.'"

I blinked my eyes in thought, "Is that why you're here for your education? To seek power?"

Sasha resumed copying more notes from the dwindling pile from my hands.

"Yes," she finally said, "The power to find him."

"To find him... But you study archaeology... Wait, did he..."

"Die?"

I sunk my lips into my mouth and pressed them. I waited for her answer.

She glared back at me briefly, "I don't know quite honestly... He joined the White Army before my birth and I've never met him. If he is dead, then the tools and education I will receive shall find him. My childhood was always surrounded by death. My family and I didn't have much, but father remained loyal to the Russian Empire. He briefly fought in the Great War and when father learned about what happened to the Romanov family, mother said he wept. 'They're just young girls...' he repeated over and over again according to my mother. Mother told me, he gripped her hand and saw a burden

of tormented sorrow in his eyes, they were like my eyes…
Blue. That's when he told mother, 'The Bolsheviks will die. I must fight for my girls.'"

Sasha took her pen and gritted her teeth to hold it. She placed her notebook down on the floor. She reached down between her chest and showed a necklace. It was a golden bronze locket. It was a perfect heart locket that was adorned with stacked layers of filigree and a delicate blue crystal heart nestled inside a bronze floral heart. She opened the locket, mechanics twisted, clicked, and turned. A beautiful melody played and raptured me. Inside the locket was a worn picture of a man in a uniform.

"That's your father?"

She nodded her head.

"That melody… It's beautiful."

Sasha snapped the locket shut, the melody ceased, and she grasped the locket into her hand.

She released the locket, and it fell against her chest. She took the pen from her mouth, and spoke, "Yes, that is my father's picture during the Great War. Mother kept this locket with her and said it brought her luck and then she passed it on to me. The melody is Debussy's Clair de Lune. Mother used to lull my sisters and I to sleep with the melody. My oldest sister Varya told me before the revolution, her, Anya, mother, and Uncle Dmitriy would attend the Imperial Mariinsky Theatre. The Mariinsky Orchestra once performed Clair de Lune. My sisters fell in love with the piece that my mother eventually received this locket as a gift from my father. Father was discharged from the service and returned to us in 1917 before the February Revolution. He made it for her, put his picture inside it, and every night she played this for me and my sisters."

The more I learn about Sasha, the more my attraction grows for her. I am a hopeless romantic sod for sure. My uncle has been inquiring about where I've been spending my long hours. Every time I tell him, "Long hours at the university library," he notices my stutter. He rolls his eyes and says, "It's a girl." My face turns bloody red of course. I can't help it and my uncle even asked me to invite her over. I have to make a visiting card... The card for a woman is usually from 2¾ to 3½ inches wide, by 2 to 2¾ inches deep, but there is no fixed rule. The invitation will be set for Friday on the 18th of September... Bugger, I just realised that I don't even know Sasha's surname... How am I supposed to write one when I don't even know her full name?

Your third-rate gentleman,
Nicholas Ainsworth

10 September 1936
Entry Nine

My tolerance level with Uncle Henry is going to burst! I know he means well when instructing me on the qualities of a gentleman, but he knocks me off my trolly... We've added more to my closet with suits and even a proper tuxedo. Uncle Henry made it clear with me and his voice was firm, "You will wear this tuxedo upon informal occasions after 18:00. It is appropriate to wear one at the theatre, at most dinners; at informal parties; when dining at home; and when dining in a restaurant..." I interrupted him, "Blimey Uncle, I know and such attire is worn at the opera; at an evening wedding; at a dinner to which the invitations are worded in the third person; at a ball or formal evening entertainment; and at certain state functions on the continent of Europe in broad daylight." My uncle's eyebrows rose, "Very good. So, you have been reading the etiquette guide. The hostess has written across her visiting card and you will give this invitation personally to Miss Sasha."

I jumbled my head to the sound of my uncle's words, "Wait, what? Hostess? Since when did we get a hostess? I thought you were just going to invite Sasha over for tea or something." Uncle Henry laughed, "No, my boy. This is an invitation to an informal dance. I've been seeing a lovely lady and she will act as hostess." Uncle Henry flashed the invitation as its contents were inside a black luscious envelope. A wax seal was embedded upon it with an elaborate letter Y and a black feather. I took the envelope as Uncle Henry cleared his throat, "By the way, you have more invitations to send out personally. Make sure you are dressed appropriately when handing out the invitations. You are representing me after all."

"More?"

"Yes, invite your professors and even your esteemed Dr Gilders. Them knowing you as my nephew, will give you respect." I stared at the addressed envelope and back at my uncle, "Why are you doing this?" My uncle warmly smiled at me, "Because I love you my dear boy. You are the only thing I have left, and I want you to be successful." I was speechless. I have never heard of my uncle establishing an informal event just for me. For me to rise and grow my reputation. I smiled knowing this growing reputation will help reach me closer to my dream of traveling across the world in search of deviant burials. I will have the respect, wealth, and power to do so. I have to play the gentleman's role. My uncle spoke again, "Come back home at 18:00, dress up in your tuxedo, and the hostess and I will instruct you on the waltz." I nodded my head and prepared to set off.

When I arrived at university later that day, I carried a packet of invitations tied with a fancy gold string. I traversed the university departments and halls. I left invitations by the faculty doors if no one was there, slipped them under the door, and handed a few in person. I bowed my head gracefully, arms extended, and said, "Greetings, my Uncle Henry Yates invites you to attend." At other times, I placed the cards on a table in the halls where appropriate or in drawing rooms throughout.

I knocked upon Dr Gilders' office, "It's open... Please come-in." The professor's eyes peered over his reading glasses with the Hebrew Bible in his hands.

"Mr Ainsworth, it is a pleasure."

"Dr Gilders, I wish to personally invite you to attend my Uncle Henry Yates 'informal dance." He received my invitation and studied the seal. "Henry Yates... The Henry Yates who donated funds to support our soldiers during the Great War?"

"Yes, sir."

"I respect the man. He raised up British morale with his exquisite parties for the soldiers and spent time at our hospitals to visit the wounded."

"How do you know of my uncle?"

He grabbed a letter opener and sliced the wax seal, "I don't know the gentleman personally, but my brother wrote to me about him. He said your uncle was a kind gentleman and visited him during his hospital admission. I couldn't visit my own brother because my life's work with traveling detained me, but your uncle kept many of the soldiers 'company. He listened to them, spoke to them, or just sat with them in silence. When the hospital was low on supplies, he gave some of his money so the hospital could afford the supplies. In some ways, he saved my brother because the hospital was able to administer the medications he needed."

I smiled about my uncle's actions. I had no idea of his kindness and here I thought of him as self-absorbed in his money. "I am sure my uncle will be pleased of your arrival." Dr Gilders grabbed a fountain pen from inside his desk, and scribbled. He handed me a card and I read aloud what he had written, "Dr Ralph Gilders accepts with pleasure for Friday, September 18."

"Keep up the good work in your studies, Mr Ainsworth."

After departing from Dr Gilders' office, I turned the corner and bumped into someone, "pardon me. I am so sorry..."

"Nicholas?"

It was Sasha. A smile creased from cheek to cheek seeing her, "Greetings," I bowed before her. She laughed, "Wow, is that a new suit? You look dashing!"

"Thank you, this is for you." I handed her the invitation. Her eyes grew wide, "Oh wow, so fancy and proper... You're full of surprises." She tore open the envelope and read the invitation to me:

There was confusion on her face, her eyes squinted at the words on the invitation, "Ms Helena Yates?"

"That would be the hostess of the event. It will be at my uncle's estate where I live."

Sasha's breath was sharp and tremulous, "I don't have the proper attire... So, I don't think I can make it."

"No worries, I can help you. We can get you a dress for the occasion."

Sasha dropped the invitation, bending down quickly to grab it, "Uh, um... You'd do that for me?"

"Yes, I would be honoured if you attended."

"Would you mind waiting for me? I was going to meet with Dr Gilders." I nodded my head to agree and waited for her about an hour.

Eventually, we arrived at a clothing store in London, but closing time dawned soon. Sasha was overwhelmed. She panicked by playing restlessly with her hands. She asked so many questions like, "Is it necessary to be in the latest fashion to be properly dressed? What is the difference between a ball dress and a dinner dress? When should jewellery or ornaments be worn in the hair?" All good questions, which I happily answered. From what I remembered I said things such as: "The well-poised woman makes fashion her servant. Others foolishly make themselves the slaves of fashion. Out of date fads should be shunned but new ones adopted only if found suitable.

Also, the formal dinner dress differs little from the ball dress, except that the skirt of the latter must be appropriate for dancing, while for the dinner dress, it may be closer fitting. As for jewellery, they should be worn at balls and dinners, but the size is merely of taste."

I paced back and forth as I waited outside the dressing room. A store-clerk woman was assisting Sasha with her dress.

"Will my locket suffice?"

"Yes, that will be good."

After I answered her question, she sauntered out of the dressing room. I was thrown into a loop, she had her casual clothes on, and smirked. "Where's the dress?" I asked.

She twirled around towards me, "The store-clerk is packing up the dress now, so you won't see it. I want it to be a surprise for you. You told me what was needed for the dress and I trust the store-clerk's opinion on it. She has helped a few women pick out such dresses for fancy events."

"I see..."

Sasha walked closer toward me, stroked my cheek, and said, "Besides, I hope it will trance you for I am in a sea of wonders." My heart jilted from her tender touch and the whisper of her words. All I could croak out was, "Sea of wonders?"

She laughed at me, "Yes, a quote from Stoker's *Dracula*: 'I am all in a sea of wonders. I doubt; I fear; I think strange things, which I dare not confess to my own soul.'"

I groaned rolling my eyes, "Not bloody vampires again..."

"I couldn't resist. Vampires are beings of seduction and are mesmerising."

Her words were flirty by how she conveyed them so playfully, "what are you getting at?"

"Ok, time for one of the confessions of 'my own soul, 'I like you and I want to impress you." She kissed me on the cheek. My face withered pale. I didn't know how to react. She kissed me on the opposite cheek from where Irene had kissed me.

My heart soars with delight. No more living in doubt on what Sasha's thoughts are about me. I shall be ever so slow and gentle with her. I deeply appreciate her openness with me. It's different and gives me time to heal. I paid a fair amount of money for her dress. I was even late for my dance lesson for the waltz... I practiced upon Uncle Henry's bird while trying to lead: step forward with the left foot, right foot step sideways to the right, bring back with the right foot, step back with the right foot, step back sideways with the left foot, and bring your right foot next to your left foot. Uncle Henry would yell: "No, wrong! Step back with the right foot," or, "wrong, footwork..." Uncle Henry's bird, Helena is a pretty thing. Short blond hair, green eyes, and smooth skin. She's an American which surprises me. She has a high squealing voice and calls me "honey." Eh, Uncle Henry joked with me by saying, "I'm doing a lot better than our lovely king of England, Edward VIII with his American birdy." It drives me insane, but it will be worth it once I dance with Sasha at the party. I eagerly wait to see her.

Yours Truly,
Nicholas Ainsworth

17 September 1936
Entry Ten

bsent from writing again. I find writing in this diary is helpful because of the annoying preparations for the dance. After long hours of study, a few random exams, and assisting Sasha with our project; I come home and help out with preparations. Helena and I have been going over the guest list by creating a list of our own to confirm who is coming and not. Impressive enough, two-hundred guests so far. My uncle chuckled, "That's pretty normal with my reputation. The last one I held here was when your mother first met your father. The guest attendance was about that size." My eyes grew wide at my uncle's confidence and easiness about all these guests arriving. Helena whispered to me that my uncle is like a British version of Jay Gatsby.

"Who?" I asked sitting next to Ter.

"Jay Gatsby, honey... You know the character from Scott Fitzgerald's novel, *The Great Gatsby*. Your uncle is so handsome and romantic... Like Jay!"

"Sure."

I didn't know what else to say, but bloody hell, is she really just into my uncle's money or is it the fact that she's into the British gentleman? Probably just for the money like many of the past ones who stayed here. Then again, if my uncle wasn't the way he was, he could have himself a nice lady. Some of those ladies wanted to be with him, but if only he could learn to control his attraction toward other women. Of course, I am one to write about such things. My attraction towards Irene and Sasha. However, I cannot keep beating a dead horse because horses are for courses. I am better suited for better things like Sasha. I am in a different situation and growing into a striving gentleman. Pretty soon, I will be sixteen come January. I wonder how old Sasha is. She is older based on what she's told me about her past. I just hope she's not too old... I don't know how my uncle will feel about me courting with an older woman.

Besides all this pish-posh, I have been working in solitude on a similar systematic study for deviant burials. I haven't told Sasha yet because there is nothing concrete, but my approach attempts to cover the whole of Western Europe from the first to fifth centuries. I want to confirm that deviant burials can be discovered well beyond Britain. Dr Gilders has been noticing the connection between Sasha and me. We've been sitting next to each other during his lectures and talk before the start of his class. I asked Dr Gilders if I could meet him to ask him about deviant burials.

"Deviant burials by what means are you seeking?" Asked Dr Gilders intrigued.

"I want to discover if deviant burials are beyond Britain." I handed him some of the notes that Sasha and I put together. He studied them over, gave them back, and said, "I must warn you. Applying concepts derived from later times and completely different cultural contexts is a risky exercise."

I bit my lips in confusion, "What do you mean professor?"

He exhaled and laughed, "Vampires... They're creatures of the night in folkloric sources as diverse as Babylonian literature. For instance, the shroud-eating Nachzehrer of Germanic tradition, and the Chiang-Shih, 'hopping vampires 'of Chinese legend, notions of corpses rising from the grave have long been documented.

However, what archaeological datasets reveal is that these ancient accounts are just stories that our ancestors told each other on dark and stormy nights. Many of them were genuinely scared, taking time and trouble to ensure that the dead stayed where they belonged."

I cleared my throat while shaking my notes in hand, "Indeed, but what Sasha and I are interested in is to actually get to the bottom of these strange practices and resist misdirection because as archaeologists, we have to develop new systematic approaches. The best way to do this is by collating deviant burials into datasets. We're not trying to prove if such blood sucking creatures exist, but to probe for historical influences on mortuary practices instead of flights of fancy."

"I see... The threat of vampires still captivates us today and that makes it more difficult to pin down your discoveries. After all, the science to debunk these myths is quite a bit stronger than it was centuries ago. Perhaps the undead stir up our deepest fears about our own mortality? Maybe they simply make for great cinema? For instance, I had the pleasure years ago to watch Nosferatu when it came out June of twenty-nine... Who the hell knows?" My eyes shifted to the floor with an utter groan of disappointment.

I am disappointed in Dr Gilders' lack of enthusiasm for the proposed investigation and project. Sasha and I have worked so hard for this... I must get Dr Gilder's approval for this project. The three of us could fund a project to go on an excursion to one of the many deviant burial sites to collect data. It's for the protection of archaeology! To debunk public fascinations with the undead such as Irene's romantic intuition about vampires. Well, here you go Irene... Real proof to show you the real truth about mortuary practices. To say to her: "Thanks to the process of decomposition, the corpse would be found transformed from its previous cold, pale, and stiff state. Fresh-looking blood would be seeping from the lips; the face would be ruddy; the body would be engorged, and have a 'fresh, new skin 'that made the nails and hair to appear to have grown. The corpse might even 'gasp 'if a stake was driven through its lungs, releasing foul and noxious gases!"

Your Humble,
Nicholas Ainsworth

19 September 1936
Entry Eleven

What a night! Where do I begin? I have so much excitement built up within me. Sasha was the first to arrive at the event. One of the servants we had on staff, opened our doors. She was glamorous. Her long auburn hair touched past her shoulders on her right side. She wore silver earrings that dangled, her skin appeared smooth, and she wore her locket necklace. She wore an evening dress. It was a black silk satin and crepe chiffon with a fringe overskirt. The dress was long enough and appropriate for dances. Her black heels reverberated against the marble stone floors. We saw each other with a smile, I bowed down, and she curtsied. After our greeting, she offered her hand to me. I clasped and kissed her hand. Our eyes met. Her blue eyes radiated in the most tender care of my mannerism. The lights from the chandelier above us gleamed within her eyes. "You look beautiful," I said with grace. "You're quite handsome yourself, that tuxedo is delightful." She offered her arm as I escorted her to the ballroom, "That dress... I've never seen anything like it. It's lovely." Sasha chuckled under her breath, "I thought you might like it. Its fashion is from Russia. Nadezhda Lamanova is the designer of this kind of dress."

My eyes study the dress again, "Ah..."

"Did you know that until the Revolution, Lamanova held the title of supplier of Her Majesty's Imperial Court? Lamanova created gowns for the Empress Alexandra Feodorovna."

"I did not, but I can see why you decided on this dress."

"It was you who said to keep my Russian accent because it's beautiful. I took that to heart and decided on this dress."

I stopped before reaching the ballroom doors, "what is wrong?" Sasha asked in perplexity by smudging her lips. I turned to her and gazed, "I'm sorry, but before we enter... I must let you know that I will be introducing you to my uncle... I will need to accentuate your name, to be made clear..."

There was an awkward moment of silence. We stared at each other until Sasha's mouth opened, her lips parted, and her eyes gleamed.

"Oh..." she said. I nodded my head in picking up what she figured out. She laughed and suppressed it with the palm of her hand. She came closer to me and whispered her full name to me: "Tikhonova Aleksandra Valerianovna."

My head jumbled as I strained my eyelids in confusion, "What?"

Sasha laughed at my reaction to her full name, "In Russia, names aren't used in the same way as most would probably use them, especially in formal ways. For instance, in legal documents, the surname is usually written first, then the first name and then a patronymic name, which is a name based on my father. The patronymic name is important as it's polite to call somebody by their first and patronymic name."

"So, your real name is not..."

"No, my name is Sasha! Many names have a short version which is used as a nickname." My mouth was unlatched, I didn't know how to react or what to say. I gasped for air to speak, but I stopped and frolicked my left hand in a downward motion. She laughed again, brushed her fingertips against my right temple, "Aww, you're so sweet trying to do everything right, but it's okay." I muttered her name, "Tik-ho..." I bit my lip losing my words, "Tikhon-Tikho..." She repeated her name slowly to me again, "Tik-hon-ova."

"Tik... Tikhonova..." Sasha nodded her head, "Uh-huh."

"Aleksandra... Bugger..." I mumbled.

Sasha buried her face against my jacket as her shoulders rose up and down.

"Oh, stop... You're making my eyes water with laughter," she muttered against my coat.

Suddenly, the ballroom doors whipped wide open by the servants. Sasha's head bolted up; it was red from her laughing and I continued to escort her. Uncle Henry was smoking a cigar, "Mr Yates, may I present Miss Tikhonova!" My uncle quickly removes his cigar, "How do you do, Miss Tikhonova?"

"I am delighted to meet you, Mr Yates. You may address me as Sasha, please I insist." My uncle nodded his head, "Very well, Miss Sasha. May I present the hostess, Ms Yates." Helena heard her name called as she sauntered over, "Oh, I am very glad to meet you!" she squeaked. Helena wore a dark satin red ballgown with segments of glitter sparkled upon the chest area of the dress. "Nephew, I trust you and Miss Sasha will enjoy your evening. It's time for me and the hostess to greet the incoming guests. When one guest comes; another is to shortly arrive." They both exit together as my uncle escorted his bird.

Sasha and I stared at each other until her eyes caught something else, "Oh, what's that?" Sasha paced towards the direction she was looking as I followed. I observed the giant oil painting she was staring at. The painting was of a man with dark hair, clasping the woman's hand with his. The woman wore a white dress, had red hair swept up, and tied in a round bun. She had white pearls around her neck, and she was bent backward for they were passionately kissing. "The Kiss by G. Baldry..." I walked behind Sasha as I said the words and then whispered in her ear, "It's a nineteenth-century painting."

Sasha's shoulders rose, she shuddered as my breath tickled her ear, "Oh... It's very sensual... Almost vampiric." I rolled my eyes, "Vampiric? Ugh..." Sasha tapped against my shoulder as I shook my head at her observation of the painting. "Now, now... Hear me out..." I crossed my arms and raised an eyebrow, "The gentleman in the painting is the vampire. His eyes are closed, but the right side of his face that is more towards the woman he is kissing, is lighter in complexion than his left side. The left side is darker and mysterious just like his hand that is clasping the woman's. The contrast in the light and dark side illustrates the gentleman concealing his vampiric identity. He has his other hand upon the woman's shoulders because the kiss is the mechanism for the trance. After the kiss, the woman will be in a complete, vulnerable, and hypnotic trance. The gentleman will slowly place his lips upon her neck, especially when she is bent backwards in the position the image is painted in, and..."

As Sasha was telling me her interpretation, her words became passionate, strong, and powerful. After she said, "And..." She fell backwards as if she fainted. I was terrified of her falling that I caught her. She placed her hand over her forehead and dimmed her eyes at me, "Oh, embrace me... Embrace me the kiss of death." She put weight behind her in my arms like a corpse. I sighed because of the dramatic effect of her voice when she asked for 'the kiss of death.'

"Oh, you're very funny and a gifted actress too!" She laughed and wrapped her arms around the back of my neck, "Are vampires a sensitive spot for you? I can be sharp and witty with my remarks." Her voice was smoky and flirtatious as I remarked, "Oh, vivacious and gifted... A deadly combo." I grinned as she brushed her hand across my cheek, "Ha-ha, I like the emphasis and hint on 'deadly.'" The temptation to kiss her wallowed in my mind. Her light sapphire eyes glazed a fierce, uncompromising intelligence. My neck leaned forward, but as our lips barely touched, a voice shouted, "Mr Ainsworth!" Sasha and I bolted up from our moment, "Dr Gilders!" I said gleefully. Sasha and I sashayed to the professor as him and I shook hands. Sasha offered her hand and Dr Gilders clasped her hand with his to acknowledge her, "I am delighted to see you Sasha."

"Dr Gilders, did you have the pleasure of speaking with my uncle?"

The professor turned with a smile, "Yes. I thanked him for what he did for my brother. By the way, I believe he and the hostess would like you and Sasha to lead the waltz."

"What?" Interjected Sasha, her eyes grew wide with terror. Guests floundered inside the ballroom like a bunch of sheep cattle. We glared over to where a group of musicians were preparing to perform.

Sasha gripped my hand and squeezed it, "No... No, I..." I turned to her and placed my hands upon her shoulders, "It's quite alright. We can do this."

"I've never danced before..." She whispered softly.

"Ladies and gentlemen, it is now time for the waltz! Our lovely musicians shall perform Chopin's The Minute Waltz in D-flat major." Shouted Helena. A crowd gathered around us as I clasped Sasha's hands into mine and pulled her close. Sasha's breath was tremulous, shaken, and her body wilted like an autumn tree. She stared at me like a frightened puppy, "Follow my lead and keep your eyes on me..." As soon as I said those words, the music played, and everyone danced to the melody. Sasha and I were caught in the centre of the room as her eyes stayed focused on me. The song passed by quicker than a summer breeze as the musicians performed a new composition. The crowd broke further apart from us as we had more room. It's a piece I have never heard before in my life. It was a moody, ambient melody. It was ethereal in the sense that it made me feel like I'm in an empty palace and there is a beautiful lady. One who keeps dreaming of a handsome man in beautiful places, but he turns out to be death. What a morbid thought, but death stops everything. It stops family, desires, and happiness. As I gazed into Sasha's eyes with this thought, another thought occurred to me. What death cannot touch is the love from that person and the memory. Those passed on to the next generation continues to live on through them. Death is not the end, for it is merely the continuation of a journey. The melody continued to play, a small gap within the crowd was exposed. I caught glimpses of our figures dancing within the large mirror. An image that will remain forever in my mind.

When the piece ended, my ears were swept up by Sasha's muffled laughter. I shifted my attention at her and saw her smile graced from cheek to cheek. We embraced; my fingertips ran through her hair and they tingled from every touch. Her natural scent whisked me away to an unreal mystery and paradise. The mixture of lemon, orange, tuberose, rose, and honeysuckle basked my senses.

"Thank you," replied Sasha. I smiled at her, caressed her cheek, "Thank you..." The urge to kiss her again settled in my mind, but our moment was interrupted again by my uncle. He asked Sasha, "May I have this dance?" She stared back at me as I nodded knowing it was appropriate to dance with a variety of people. Sasha agreed, "Yes, thank you, I'd love to dance." My next dance partner was Helena. As we made eye contact and danced to Johann Strauss II's The Blue Danube Waltz, Helena whispered in my ear.

"You and Sasha were glowing honey."

I blinked my eyes and scrunched them.

Helena clucked her mouth, "Oh, trust me; I know you're dizzy with a dame."

"Dizzy?"

"Someone who is deeply in love with a woman." I suspired a sharp breath, "It's okay honey, she's dizzied for you too. It's how your uncle makes me feel." We continued to dance in silence as she spoke again, "I came here after the U.S. stock market crashed, it was an amazing time before then. Lavish parties in the heart of New York City, flappers, and so much more. It was a golden paradise but out of all the parties, booze, and fun your uncle is my paradise. I met him ten years ago in New York. He's so charming, that accent, but he's more than that. I was foolish to push away the man who enamoured my soul, entangled within my bones. He is the man who saw past the dirt and darkness, who resuscitated my heart and brought me back to life." Helena leaned closer to my ear and said, "She's a keeper Nicholas. Don't let her go."

When I gazed upon Helena, her eyes spoke a sincerity that I never understood until now. Ever since Helena has stayed with me and my uncle, there has been no other woman in my uncle's company. Not one... Whatever happened all those years ago between Uncle Henry and Helena, it makes me realise what my uncle was trying to teach me earlier, "Be careful who you fall in love with," and, "People are never the way they were before to shape who they are today." My uncle was hurting... When he came back from the U.S., he was a changed man. He fell in love with Helena. Despite all those birds my uncle eloped with, he always thought about Helena.

The party ravaged on, drinks flowed, the music played on, and all the guests settled in at random locations on the first-floor conversing. Sasha and I stayed close by each other's side. Dr Gilders was a little drunk and tipsy, "Mr Ainsworth, may I have a moment?" Dr Gilders teetered as he glanced upon Sasha and me. I looked back at Sasha, "No worries, the lady may be present for our conversation considering its academic nature." The doctor gestured his hand to follow him to the sitting room where we could speak privately. He stumbled as we made our way to the sitting room. As we all walked in, the doors shut behind us. Dr Gilders pointed out a sofa on the left side for Sasha to sit. As she sat, Dr Gilders plummeted down upon one of the chairs by the fireplace, "I know it seems bad form given my indisposed state, but I assure you, I am well enough to carry on this conversation." As he said this, I sat next to Sasha and we listened to what he said next, "Deviant burials. I would like to hear what you two have gathered so far. Specifically, I would like to hear Sasha explain her part in this research. I have heard and read Mr Ainsworth's perspective."

"I discovered something rather peculiar... This past Saturday, I took a train to Oxford to find more on the subject of deviant burials. I read a recorded account of an event that happened about twenty-seven thousand years ago, in a stone-age village fenced in by mammoth bones, three young people were buried together, their bodies covered by burnt spruce logs and branches. A woman, disfigured perhaps by some congenital abnormality, was placed in the middle. To her left, a man was laid prone, his face in the dirt. To her right, another man had his hands angled awkwardly onto her groyne, where red ochre, a pigment with ceremonial significance, was sprinkled. A thick wooden pole was driven through this man's own groyne and thigh, pinning him to the ground. There was no documentation of where this happened, but I wonder from your knowledge if you have any insight."

I straightened my posture as I was drawn in by Sasha's story. Dr Gilders crossed his arms while nodding his head in thought, "For archaeologists, including researchers, such burials are like prehistoric murder-mystery puzzles. What you described is either a gravesite that is atypical, unexpected, or just downright weird. Questions I would inquire about such a site is would the man's position be a mark of disrespect? And is the other man's 'staking 'evidence of an ancient fear of the 'dangerous dead; 'the belief that corpses would rise from their graves to cause mayhem and hysteria?"

Sasha's voice trembled into an excitement at Dr Gilders' observation and questions, "Yes, which is why I told Nicholas earlier that historically, archaeology hasn't paid much attention to deviant burials because such sites involve peasants and criminals and are often discovered in excavations where time and resources are limited, precluding detailed analysis." Sasha played with her hands upon her lap and waited for Dr Gilders to respond, "And you two hope to broaden focus beyond the lavish mortuary practices of the elite and push the field to take a much keener interest." Sasha smiled brightly with vitality and squeezed her hands into fists upon her lap. Dr Gilders placed his hand underneath his chin, played with his beard by digging his finger underneath. "You two need to gather more evidence. I find the subject amusing but as a man of logic, you need more data. How many burials have you two compiled?"

Sasha and I stared at each other, "About one-thousand-five-hundred burials so far..." added Sasha. My leg thumped up and down in excitement. This was the moment I felt like I've been waiting for. The moment when Dr Gilders said he found our subject amusing. The professor's eyes glared, "It's a good start, but you will need to collect more numbers for your spreadsheet. I'll give you both four years to compile and collect such data on burials. By that time, both of you should have your degrees and that will give enough time to gather money for a possible excursion. As I promised Mr Ainsworth, that if he were to prove himself, he could go on an excursion of his choosing. Based on the data you both will collect; we can pinpoint which locations to travel to." As Dr Gilders said this my leg became more erratic. An unbound energy morphed into the fibre of my being. Sasha gripped onto the top of my leg, dug her nails into the fabric of my trousers, and squeezed it for me to stop bouncing my leg.

My leg twinged from her grasp, "We thank you for the opportunity professor…" I grunted gritting my teeth. "Very good." Dr Gilders stared at the clock upon the mantel. His eyes popped open and his mouth was ajar, "Ah, it's late. I better get going. I shall bid the hostess a farewell and I look forward to observing both of your performances during classes." The professor shot from his chair, and stumbled with a bow, "Have a good evening…"

After the professor departed from the room, my face was red from Sasha's grip as my lips sunk in. She stared at me and jolted her hand away, "I am so sorry…" I gasped out air after her release, "Cor, that hurt…"

"It's my biggest pet peeve… Nervous habits like that give me anxiety…" I rubbed my leg, "Duly noted…" Once I had said this, a solo grand piano echoed from the ballroom and played the beginning notes to Debussy's Clare de Lune. I rose from the sofa as Sasha gasped a sharp breath from hearing the melody. We made eye contact, I offered my hand out to her, "Care for this dance?" Sasha's eyes sparkled and glistened, "Here and now?" she barely uttered. "If the lady wishes it so, I would be honoured with this private moment with you." She offered her hand as I grasped it and we waltzed to Debussy's musical score. The entire time we were both silent, entranced with the melody which raptured us both. The room seemed to disappear around me as my attention was completely fixed on Sasha and the sensations of our touch. The atmosphere was tense but delicate. Every motion and twirl suspired Sasha's breath and passion entangled us both. As the last few notes ended, my hand caressed her cheek and our lips locked with a tender kiss.

It was so magical that night.... My first real kiss which will forever be engraved within my memory. Eh, I just realised the sun is dying from the view of my window outside. All I've done today was study and write about my experience last night. I need to stretch my legs and get out of this room. A nice evening stroll around the Royal Parks shall suffice.

Warmest,

Nicholas Ainsworth

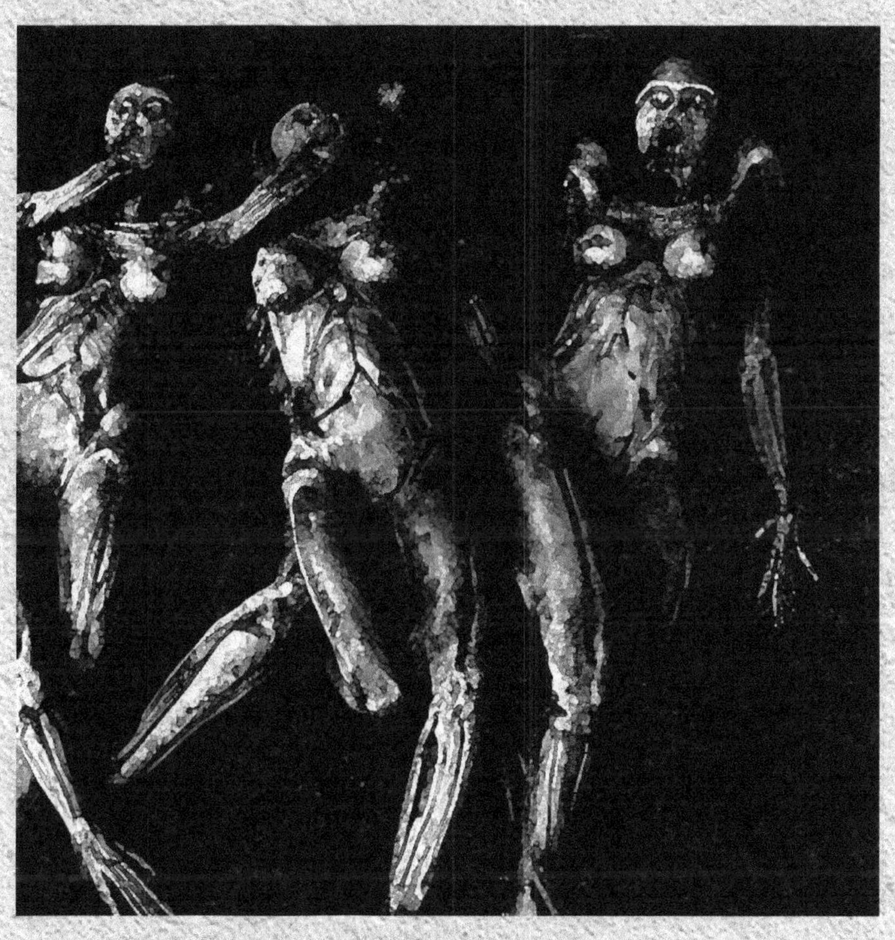

5 October 1936
Entry Twelve

I've been absorbed into my own little world with academics, research, and chaos in London. Sasha and I have been progressing slow on our endeavour, but we have two-thousand deviant burials recorded. We've been enjoying our time together with some mishaps. I finally mustered the courage to ask her age... I was terrified when we were visiting the University of Cambridge's library archives. She noticed the expression on my face as a despondence seeped into my brain.

"What's wrong?" Asked Sasha.

My eyes closed shut and I jammed my hands into my pockets, "Sasha...?"

I bit my lip and sighed, "I'm not sure how to ask this, but as politely as possible... How old are you?" Sasha breaks into a breathy chuckle, "Eh, I am seventeen, but I will be eighteen this December."

"Ah, bloody hell..."

Sasha's head jumbled, "Okay, not the reaction I was expecting. How old are you?"

My eyebrows sparse, "Eh, fifteen..."

Sasha shuddered her breath, "Oh..." She panicked, dropped the research papers, and they scattered everywhere, "Am I too old for you? What is the age of consent? How long until you are of age? Should we..."

I interjected as she ranted these questions and paced back and forth, "Stop..."

Sasha became upset as I embraced her and she murmured against my chest, "You act mature for your age..."

A short laugher broke, "Well, thank you... You're not too old for me. I believe age of consent is sixteen and my birthday is in January." Sasha whipped her head up at me, "So, you'll be sixteen this coming January?" I stroked her cheek, "Yes, I will. And besides, you're worth the wait." Sasha embraced me tightly, her face buried against my chest, and she moaned relief. "You're so sweet. No one has ever told me I was worth waiting for." She wrapped her arms around my neck, "You're worth waiting for too... I've never given myself to anyone before. I've never felt this way and I'm trying so hard not to rush it." She graced her fingertip against my chest and stared at me, "Am I your first, too?"

My lips sunk inside my mouth, I thought about Irene and the kiss she gave me. "I'm not?" Sasha's words broke my memory of Irene, "Not officially, but you are the first in my heart." She smiled at my comment, "May I ask what her name was?"

"Irene."

"Hmm... Pretty name." Despondence radiated from Sasha's countenance, "Childhood bonds are strong especially when moulded from love and innocence. It holds a place in the heart that none can reach." I brushed Sasha's hair through my fingers, "I broke her heart... I told her that her and I could never be together because of the distance and the passage of time." The hand that was stroking her hair was caught by Sasha's hand. She clasped my hand and held it, "I understand why you did what you did because it wouldn't be fair to you or her to hold on, but there is always a possibility for such love to rekindle. Look at your Uncle Henry and Helena. They met in the United States of America and defied distance and time. This girl is probably of your country given her name." My other hand stroked her back for comfort, "Sasha..." I said. She glared at me, "Please, you do not need to worry. In all that I am, you're the defender living in light."

"The defender living in light?"

I smiled warmly, "You're the defender of my heart which breathes and radiates its living light into my soul."

Sasha's body faltered as she turned, "Eh, I'm sorry for doubting you. I'm just not used to this... I usually don't think I deserve nice things because of the shadows which have devoured all I ever loved." We broke our embrace, "Ugh, look at this mess..." She squatted down and was gathering all the scattered papers across the floor. I assisted in helping her collect the papers as I asked, "Speaking of shadows, how did you escape Russia?" Sasha's face stiffened pale, her eyes focused on the papers that are scattered, "I never did finish telling you..."

"I understand if..."

"No, I want to. It's just difficult to talk about but I want to share it with you because it does tie into my interests with archaeology." We finished collecting all the papers and leaned against one of the walls in the archives and she began her tale.

"The night I fled my execution, a frenzy possessed me. I had no inclination of where I was going, I just knew I needed to get away from the shouting and dogs barking. While running, I tripped over my own feet and stumbled into a mass grave. The stench was unbearable, rotten, and made me nauseous. The grave was too far into the ground and I wasn't tall enough to climb above. My fingernails collected the dirt as I slid back into the bedded grave. Corpses laid all around me. Their eyes all stared at me and blood congealed out of their mouths like they were still alive. Purges of bloodstained fluids oozed from their bodily orifices. Some of the bodies displayed their superficial veins of skin and had distended abdomens. I tried pushing them away from me, but they were difficult to move. Their knees and elbows were slightly flexed, and their fingers and toes appeared unusually crooked. I thought their hair and nails were growing... I was terrified and shuddered in complete terror. I thought about the vampiric tales my mother used to tell me while we were in hiding. It was like those tales became true, and I was trapped. I laid there frozen and gazed upon the night sky. I did not want to look at the bodies all around me. The stars gleamed from the night, it was the only thing with the forest trees that kept me calm and still.

Darkness seeped into my mind, snow fluttered with their white tuft flakes, and the air was chilled. I did not know how long I had stayed there until a light flashed upon my face. It was a flashlight and a man's voice spoke, 'This one's alive!'

In the darkness the flashlight dissipated, and a black shadowed object was in front of me, 'reach. 'The man called. My arm reached for the object in front of me. It was the wooden end of a rifle as the man pulled me up. He swung the rifle against his shoulder as a strap held it around him. 'Come...' He lifted me up and carried me out of the forest. The warmth of his body was soothing, and I had fallen asleep. My eyes awakened to the sight of fire dancing nearby. I was wrapped up in blankets and over the fire was a pot. Heat radiated from it and various warm, cosy smells delighted my nose. The man stood over the fire and stirred whatever it was inside the pot. His boots shifted at my direction against the wood floors. I pulled the blankets closer too terrified to budge. 'It's alright Malenkaya. You are safe here. The rabbit's stew should be ready soon. You are very fortunate to survive the Kovalevsky Forest; rest...' His voice was soothing, sincere, and all the comforts around me drifted me into a sleep. The man was kind, he woke me up and offered me food. I was revived and more aware. He explained to me, 'I've been searching around the forest for my wife. She was brutally murdered by the Reds and they dumped her body somewhere in those woods. I want to give my wife a proper burial before my departure of this wretched country, but here I found you amongst one of the mass graves. Those blue eyes of yours gave it away.' I did not speak as I was finishing the last of my serving of the stew, 'Ah...' His eyes caught my locket and he reached for it. I jilted away still terrified, 'It's alright Malenkaya; I will not harm you. Where are your parents?' As he asked me this, memories flashed of my family's execution. I sobbed and curled my body close to me, 'Oh, I see... Malenkaya, you shall come with me to the United Kingdom. My wife and I have always wanted a child of our own, but she was unable to carry any children. I'm Edik.' Edik cared for me, he protected me, and gave me shelter. He eventually found his wife and buried her beside the cabin where we stayed briefly outside the forest. He and a group of his friends made arrangements to escape Russia with false and illegal documents. All of his friends stayed behind to fight against the Bolsheviks, but Edik and I took the train. We took it as far as it could until we switched over to a ship and sailed across the English Channel. We arrived in the small town of Chatham. We stayed there briefly but being an immigrant, it was difficult for Edik to find a job. So, we moved again into London where there was of a higher chance of him finding work. Still, no luck after almost two years of scraping by. With a heavy heart, Edik gave me up to an orphanage because he could no longer provide for me. I've been at the orphanage since then. I have been fortunate that they have kept me this long, but I know when I become eighteen, I will be on my own. Every day, I stare out at that window hoping that Edik will come through those gates and adopt me. He hasn't come..."

Sasha's head faltered against the wall as she groaned. My heart sunk from her predicament, I wanted to help her, and save her: "If Edik doesn't return to you. My uncle and I can take you in." Sasha gasped, she bit her lip, and shook her head, "No, I couldn't have you and your uncle do this. I appreciate it, but I will need to find my own way." My cheeks bulged, "Sasha, I respect your will to find your own way, but I don't feel comfortable knowing the possibility of you roaming London."

"Have faith in me. London is not too bad. I've been in this area for years." She nestled against my chest, "Besides, it's said home is where the heart is... As long as your heart is beating my place is with you." I wrapped my arms around her, nuzzled my cheek against her head, and her scent of lemon, orange, tuberose, rose, and honeysuckle basked my senses.

My affections grow for Sasha, but I worry about the predicament of London. Yesterday, Cable Street and Whitechapel in the East End of London had a demonstration. The British Union of Fascists were organising a march to take place. Thousands of marchers dressed in their black-shirt uniform engulfed the East End. The main confrontation took place around Gardiner's Department Store in Whitechapel. Dr Gilders arrived late today for class. Almost fifteen minutes. He was pale as a white sheet, his eyes wide, and sweat trickled down his face. He stood before the class, gasped a sharp breath, and stared at all the students. His voice quivered as he addressed us, "My apologies about arriving late class." He wiped his brow with a cloth from his pocket as he trembled, "As some of you may gather, I live in the East End area. I advise you all to avoid Cable Street and the area in general. I was caught in the middle of what seemed to be twenty-thousand anti-fascists demonstrators. So many policemen and mounted police attempted to clear the road to permit the march. The demonstrators fought back with sticks, rocks, chair legs and other improvised weapons. Rubbish, rotten vegetables, and even chamber pots were thrown at the police by women in houses along the street. The BUF marchers were dispersed towards Hyde Park instead while the anti-fascists rioted with police. Many were arrested, some escaped with the help of others. Some were injured on both sides including women and children. I do not feel safe returning home because of the destruction."

Sasha's face withered pale. She tapped her pen against the long table as she heard Dr Gilder's story about the riots. She closed her eyes tightly and bolted from her seat. She flounced quickly, exiting toward the backdoors of the lecture hall. Dr Gilders didn't seem to notice Sasha disappearing. He shifted his body toward the blackboard and wrote the agenda for his lecture. The sound of chalk reverberated across the hall as I exited the hall to follow Sasha. My dress shoes echoed throughout the halls. I discovered Sasha curled close to her body, her face buried against her knees, and her body leaned against the hallway walls. I sat next to her, "What are you doing here, Nicholas?" she mumbled. My eyes shifted to her, but she did not look at me and kept her forehead against her knees, "I want to be here for you." She chuckled under her breath, "You need to focus on your studies. You shouldn't have to worry about me..." I stroked her shoulder, "Academics are important, but the knowledge gained from academics will always be there. You will not always be there." Sasha slowly lifted her head and her eyes glistened upon mine, "I've always been alone. You don't need to be chivalrous." I smiled warmly at her and parted her hair that fell upon her face, "I know you are capable of doing things on your own, but that doesn't change how I feel and what I would do for you." I caressed her cheek, as my touch made her smile, "Here I was trying to get away from such violence. I thought I would find it here, but the riots of the East End... It reminds me of the day my mother spoke of and how the Revolution started. Red Sunday, when unarmed demonstrators led by Father Georgy Gapon, were fired upon by soldiers of the Imperial Guard as they marched towards the Winter Palace to petition to Tsar Nicholas II. Now, in London there are riots... No matter where I go, death, violence, and destruction follow me. The orphanage where I live is close to the East End and I am afraid."

We clasped our hands together, "Stay with me..." I whispered softly.

"What?"

"Stay with me..."

"But..."

"At least until the riots are more under control."

We gazed; our eyes locked, and she ran her fingers through my hair to the back of my neck.

"I don't think your uncle would think it proper..."

Her touch made my body tremble, "Why? It's for your safety." I uttered.

She sighed and bit her lip, "Nicholas, I can't stay even though I desire so. I am still very much a stranger to your family. I've only met them once last month. I would feel better if you escorted me home."

Taking her home was eerie. Dust and debris scattered among several streets of East London. Some of the streets were still blocked. Bricks, scraps of metal, and wood shrouded the roads. It was silent and dead. It was as if Sasha and I were the only living souls amongst the ruins. Buildings abandoned and destroyed as we observed a cat cross the path in front of us. We were silent and did not say a word. Sweeping echoed throughout the area, and hooves reverberated upon the roads. The police and community were still cleaning up the mess. The sunlight hid behind the clouds, but the sky's tinted blue still loomed. The road ahead of us was vailed by the light and dust. From the distance, the shadow of massive iron gates took form. As we got closer, I observed it was the orphanage. It looked desolate, empty, and hollow. Sasha pulled the gates as they creaked and squealed. She stopped as she stepped only halfway through the gate. Her shoulders sunk sullen and she turned to me. She closed her eyes tightly, and gasped, "You probably think less of me..." she said.

"What?"

"I know being near Whitechapel, it's not the best place. It's not as nice as your side of the city. You deserve a proper, lovely lady like your Uncle Henry and not a poor girl like me."

I lunged my body forward, but she shuts the gate.

"Sasha, wait!"

I pried the gate wide open and flounced after her. I gripped her shoulder and turned her around. Sasha's feet stumbled as she faced me, but she did not look at me. "I desire no one else because there is no one else like you. It doesn't matter to me where you're from and the area. What matters most is how you shine and treat me. I couldn't ask for anyone better because what I see in front of me is a genuine and intelligent woman. I am fortunate to have your affections which I do not take for granted." She warmly smiled at my words, "You're so good to me. You did escort me here despite the possible danger and I feel no one else would do that for me except one who truly cares for me." I nodded my head with a smile as Sasha suspired her breath, "I'm sorry about these walls and defences. Every person always has something to work on about themselves and vulnerability is mine. I deeply appreciate your patience with me. I feel sometimes though you have the urge to swoon right into a relationship."

I smudged my lips; bashful about the idea of swooning for love, "Eh, yes... I'm sorry about earlier when pushing you to stay with me and my uncle." Sasha embraced me after my words, "Thanks, I know your intentions are good, but that's something I wouldn't be ready for. I was and still am in an angry frame of mind. I'm still fragile from a lot of things and I know you are too. I have to find myself, and I know it's going to take a while. I'm in the middle of a very important self-discovery, journey, and I'm slowly learning how to love myself. Which I think is the hardest thing any of us will ever do."

There was a pause. We both stared at each other as a thought brewed into my mind. My hands rested upon the front of her shoulders and my eyes glared down and spaced out. My eyes met hers, "Do you wish for space?" I mumbled.

Sasha's mouth slightly parted, "No... I want you to know that I'm so glad I found you and that you're in my life right now. I want this for both of us. I know you're a safe space for me... I still have a hard time opening up. I am so sorry you're the one suffering for it. I know and appreciate that you're there for me in any and every way. You seriously don't know how glad I am for you. I'm also here for you, and I hope you know that."

I do know and feel she is there for me. I feel a connection with her, and I feel she does too. A relationship is something I desire to work on with her and grow together. It's not my intention to push her to open up but to support and encourage her with my feelings and emotions because actions speak louder than words. I use both actions and words. There is validation in how we both feel. I respect it. I'm glad Sasha is opening up at her own pace because in her actions of doing so, it allows me to know where to stand with her. Patience is a challenge for me because I am the kind of person who goes after what they want because like what she told me... I really want this too. A deep, intimate and romantic relationship are what I would like, and I know I would be honoured to have such a connection with her. Bugger, I'm not perfect at patience but it will be worth it.

Your Ernest,
Nicholas Ainsworth

11 October 1936
Entry Thirteen

It's 07:00... Dawn is gleaming through my window and its rays 'part the shadows in my room. My head throbs; I must jot this down as I cannot get this horrid nightmare out of my head. I can recall only segments as my watch keeps ticking. First, I was in Yorkshire. The sun shone brightly, the green fields were luscious, and the sky aqua blue. In the field, there was a boy. He looked like me as a child. The same darken brown eyes and flabby cheeks I once had before maturity. The boy's hair was white-ashen, and it made him appear older. I knew that wasn't right because my hair as a child and now is brown. We stared, he looked as if he wanted to talk but he couldn't speak. His eyes wallowed in sadness and his lips pressed tightly against each other. I knew he wanted to say something, and I asked him, "What do you have to tell me?" His eyebrows rose, his eyes grew wide, and he pointed at me. This dread came over me. I turned to the direction the boy pointed, and this young woman flashed before me in a white dress. She was right next to me and lunged forward. I caught a glimpse of her sallow but tinted face. I couldn't see her facial features clearly. Her long hair dangled against her cheeks, she gripped onto me, her nails dug beneath my skin and mustered a smouldering sensation. I jolted and thought I had awakened from my dream, but my surroundings were in my old Yorkshire bedroom. The room was pitch dark and only the visage of my door appeared. I desired my parents and wanted to see them. I knocked upon my door but as I knocked, the young woman's image appeared before me. My subconscious mind gave the instinct that she followed me into the segments of my dream. She flashed forward, almost like she had superhuman speed. Immense pain shattered my body and its numbness pulsated throughout. Blackness swallowed me, but I awoke to my current bedroom. For a moment, I did not know if I was still dreaming until my daze of waking subsided. My hands trembled as my mind recalled the young woman chasing after me. It horrified me because I have never had a dream of such a being lunging after me. I've never had such a dream where an entity of some kind followed me through dreamlike segments. This is the second time, where I can recall a dream in such detail. First, Irene dancing with me at Whitby Abbey and now this mysterious woman in a white dress. I usually cannot remember my dreams. As I glared around my room, I noticed a dry bloodstain on my pillow. I patted down my face, cheeks, and neck but there was no blood upon my fingertips. I must have had a bloody nose as I slept. The side I sleep on matches the side of the pillow where the stain is. This dream disturbs me, and I wish I knew what its meaning was.

Yours Truly,
Nicholas Ainsworth

4 November 1936
Entry Fourteen

Wretched news from Yorkshire. I was studying in my room when Uncle Henry entered. He knocked upon my door, opened it, and said, "Nicky..." I peered over and saw despondence. His eyes watered trying to fight back tears. I've never seen Uncle Henry in such a condition as he squeezed a piece of paper in his hand. He presented it to me, and I received a letter. Here, I have pasted the context of this letter on the next page:

Dear Yates Residence,

It is with a heavy heart that I write to inform you that Ms

Addison Ainsworth passed away on the morning of the 2nd of

November. I discovered her deceased by means of suicide. Crime

investigators and policemen confirmed the method used to end her life.

Proper funeral arrangements must be made, and your residence is the o

kin left to attend such matters. Please come as soon as possible to

organize, conduct, and enact her will and testament. The Duncan fan

will wait for your arrival at our residence. Ms Ainsworth was a rare

gem to my family, and it is with great honour that my family support y

in your time of grievance.

My family's condolences,

Irene Duncan

That is Irene's handwriting. My stomach churned sour, I dropped the letter from my hand, and groaned. I shrieked another groan, a painful sorrow I had not known. I wept in front of my uncle. Suicide, how could she? My mother was stronger than that. How she handled father's trauma after the war while I was growing up, mostly raising me. She taught me to be strong and driven. I cannot believe nor think in her nature; she would commit such a deed. I didn't see any signs; I've never known the battles raging on within her head. I was blinded, lost in my own little world. I was oblivious to everything. My uncle approached me, placed his hand upon my shoulder, and I clasped my hand on top of his. He squeezed my shoulder and we grieved.

My uncle and I shall drive back to Yorkshire to handle the necessary arrangements. I've told Sasha today about the news of my mother. She embraced me as her tender hug jolted swarths of emotions. I clutched her close to me and my tears stained her outfit. She wore a dark green wool tailored dress with long, tight sleeves and slightly bloused bodice. The dress gently flared but was worn at mid-calf, had side pleats and with a wide belt. She whispered to me, "Let me come with you for support. I don't want you to be alone." As she had said this, she was stroking my back, "I appreciate it, but you need to stay here and continue our project. We've come so far on it with almost two-thousand-five-hundred burials recorded." We broke our embrace and stared at each other, "Our research can wait for a bit, you're more important." Her voice was quick and firm as she bit her lip when she spoke, "There's something bothering you, what is it?" I asked.

Her eyes lingered to the ground and she fiddled with her hands, "You're going back to Yorkshire..." she muttered.

"Irene?"

She nodded her head.

My hands graced Sasha's shoulders, "I have feelings for you, Sasha."

"It's not you... It's her. What if she desires you back? She is or was your childhood friend. She will try to be there for you, but I always want to be the one there for you."

I cuffed her hand and placed it upon my chest, "You feel that?" Sasha nodded her head; her eyes fell into a trance as if my heartbeat hypnotised her in an everlasting gaze. "That's called purpose. My heart has purpose and desires only you. Irene may have been my first, but she won't be my last. My heart desires you. We're partners in crime. You are here for me."

"I have to learn to trust you." Sasha's eyes gravitated into mine after her words. "It's fine," I said, "you're expressing your emotions." She smiled at me, "I've been trying to work on that and it's a slow process. It's not going to change overnight." I kissed her forehead, "It's good you're honouring your emotions. You should always do that."

I never thought I would see Irene again. This will be a test for me to know who my heart chooses. I choose Sasha, but I am terrified when I see Irene. I imagine it will be awkward. Will those brown eyes hone onto me like before?

Yours Truly,
Nicholas Ainsworth

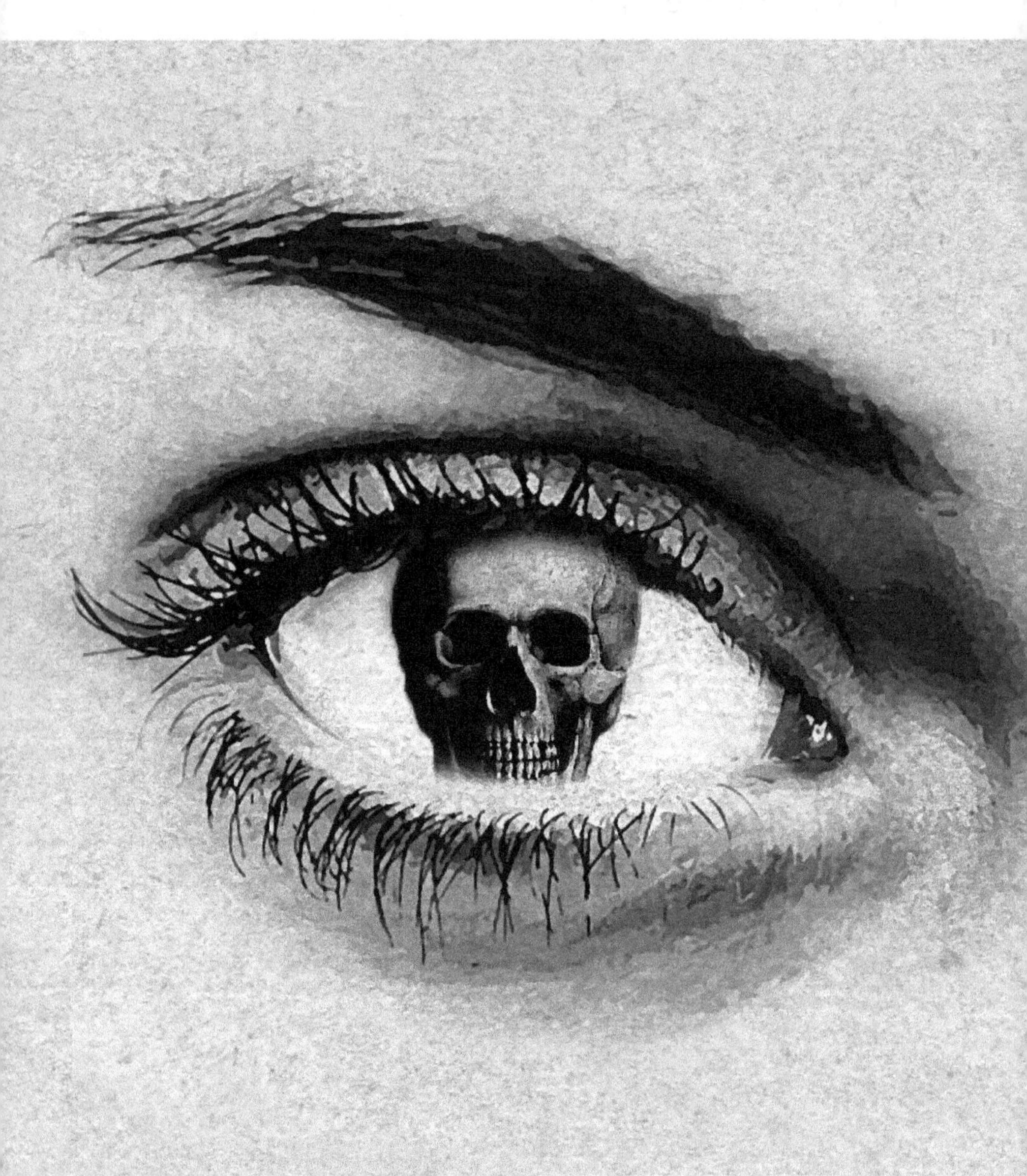

6 November 1936
Entry Fifteen

The solitude in this place is dreadful. My uncle is sorting out the arrangements with the funeral director, Helena is at the Duncan residence a few miles down, and I am here in my old home. It's been rather difficult, but the isolation helps. Most of my mother's belongings are packed in boxes. I am almost done sorting through it. I found some old pictures of memories of my mother and father. Them, dancing at the residence where I live with my uncle. Pictures of when I was but a boy as it makes me recall my dream about the young woman in the dress. It feels strange inside the place where my mother died. It makes me wonder how many homes people live in and how many have passed away in them. I saw Irene. She did not speak to me, but she only acknowledged me. She had dark circles under her eyes and the brown tint in them gloomed at my sight.

She is not the same girl I once knew. I am thinking about visiting Whitby Abbey. It's the place that inspired me to become an archaeologist but it's also the place where Irene and I spent much time. I am afraid of seeing her there, but maybe I can find answers about deviant burials. After all, Irene told me that the ruin was one of the inspirations behind Stoker's novel. Why was Stoker inspired of all places by Whitby Abbey?

Your Curious,
Nicholas Ainsworth

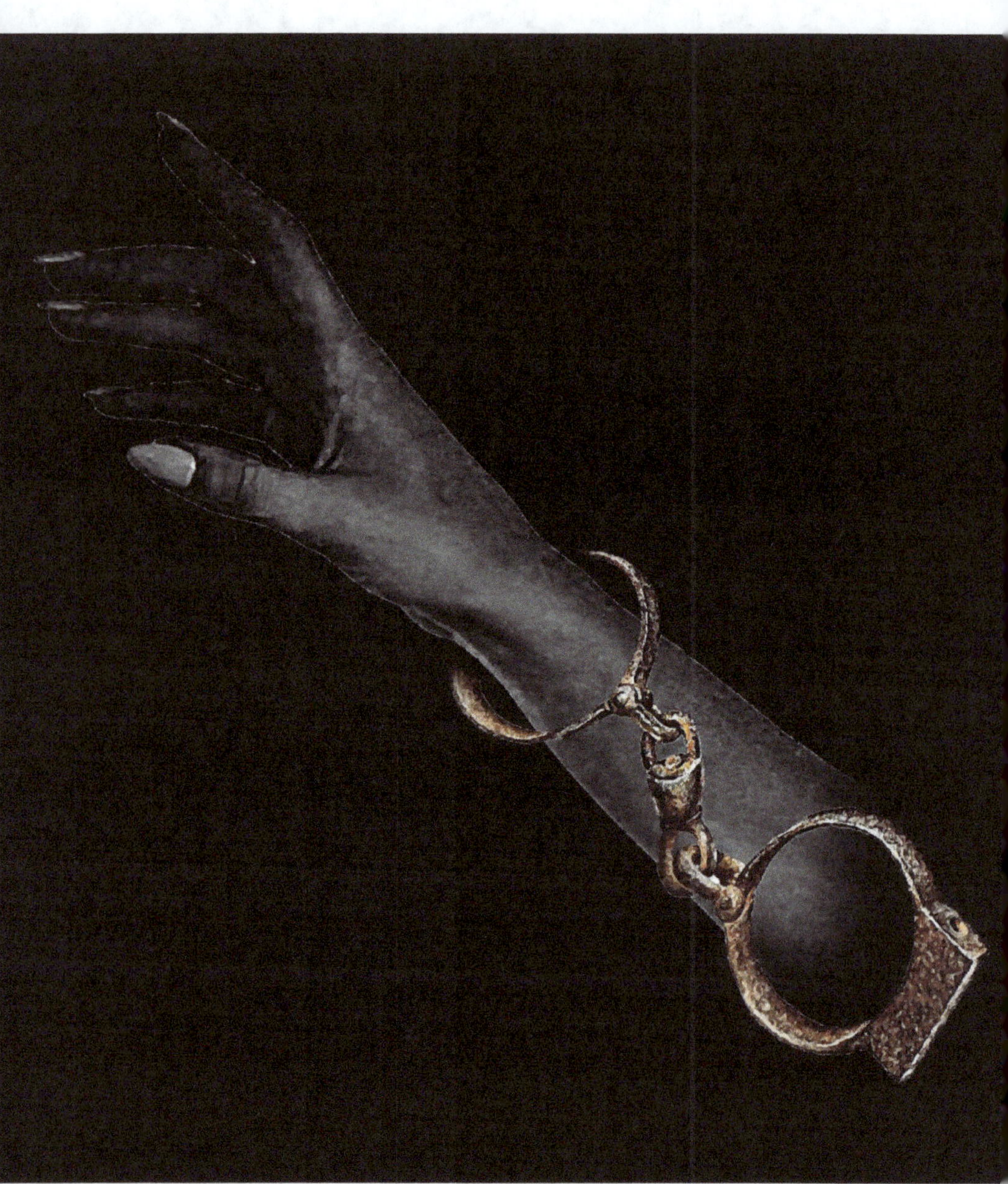

7 November 1936
Entry Sixteen

Today was my mother's funeral. Helena, Uncle Henry, the Duncans, and I attended the funeral at Whitby Cemetery, or also known as Larpool Lane Cemetery. A dirt road led into the cemetery with a medieval-gothic tower surveying the area. We walked underneath the tower's archway and into the graveyard. I carried my mother's casket. It's the most difficult thing I had to do. We all carried the coffin to her burial site. Irene stood next to me and her scent of wild bluebells distracted me. I felt and still feel guilty that my mother was alone after father passed away.

We had a luncheon after the funeral at the Duncan residence. Irene's family stayed close with my mother after I left to live with Uncle Henry. My mother always enjoyed the Duncans 'company. I believe my mother always wanted Irene and I together. She always teased me when I told her I would go see Irene, "Nick, tell Irene she's invited to come over for tea. She's always sweet and good to you." I tried to enjoy the Duncans 'hospitality, but not only was my heart too grieved, my mind was focused on Sasha. As I thought about Sasha, I stared at Irene and she was just a sad remembrance of my past. Irene is the reminder of what was once there. It makes me sad because I will never get to call, write, or visit my parents. Yet, I've had some time after moving away to do such things. I wish I had written if I knew my mother were to die. Maybe, if I wrote to her, she would still live and be here... It's my fault, I should be more mindful about others instead of my own selfish desires on education.

After the luncheon, I told everyone I wished to be alone with my thoughts. I departed and travelled to Whitby Abbey. By the time I arrived, the sun was dying beyond the horizon. The mixture of orange, red, and tints of pink painted the sky's canvas. There it was high above Whitby and dominating the whole town, stood Whitby Abbey, the ruin of a once great Benedictine monastery. Below the abbey and before me stood the ancient parish church of St Mary, perched on East Cliff, which is reached by a climb of one-hundred-ninety-nine steps. I remember counting them with Irene when we were children. The weather had gnawed at the graves, some of them teetering precariously on the eroding cliff edge. Some of the headstones stood over empty graves, marking seafaring occupants whose bodies had been lost on distant voyages. I scuttled closer to the abbey, the wind swept the headland and against my body. I hurdled my body closer for warmth, and my vision wavered due to the chill. Nearby the parish church, a swoop of bats fluttered from the distance and gave me a homegrown taste of such thrilling horror about my own research.

I found the fallen pillar of the abbey where I said goodbye to Irene. It was the place she gave me my first kiss. The image of her turning sallow crept into my mind. The whistling wind made me recall the rain and downpour. While in deep thoughts, a voice interrupted them, "Nicksie?" I jolted, gasped my breath, and turned around. It was Irene, she was still wearing the black dress from the funeral. It was a fingertip-length dress with unique silver designs which shrouded around her breasts. She wore a neck laced cover above the neckline and wore an overcoat jacket to shield her from the wind. "Did you follow me here?" Irene shook her head, "No, I come here often to reflect. It's so peaceful here with the wind, the roaring water, and the waves hitting against the rocky cliffs."

My eyes squinted and I bit my lip, "Were you hoping to find me here?"

Her lips sunk into her mouth, "I figured you would come here eventually. How could you not? It's where we spent most of our childhood together. Counting the stairs of the old parish, hearing your obsession over the history of the ruins, me making up stories about the dead who lie here amongst the graves, and this spot where I kissed you... You hurt me."

"I am sorry..."

Irene's chest deflated as she shuddered, "I cried, screamed, and lamented sorrows among this hollow ruin. I wallowed; tormented by your rejection. I could have gone with you. Your family knows me well enough for the possibility of such a condition, but instead you tossed me saying and I quote, 'We can never be together because of time and distance. I'll be at university and travelling the world as an archaeologist one day. That life wouldn't be fair to you. I cannot keep you and I can never love you.' Even though I can say it's your loss, deep down I know it will be mine too."

"Irene..."

She shallowed her breath again, "What hurt the most was when you said that you could never love me. Yet, here we are Nicksie. You probably thought you'd never see me again, but we're here. So, where do you stand now Nicksie?" She shrouded her eyes and rubbed them, "I am haunted by you because I haven't stopped loving you. I decided to stop showing it because I have to stop looking for such happiness in the same place it was lost. I amble through this romantic ruin, cadaverous by our memories, our childhood, and our bond. Why are you here at Whitby Abbey?"

The wind rustled against us as I approached her. "The memory of this place, I feel its shadowy impressions of us. I hoped to visit this place once more, but our experiences Irene leave only vaguely discernible echoes that I strain to hear."

"You despise our bond, then? Why do you loathe me? You've come here to torment me." Her voice echoed with built up passion, "How can I forget you when you're always on my mind? How can I not want you when you're all I want inside? How can I let you go when I cannot see us apart? How can I not love you when you control my heart?"

I don't know what overcame me, but I felt her pain because of our childhood bond. As she raved these questions at me, I embraced her. My body radiated with compassion. She squirmed, shocked by the embrace, and wallowed with tears. In our embrace, she latched her hands tightly against the back of my jacket. My nose caught her scent of wild bluebell and consumed me with an overwhelming passion. I felt déjà vu. The uncanny sensation experienced from my dream of Irene. As the dream flashed before me, I whispered in her ear, "My rejection hurts, but what hurts me the most is my regret, which is why I am here."

Irene shoved me away, gritted her teeth, and her eyebrows pressed together, "If you have regret and miss me, remember, I didn't walk away. You let me go."

"My regret was not letting you go but hurting you because you are my childhood friend. For the sake of our bond and friendship, I am here to only tell you that one of the hardest things to do in life is letting go of what you thought was real. My heart belongs to another, Irene. Our friendship is real, but a romantic relationship with me is not. Just because we can't be more than friends, doesn't mean I don't think about how I've hurt you. I'm trying to distance myself because I know I cannot have you."

"I see... This is becoming ironic."

"What?"

"Our connection with this place, the connection I feel here because of its solitude, and its literary inspirations behind it." I squinted my eyes as I smudged my lips, "what do you mean?" I asked.

"You wouldn't know because you don't believe in Romantic poets, and the ghostly stories behind this ruin. In *Dracula*, there is a moment when Mina says in her diary, 'Right over the town is the ruin of Whitby Abbey, which was sacked by the Danes, and is the scene in 'Marmion 'where the girl was built up in the wall. It is a most noble ruin, of immense size, and full of beautiful and romantic bits; there is a legend that a white lady is seen in one of the windows.' I am my own girl walled in this abbey. I fell in love with you which was a grave mistake for our friendship. I am now bricked up inside these ruined walls by means of punishment because I now realise we'd make better strangers. Like the ghost behind the wall, I will whimper, scream, and beg to be let out where I died."

Tears streamed my cheeks because of the torment and misery my actions caused her. My uncle's words rang in my head, "Be careful who you fall in love with..." I saw it then. I saw she fell in love with me. Even though as her friend, I desired to make her pain go away and be with her, my heart would not be true to itself. I swallowed and croaked, "Irene, I am so sorry for making you feel all these negative things. It was never my intention to hurt you in any way, but by being here and conveying my true feelings, I feel like a huge weight has been lifted off my shoulders."

Irene closed her eyes, and reopened them, "I am glad you feel a heavy weight lifted because I still want what's best for you despite how I feel. However, I do need time to grieve and process these emotions and where you stand because my heart is in pain, but that's because my feelings for you and such a desire for an intimate connection with you are real."

"I understand and I'm sorry to cause you such pain."

After my words, Irene walked towards me. She hugged me and during our embrace said, "No matter what, there will always be pain when it comes to the matters of the heart. It's what makes us human."

My eyes flayed and grew wide. She stared at me, but I could not speak, "Farewell Nicksie. Whomever has your heart, never let her go." Irene sauntered away. I watched her figure vanish among the remaining light where the darkness gleamed its gloaming tenebrous.

It still hurts what happened between Irene and me. She is the last connection I have to Yorkshire and childhood. I must grieve such losses, focus on academia, and accomplish my dream.

Yours Sincerely,
Nicholas Ainsworth

27 November 1936
Entry Seventeen

The research is coming along steady. Sasha and I have three-thousand deviant burials recorded on the spreadsheet. We requested an office room of our own to post the spreadsheet. Dr Gilders approved a room for her and me to use for our studies in the archaeology department. A terrible accident happened while on campus earlier today. For some time, the university has been constructing a new building. It's forming into quite a magnificent art deco building and its design was originally proposed by Charles Holden. That was before my arrival to university, but a group of university officials, led by the principal, Sir Edwin Deller, went out to inspect the work in progress. Suddenly, without warning, a skip (a large open-topped waste container designed for loading onto a special type of lorry), was pushed by a workman overhead accidentally.

It fell down and hit them. All were rushed to University College Hospital, where I hope they will be alright.

Nicholas Ainsworth

30 November 1936
Entry Eighteen

Sir Edwin Deller died of his injuries. There was a moment during the day where the university held a moment of silence. I never knew the man, but it is sad to see how his death had affected others while strolling the university grounds. Sasha's birthday is coming up December 11th and I don't know what to get or do for her. I still worry about the orphanage booting her out when she turns eighteen. She doesn't want my help though and I must honour that. She was speechless when I told her about Irene and what happened at Whitby Abbey. Her face turned pinkish-red and she muttered at me, "No one has ever chosen me over anyone else before..." She couldn't believe it because she knew of my childhood bond with Irene, but that is now severed. It feels strange, sometimes painful because I feel something from my soul was shattered that was once a part of me. To lose such a close friend is like limbo. I cannot describe it. At the same time, it is something I am glad I did because I can fully focus on myself and my goals. It is such a strange phenomenon.

Nicholas Ainsworth

30 August 1939
Entry Nineteen

've stopped writing in my diary. Writing relieved stress, but perhaps one of the biggest reasons I stopped was because I don't know what to write. I thought I might need to jot down a list of what I'm grateful for every day or write down all my hopes, goals, and aspirations for the years passed. However, as I am writing now, I believe I was embarrassed by my past self. It's like the moment when one finds any book they used to write or any painting they drew or any kind of handicraft they made when in primary school. Even looking through this diary before actually writing again, I laugh at myself. I'm laughing because deep down, I feel shameful of some of my past thoughts and activities. Such as the reminder of not being there for my mother when she was alive. At night, Uncle Henry tells me that he has heard me talk in my sleep. He says I call out to my mother as if my entire soul poured all its essence and emotions into that one word, "mum..." Though to face the past and put it behind me, I must face it again which is why I picked up this diary after so many years. I cannot live in the past, but I cannot forget it either and I cannot let it consume me. Thus, I think writing in this diary again will help mend such wounds. So, good friend, it's wonderful to write in your frail pages again.

Before I stopped writing in this diary, King Edward VIII abdicated the throne over his proposal to marry American divorcee Wallis Simpson. By May of 37, the coronation of King George VI and Queen Elizabeth happened. A few weeks later, Neville Chamberlain became Prime Minister, and also the first available in London, the 999-telephone number was introduced as the world's first emergency telephone service. On another interesting note, the London and North Eastern Railway Class A4 4468 Mallard built in Doncaster broke the land speed record for the fastest steam locomotive, reaching 203 km/h. Bloody impressive, but what's more impressive is the research of the long-time project Sasha and I started years ago. We've reached a final result of a staggering 25,000 burials. We plugged all the data into our vast spreadsheet. Its magnificent display is shown in our office space within the archaeology department. We drafted pins, strings, and plot points across our map of Europe. We shall travel to all the plotted locations soon. Yesterday, Dr Gilders got all the funds approved for such excursions. All is set and we just need to make the necessary travel arrangements. Such funds were not possible without my uncle's influence. That informal dance event worked off drastically and the research Sasha and I put together captured the attention of the majority of the department. Actually, I can see why now I haven't been writing because I've been tranced into my passions for archaeology too. Sasha and I shall graduate May of 1940. She is my best friend, lover, and my companion. A few weeks before my sixteenth birthday, Sasha got adopted by a family who lives on the West End. She now lives not too far from Regent's Park. Her stepfather is Dr Percy Patel at King Edward VII's Hospital Sister Agnes which is a private hospital. She is fortunate and form what Sasha told me, Dr Patel's wife miscarried, and the miscarriage caused other several failed attempts at conception. They decided to adopt and out of all the orphanages and children they met, Sasha drew them the most. Sasha believed it was the moment when Mrs Patel caught a glimpse of Sasha being bullied by a few of the girls before they lined up to greet.

I met Sasha's stepparents. I thought my place at uncle Henry's would be intimidating but the flat where they live was intimidating. Pure white marble in the early Victorian style. The steps to the entrance was bricked, spacious, and wide. Before the steps were two marble stoned lions. The inside was a decorative and furnished wood. Dr Patel has his own private medical library where he obsessively spends countless hours conducting medical research. He and Sasha get along well because of their passion for education and academia. The good doctor allowed us to borrow some of his books about human anatomy. He took a keen interest in our project. He said, "The human body is a flowering pathway. Things are in dynamic equilibrium and when something alters that equilibrium greatly, it begins a cascade of other events that are traceable. It tells a story!" This traceable cascade he speaks of is why he supports the project about deviant burials. I cannot wait to discover these deviant corpses and see what stories and secrets they hold!

Uncle Henry and Helena are finally married. They got married last year. I cannot believe Helena revoked her

American citizenship. She did not want to go back after spending so much time here. Jokingly, my uncle remarked, "Now, it's your turn!" Sasha caught the inside joke and she turned red while I stuttered. The thought never occurred to me for Sasha and me to possibly make such a step. We've been a couple for four years. Yet, it's a conversation she and I never had. I mean, we've sneaked a few passionate kisses here and there, but not once did we speak of engagement. I guess her and me have been too engaged in our education or, perhaps I have been too blind to notice.

Your Studious,
Nicholas Ainsworth

3 September 1939
Entry Twenty

War! Honouring our guarantee of Poland's borders, Great Britain and France declared war on Germany.

Newspapers scattered everywhere across the Green Field on the University of London. People cheered and celebrated our country's call to arms. Sasha and I ambled the grounds when someone shouted, "War, we are at war with Germany!" Large masses of students gathered and threw papers of all kinds across the field. Sasha and I stared at each other, fear gripped her, and made her ill. She shook her head, "It's over..." she said and rushed towards the direction of the Senate House. I followed, but stopped her, "What do you mean, over?" I cried. She turned her body in my direction, "It will be impossible to travel and continue our research with deviant burials!" I gripped her hand, "Sasha, we can't give up and stop now. We just got the funds approved. All we need is to decide the location to start."

She pulled away and broke my grasp, "And where would we go Nicholas? I will not travel further across the European continent when there is another Great War! Edik and I gave up so much to get away from such death." I gritted my teeth, "We must go Sasha! We will never get another chance. The war will disturb the burial graves we marked on our spreadsheet." Sasha exhaled her breath short, "I am sorry Nicholas. I want to continue but it's not the best now since we're at war. This is the safest place we can be." I flailed my arms about and darted towards the direction of the archaeology department. Sasha chased after me, her flat heels clicked along the stone floors of the courtyard, "Wait, Nicholas! Where are you going?" She shouted at me, but I did not listen to her. Nothing can stop all the hard work she, and I did over the years. No bloody war would stop me! I arrived into Dr Gilders' office and barged in, "Professor!" I cried, "I know..." he responded glaring out his window. A few papers fluttered across his window, "Britain is at war and I am afraid this puts a damper on our travel plans. With Poland under German control, I do not feel safe traveling. Not only for our well-being, but I am Jewish."

"Sod those Germans! This is our chance…" After my words, Sasha dashed in front of the door. She was catching her breath, took her heels off, and rubbed her feet. "Nicholas, you're mad! Please, we can resume our research after the war." Suspired Sasha. I shook my head, "We can still do this! Instead of traveling to all the locations we plotted on the map, let's choose one that has not been occupied by the Germans. I'd rather take the chance of going to a burial site that has a higher probability of being undisturbed by the war. We can just go, record data, and leave. I'd rather go now before everything gets worse."

"No, Nicholas!"

"Sasha, enough! You can choose to come along or not!"

She inhaled a sharp breath, my eyes caught her face moulded into a flustering rage, "You're a tupitsa!" My eyes shot wide at her word, 'tupitsa '[translation: dumb ass] and Sasha's Russian accent was much thicker in her rage.

"Stop it both of you!" Roared Dr Gilders slamming a book down upon his desk.

"Both of you are acting like children with toys and such behaviour will not be tolerated at this university nor in my office! Sit down both of you!" Sasha and I both glared at each other and plodded down on the chairs. She crossed her legs and rested her hand under her chin. Sasha's elbow rested upon the arm of the chair. I crossed my arms, rose my right leg and plopped it on top of my left knee. We both groaned at the same time in anger, but as we did so, we looked at each other puzzled. I sunk my lip into my mouth, and I was too angry to laugh at our reactions.

"Hear me out, both of you." Commanded the professor. "Sasha makes an excellent point about traveling abroad when another war has been waged. I, myself, do not feel comfortable with travel, however, Mr Ainsworth also makes an interesting point. On one hand, if we desire to collect such data, it needs to be ideally now, so the sites are not disturbed by the destruction of the war. Thus, I am open to traveling to one location only, but it must be a location that is in Eastern Europe and not the west. The location must also be unoccupied by the Germans. Let us go to your study room and have a look at the map."

We arrived in our study room down the hall. A large map of Europe showered with pins were connected with strings to all the locations we found of deviant burials.

[Every time I think of this map, my heart radiates in the proudest manner.]

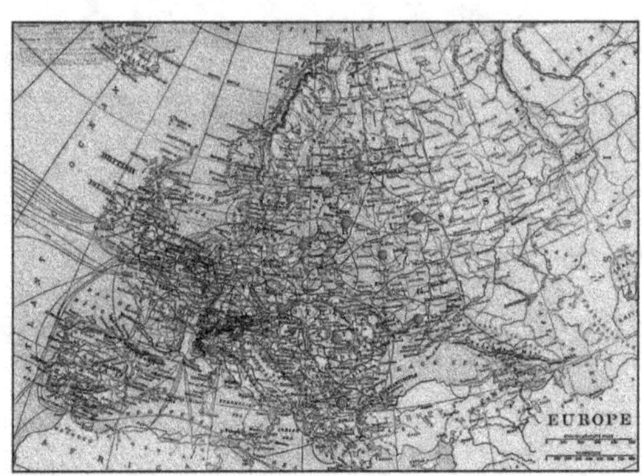

I gestured my hand toward the map, "Sasha, would you care to choose a location?"

Anger flared, she frowned, and shook her head, "no, because I do not wish to travel."

My eyes glared back at the map. I saw Poland, but that was occupied by the Germans only a few days ago. My hand graced and followed the pins and strings on the map. I traced a route to a location. From France, my hand traced Italy, Yugoslavia, and I stopped. "Here," I pointed. My fingertip tapped against the location of Romania.

"The Transylvanian Alps?" added Dr Gilders. He thought about my choice and ambled closer to the map. "Yes, a location that is not occupied by the Germans and yet is far out enough to possibly gather valuable data."

I heard a quick shuddered groan from Sasha, and she ran out of the room.

"Sasha!" I shouted while extending my arm in her direction.

"Nicholas, I will see what arrangements can be made for travel. Come back to my office in a few weeks."

I nodded my head and rushed out of the room to find Sasha.

I stopped her at a landing between the countless levels of stairs. I gripped her arm, "Sasha, I realise you're upset, but we cannot stop now..." She shunned her arm away from my grasp and her voice strained in resentment, "Nicholas, is that all you care about? We are safer here where there is no war. I will not go!" Her bitterness was harsh, but I remained cool, calm, and collected. I inhaled from my mouth as my breath exhaled out of my nose and eased the tension in my shoulders, "I understand your reasoning, as I can see the ins and outs of this situation but thinking on a deeper level than just the surface, we must act now. We don't know how long this war will rage and I don't want what we've built together to flutter away and fade like so many dreams and ambitions." Sasha shielded her eyes, shook her head, and held her breath. Her shoulders rose but stayed frozen. They fell once she spoke, "You forget that this was my dream to begin with and I don't feel comfortable travelling at this time. Please, Nicholas, have patience and don't go. I cannot bear the thought and torment of you across the English Channel as I am here safe. I cannot bear the risk of you dying over your ambitions especially when I am the one who inspired and influenced you on deviant burials. If you're not very careful, something of the kind may happen to you..." She embraced me and buried her head against my chest. Her ear pressed against my chest; she listened to the sound of my heartbeat. I can, even now, still feel the tightness of her embracement. It casts a lingering unease. My heart radiates warmth and understanding of her love for me and my safety, but I too must think. It is out there; I must collect physical data. I must be reticent to discover such doctrine and research. Yes, reticence conduces to effect, blatancy ruins it, and there is much blatancy between Sasha and me. I understand her view, but it lacks, which is a fatal mistake; I have no patience with it. At the same time, I shouldn't be mild and drab. I will not let malevolence and terror, the glare of evil faces, the stony grin of unearthly malice, pursing forms in darkness, and long-drawn, distant horrors stop me! I will travel with Dr Gilders to Romania without Sasha. I answer that I am prepared to consider evidence and accept it if it satisfies me.

Your Gentleman-Scholar,
Nicholas Ainsworth

NEWS
NEWS
NEWS
NEWS
NEWS

18 September 1939
Entry Twenty-One

During time at university, I've taken Latin for the past two years. I was in lecture as Dr Gilders crept through. He politely interrupted the Latin professor and asked to see me. My Latin instructor granted permission and dismissed me. Dr Gilders and I ambled through the university's halls. He briefly glared at me and jammed his hands into his pockets, "Mr Ainsworth, please excuse me from drawing you out of lecture, but I felt it was necessary due to the circumstances." I nodded my head and listened further, "While it is not my business to know, I've noticed you and Sasha are at unease during my class. I imagine it has to do with differences you two share about the excursion to the Transylvanian Alps."

I cleared my throat, "Yes, she will not go, and she is angry that I am going on without her, but these academic pursuits cannot wait."

"Indeed, which is why I've come to tell you, we depart this Friday on the 22nd. I wanted to know if Sasha was coming, but both of you have been silent." My lips sunk and my eyes shifted to him, "And now you know." The professor and I will depart London from King's Cross. I have to make it to the station at 10:30. It will be early but not too early. I must tell Sasha, but I don't know how she will handle it. After all, she is right... This was her dream to begin with, a part of me thinks I should have waited, but what is done is done. I cannot back out now. Too much is at stake.

Nicholas Ainsworth

22 September 1939
Entry Twenty-Two

I am on the train... So many emotions are running through me. I am doing all I can to contain them by writing. I am so grateful I've brought this one comfort as I imagine I will spend a great time alone. I appreciate Dr Gilders is with me but socialising with him is tricky for me. It's not him personally, but it's Sasha. Her and I are so close that she is someone I tend to trust with matters a lot. Especially for this pursuit and journey on deviant burials. It makes things harder. At the same time, I chose to spend time on my own for this. That way, everything is on my terms, there's nothing unexpected that might happen, and I'm in control. This is important to me, as I don't enjoy the pressure or unpredictable elements; however, I am comfortable on my own which is a valuable trait to have and it will help build a great foundation for the work I shall conduct.

Cor, I feel selfish just as I did when I left Irene for university. Though this time, I was not as naïve as to say, "I can never love you." Sasha and I are no longer together, I think, but I know our bond will never be the same. Her face, I saw it briefly through the window as the train departed. She was there on the platform as I caught glimpse. I tore her heart... To be fair though, she tore the ticket which I purchased. The day after Dr Gilders told me when we'd depart, I bought a ticket for Sasha. I presented the ticket to her as I told her when the train was leaving. It was difficult, but I gave her the opportunity to come along. She tore the ticket right in front of my eyes, angry that I was not considerate to wait, and she felt I was not compassionate with her feelings. She called me heartless, a monster because of the pain I've given to her for not listening. She is disappointed and claims I stole away her dream. I will not allow her to steal away this opportunity from me! It is a cruelty that will haunt my days if I do not pursue this expedition of discovery now! Dr Gilders studied the torn and shallow expression on my face. My eyes lingered to the window, I observed my own reflection, and my brown eyes seemed to churn darker into a sombre despair. I sunk my lips into my mouth, "Mr Ainsworth, it was Sasha's choice to not come as it was your choice to go on with this excursion. During my elaborate career as a scholar and professor, I have learned something of value. I once read by Sigmund Freud that 'Love and work are the cornerstones of our humanness.' Do not drown in despair but allow yourself to feel." I chuckled under my breath and pondered the professor's words. Allow myself to feel... It is a difficult matter to engage with. One can feel many things at once where it is not clear what to actually feel. I am in this state, I feel guilty, but this must be done. Sasha's words from university, 'If you're not very careful, something of the kind may happen to you...' I have no clue what she meant by this as I can only interpret a few instances. She is afraid of death for certain, but I will fear no such thing.

Nicholas Ainsworth

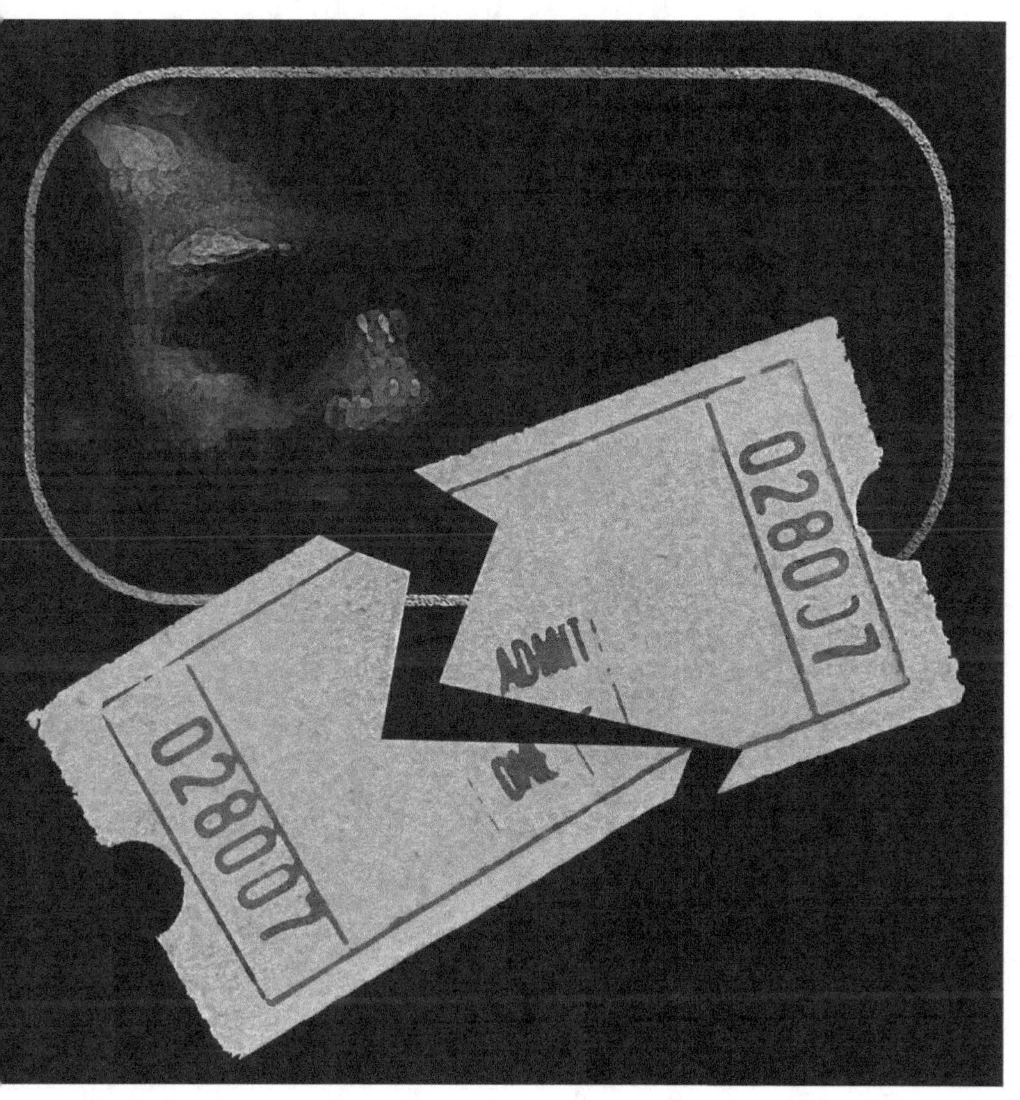

0280011
0280007
ADMIT

13:30

Entry Twenty-Three

Dr Gilders and I are on a ferry from Dover Ferry Port and on our voyage to Calais, France. It is approximately twenty—seven nautical miles and it's the shortest sailing to France. Dr Gilders tells me it's not the shortest point between the two countries though as he argues that the shortest distance across the English Channel is from South Foreland in Kent to Cap Gris Nez in France. The good professor gave me a language book and a bilingual English-Romanian dictionary to learn the Romanian language. This is in my satchel and it will be useful as we travel and make our way to Romania. Also, in my satchel is a sealed envelope with my academic records inside to apply to the University of Bucharest. Dr Gilders advised me before we departed to have my transcripts. It will be necessary if we have any issues gaining access to the university's resources when we conduct to our research phase. The sharp breeze is brisk as my hand while currently writing is pressing hard against this page to write. The wind flaps against my ears as I sit, and Dr Gilders is admiring the scenery. The croak of seagulls sings in my ears and the scent of saltwater basks my nose. It is rather stale, sulphury like dimethyl sulphide, and its scent reminds me how bacteria digest dead phytoplankton.

Such a smell recalls the brief dream I had shortly after writing my entry on the train. There was this gothic-architectural abbey, but I can only recall the parts of the inside. It appeared to be abandoned, much of its hollow winds whistled and gone to decay. Much of its structure collapsed, moisture and dampness of the weather obscured its stones to a moulded grey. I remember distinctly the frayed, shredded, and red curtains dangling by the balcony entrance. The sky in view of the balcony was painted peaks of grey with the tints of the light's delicate colours of red, pink, orange, and yellow. It was magnificent and breath taking. Suddenly, a sense of dread seized my being. A feminine figure in a dress, but I do not know of what kind. It was following me or stalking me which I felt parasitic and negative. It flashed in front of my face, blue like an ominous spectator, and its face resembled Sasha's.

What disturbs me is that Sasha in reality is alive and yet somewhere in my brain portrays her as a spirit. I was frightened by it as if it's pressuring me to do something but at the same time, I am not sure if I should be frightened by it. The ghost's face was plain and conveyed no emotion of any kind. And after some time in reflection and writing this down; I don't know how to react or feel about such a vivid dream.

Your Seafarer,
Nicholas Ainsworth

18:30
Entry Twenty-Four

What a day of travel! Dr Gilders and I have acquired accommodations within Troyes. It is a town within the capital of Aube and in the Grand East region, north-eastern France. It is located southeast of Pairs and directly south of Reims. I have a window view of the dying light. Its rays warm my hand and this page as I am writing. It reminds me of Sasha's tender touch... She was and still is my defender living in the light. I'm missing her, but I cannot wallow in these feelings because it was her choice not to come. She is the one missing out, not me. Dr Gilders has been assisting me in learning Romanian as he is quite good. I've asked him where he has learned his Romanian even though he is not fluent, "Travel, Mr Ainsworth. Travelling the world during my studies has granted me the skills and capabilities to learn such languages and appreciate them. Every gentleman should travel to marvel and appreciate what is around him. Marvel at the natural world and its beauty in which it contains."

As we were speaking, I noticed something in his inner-vest jacket. "What is that you carry professor?" He pulled out the object and placed it upon the table in our room. "My brother's old pistol from the Great War. After he served, he wasn't the same. He was always haunted by something and stared at white walls within his flat. I would come visit him despite his silence and not being able to carry conversations. One day, he left the door to his flat unlocked and unlatched. This unnerved me as I scuttled around. Somewhere I heard a clicking sound followed by a clank. I followed the echoes and there was my brother, sitting cross-legged upon the floor. He held his military pistol in his hand, cocked it back, and let the slide lung forward. He did this repeatedly in a trance, he was slouched, and his eyes glazed in a sombre gloom. 'Sean... Sean... hand me the weapon, 'I mumbled gently. He stopped pulling the slide back; his breaths shallowed, and his limbs shook. He cried out my name, 'Ralph... Ralph...' He broke into a sob and pressed his hands against his ears. He rocked back and forth as the gun was still in his hand and against one of his ears. He was humming loudly as if trying to cancel out whatever it was ravaging inside his head. I embraced him quickly, he dropped the pistol, and I tossed it away with one of my hands. He wailed and his tears stained my dress shirt upon my shoulder. I took this pistol away from him, I've kept it, and supported him by saying to him, 'one day at a time...'"

Dr Gilders stopped speaking. He rubbed his thumb and index finger under his eyes, and his lips sunk. "I'm sorry Mr Ainsworth... It's just speaking about my brother brings heartache as he later drowned in the Thames River. It was labelled as an accident whilst he worked on one of the boats that would transport freight." I nodded my head as Dr Gilders' eyes wandered to meet mine, "So, I have taken the liberty of carrying this pistol for our protection. I am paranoid about the Germans, or, who knows what else we may find." The way which Dr Gilders spoke chilled me. It was grim and monotoned. I understand his fear for the Germans, but his phrasing of 'what else 'troubles me. What else could be out there during a war? I don't think any natural wildlife will be prowling about... Back to my studies.

Yours Truly,

Nicholas Ainsworth

163

164

23 September 1939
12:30
Entry Twenty-Five

Most of the day has been spent travelling and studying in between. The doctor and I are in Grenoble, France which is roughly some 480 km... Perhaps, even more from Troyes. We are almost to the boarder of Italy as we wish to avoid Switzerland and Austria. The further we travel away from the UK, the more I ponder whether Dr Gilders and I shall ever return. When we reach Romania, I wonder how long we shall be gone. Backpacking all this equipment is draining, but it shall assist in building stamina I suppose. Dr Gilders and I are making the habit of speaking in Romanian to each other. My Romanian is still no good as compared to his, but I am learning. It is proper to learn the language of the country one shall stay for long periods of time. The countryside of France almost reminds me of Yorkshire. I miss the luscious fields of home. The calmness and serenity which it grants is no comparison to the bustling city of London.

Nicholas Ainsworth

18:45
Entry Twenty-Six

From the sensuous sound of water lapping against the walls of Venice's ancient palazzi to the intoxicating fragrance of citrus blossoms in Sicily, Italy is a country made for lovers. We are in Verona, Italy! I am disappointed we won't be able to visit Venice or Sicily, but perhaps it is for the best. After all, this country seems to divide its living space with Cupid. Dr Gilders and I have observed young women at bars who often serve cappuccinos with foam poured in a special way so that it looks like a heart and conversations about love rank high up there with food and football. Eh, of course... I believe there is a link between food and love that is very strong in Italy. It has a romance in its countenance. Dr Gilders rambled on to think back to the ancients when Eros and Aphrodite were literally role models for Italians. As for me, I cannot help but think of

Sasha. Italy for me, symbolises freedom, abandonment, and indulgence. Freedom to love and indulgence for pleasure. Abandonment because I feel I am rewarded with what is called a romantic epiphany moment: It's supposed to be an overwhelming sensation of perfection and happiness. Everyone here seems to have mastered such a miraculous art of being happy and of making others happy, but yet I shall replace "happy" with "romantic" because that diction appears just as truthful.

For me personally, I get a jolt of adrenaline observing the city's surroundings. I find Verona very alluring and attractive; there's something about traversing among the stone roads and buildings between the charming alleyways with its bright white sunshine and stoic people that is pure magic. Our temporary villa basks in the golden sunlight as the light hits the church dome from within my view. I gaze upon it through the window as I am writing, and such an image will remain vivid in my memory. The sun is setting beyond the horizon and no matter how many times I see this beautiful play of evening light, the romantic impact is just as strong. The light's rays are of auburn and its tender glow reminisces my defender living in the light. I abandoned her... That is my "romantic" epiphany moment, knowing I abandoned Sasha with my selfish indulgence and impatience. I desire her here... She would love to see such beauty and I long to see how such light dances upon her hair; the golden and red.

Forlorn,
Nicholas Ainsworth

Entry Twenty-Seven

The weather is gloomy. The rain clouds block all the light from the sun. It's just downpouring and we are chilled to the bone. I have not written in about a day because of the treacherous travelling conditions, but it is such a triumph of being closer to Romania. It gives me a glimmer of hope! We are now in Yugoslavia and its capital Belgrade. We found an inn that was kind enough to let us have a room for one night of rest. It has not been kind here. The people seem to be on edge and at unease. The country seems growing intolerable by the aggressive attitudes of the totalitarian regimes. The political scene here is maddening, there is support and pressure with Fascist Italy and Nazi Germany. Dr Gilders is silent, short tempered, and agitated. He despises being here because of the fascism and tension. I don't blame him, but it makes me nervous how he keeps a close hand on that pistol. He tries not to make it too obvious he is carrying arms, but it makes me paranoid. Even as I am writing in our room, he paces back and forth. His hand fondles the handle and sighs breathlessly. I constantly hear the ticking of my watch and I...I—can't think at the moment. I shall write at a time when this dread eases and Dr Gilders stops pacing.

Ainsworth

27 September 1939
Entry Twenty-Eight

The Transylvanian Alps, or as I've heard the locals call it "Southern Carpathian," is the mountainous territory of south central Romania. We are here!

The alps cover the Carpathian Mountain arc from Prahova River valley to the break in which the Timis and Cerna rivers flow. It is most sublime. These alps are classified into three groups of ranges. These beautiful mountains are more elevated, more blocked, and are closer to each other than those mountains in the eastern and western part of Romania. This is exhilarating to me! Hiking these mountains is the crowning moment of a lifetime! And though they are close to each other, accessibility is a challenge ready to be conquered. From our map, Dr Gilders and I calculated that the Transylvanian Alps reach roughly 360 km across central

Romania from the Danube River at the Iron Gate. We estimate the highest peaks are Moldoveanu and Negoiu.

Before these alps, is a very luscious forest which a few locals go hunting. There are also glorious glacial lakes. Dr Gilders and I have made camp somewhere among the mountain range of Moldoveanu. This range is composed of crystalline massifs which sparkle and glitter like diamonds under the sun or moonlight. It is cold, frigid, and windy. I am huddled in my own tent with a lantern burning next to me. From all the research Sasha... and I did, there may be a deviant burial located somewhere within the summit of this mountain or upon Negoiu. I am most eager to continue our journey and collect data. Dr Gilders has his own separate tent and said if we ever need more supplies, the nearest place is Brezoi.

Nicholas Ainsworth

28 September 1939
Entry Twenty-Nine

The wind howled and whispered through the night. I did not get much sleep due to my surroundings but mostly because of my excitement. Dr Gilders in the morning brewed a pot of coffee over the fire. I've never had coffee before, but its scent delighted my senses. I tried a sip from my own cup, but it's so bitter! Still, I slumped it down my throat for energy. I knew it would be a long day of hiking and it sure was. Throughout our time climbing up, the clouds shrouded the entire sky and I could not tell if it was day or night. Along our way, we found valuable resources like coal, iron, and lignite deposits, which would be useful metals in any industry. I can see due to its valuable resources, why scientists would come here for exploration and discovery. Dr Gilders and I did not speak much during our first day of the excursion. The bitter cold kept us focused upon our task. We struck bright orange markers to track our path. This way it's much easier to find our camp and progress further into our exploration. That's all we did mostly was track our path and hiked back to camp. With these markers, it shall save us time. I wonder how Sasha would take these algid temperatures. I miss her... I miss her touch, warmth, and tenderness.

Your Frosted Dweller,
Nicholas Ainsworth

29 September 1939
Entry Thirty

We are sparingly grounding markers as we go along the path to the summit. I believe we will reach the summit soon or in a few days. We've been taking our time to keep sharp eyes on any deviant burial sightings. I need to keep myself mentally aware of what I am looking for when it comes to deviant burials. I shall start with the basics of what I have learned in my studies. I am surprised I haven't really recorded my knowledge in this diary. I get lost in my own little world too much where I annotate constantly in my academic books, but I shall take this moment as a worthy exercise. First, the term 'deviant 'is used to describe burials which deviate from the normative burial rites of a given society, or at a given point in time. I suppose the issue is how the term entails a negative connotation. However, through all the data collected on the spreadsheet, I've a hunch that many "deviant" burials are not in fact burials of people viewed as deviant, but burials given to people based on their circumstances of death. Thus, it is important to note that we cannot assume that such remnants are observed as deviant in any way. We must have an open mind.

Since the nineteenth century western culture and science have interpreted deviancy as an embodied social trait. It was also around that era when the term was applied to medicine, people and even behaviours. For instance, a 'social deviant 'is seen as someone who is somatically different from a 'normal 'individual with a 'normal 'body... [what is bloody normal anyway?]. It was during that century, too, that there was a push in the realm of science to be able to categorise bodily traits as either 'normal 'or 'pathological. 'Normal would entail traits of healthy or secure while pathological would be abnormal, unhealthy, or dangerous and deviant. Studies were often performed on criminals or others to prove that moral character was tied amongst physical appearance and the biology of the body in some form. The original use of the term was actually paleogeographic, meaning 'statistically missing.' For instance, if such remains are found to be missing from cemetery records it would often be found that they were buried in a "special" way, but they would still be invisible in the sense that they were not included in the records. I hope to show a new archaeological meaning and shift on less of an 'invisible ' sense and more of a 'visible 'sense, in that these burials should be studied as special burial practices that are unique from common ones. This would be essential to the phenomenon of deviant burials within the context of their specific culture and time period. So, in searching for such deviant burials in these mountains, I must keep a keen observation for unusual places such as wells, kilns, or pits. If such sites are found, I need to observe any unusual positions such as prone positions or hands tied. Also, any mass burials without any historical documentation of epidemic or war. This also includes strange ritual activity such as cut marks on bones or unusual artefacts associated with the remains.

The glass dome from my lantern is frosted. Bloody hell... I'm too distracted in describing my knowledge and research for deviant burials that I did not see this happen. Only the swift rush of wind sweeping into my tent snapped me back to my surroundings. It is getting too dark to write now. Even with my lantern frosted, the flame in it dims. Need to sleep...

Nicholas Ainsworth

10 October 1939
Entry Thirty-One

This is becoming quite dangerous... I have so much anxiety with the treacherous conditions of Mt. Moldoveanu. We came across wolf tracks imprinted upon the trail as they disappeared straight over the edge of the precipice. I was at a loss because we've been here for quite some time. Dr Gilders and I descended from the summit at about 8,346 feet which I believe is the highest peak in Romania. The trail was stony, a knife – edged with thousand – foot drops on both sides. It ran along the spine of these alps. Yet, this trail was beautiful because of its steep, grassy slopes with wooded ravines which dropped away from the south. However, to the north from the muddy trail, sheer black cliffs plunged down shrouded with mist. We found wolf tracks, huge prints with claw marks as they were dug deeply into the mud. There was a trail of these imprints from the south and right over the edge. I shuddered with terror; the thought that this wolf simply leapt into the abyss, like some kind of supernatural creature...

Eh, here I go again letting ghostly rubbish grip onto me. I'm sure Irene would laugh and take pleasure at my imagination. No, I am a man of logic; a man of science and archaeology. This deathly cold is clouding my judgement and sanity. My sleeping bag barely keeps me warm; it is no better than a blanket... A few of the locals have warned us from Brezoi and said that hiking is difficult in these mountains, with dangerous terrain and fast changing alpine weather. Ill prepared hikers die in the "Făgăraş."

Nicholas Ainsworth

11 October 1939
Entry Thirty-Two

It was twilight when we spotted wolf tracks again! At first, I thought they must be dog tracks, but upon closer examination, I realised they are not and could have not been made by any animal other than a wolf. The tracks are simply too big, bigger than my bloody fist, and the rear paws land squarely in the prints of the front paws. For a few minutes, I stared down into the darkness of the north side, looking for a moment and nothing. Dr Gilders and I were using our lanterns by the moment we found a low stone wind break. It started to snow as the trail was slippery and we stepped cautiously along the cliff edge. A rush of wind brushed against us, it was like walking atop the parapet of a castle, and the stone walls dropping away beneath our feet. I caught glimpses of some cottage far below us on the north side of the ridge. A dark stone hut beside a black lake, that looked to be a place that the sun never reached. It was like a giant, rained, and stained mausoleum.

A couple of hours passed. Farther along the trial, it was steep up and down. Dr Gilders and I spotted a Carpathian animal; chamois, a herd of five on the rocks below us. They grazed upon the tall tufts of grass atop the stone towers. They were distinctive, with a flicker of white on the hindquarters of their black bodies, a face half-white and half-black, and two narrow, curled black horns. Howling erupted and wailed across the rocky cliffs. It chilled and tingled my spine. My teeth clattered from the bitter cold and the chamois were spooked. They scattered instantly, leaping off the towers in different directions, bouncing off ledges and leapt into space.

When we arrived back into camp, Dr Gilders observed my frail and sallow complexion. We sat by our fire as he spoke gravely, "The Transylvanian Alps are home to one of Europe's best – preserved ecosystems. We should remain cautious. The wolf is the most potent symbol. There could be as many as thousands of them in Romania. Not to mention Eurasian brown bears or lynxes. I've read the Eurasian wolf, Canis lupus, is of moderate size, seventy-five to one-hundred-thirty pounds, and ranges over millions of square miles.

Wolves here are a commonplace especially from antiquity through the Middle Ages and into the nineteenth century. To this day, the ensign of Transylvania is a wolf's head, the snapping jaws wide open, with the body of a dragon." I clasped my cup of tea as it warmed my hand, "I imagine stories of wolf attacks are part of the facts and folklore around here" I said. Dr Gilders' eyes gazed into the fire, "Indeed, but do not worry too much. Healthy wolves rarely attack humans, but rabid wolves are horrific beasts of every hearthside story, with good reason." I sipped my tea, "I am glad you brought that pistol then..."

The professor smiled, "Yes, such scientific explanations offer a rational counterweight to the horror, spooky factor, which is palpable here, even if we don't get unnerved by ghost stories." I am glad Dr Gilders is here with me. I do not think I could conquer the trials we have faced thus far in this vast desolate void.

Nicholas Ainsworth

The Antiquarian

15 October 1939
Entry Thirty-Three

We found nothing on Mt. Moldoveanu. We hiked in heavy fog all day, reaching the summit of the 8,317-foot Negoiu, the second highest peak in Romania, around 16:00. Thunder boomed all round us and lightning zigzagged through the black clouds. I knew we had to get off the summit immediately. In the midst of the darkness and atmospheric discharge, Dr Gilders motioned me with his hand and pointed. Flashes of lightning revealed shallow, dry soil and a mound. A gush of wind swept us as we approached the mound. There were cracks scattered upon the soil from its limited nutrients and its inhospitable habitat. Specialised plants peeked from its surface because of their adaptation too little or no soil, the harsh climate conditions, and low water supply. The unforgiving winds even dried out their needles! Although all these factors made the summit habitat seem too difficult to survive, a select few plants persevered. We marked the mound with a bright orange pole and with our shovels began to dig. We dug restlessly as the roar of thunder rumbled and lightning cracked across the sky.

The moisture in the air was thick and heavy as tiny droplets tumbled upon my head. My heart raced erratically, my palms sweated, and my back strained while hunched over. The ground was hard, and my breaths gave out short, sharp chest pains. We did not stop digging, I was possessed by an insatiable vivacious desire. I gasped, the water drops danced upon the spot, made the soil manageable, and dirt scattered across the wind. Some of the dirt flew at my face, but I did not care. I spat out dirt, my eyes strained, and blinked rapidly to combat against the dirt. I spaced out until Dr Gilders' hand gripped and squeezed my wrist. I stopped, dropped the shovel, and stared into the pit. There it was, a skeleton buried face down. I knelt down, reached out my hand, but Dr Gliders swung his arm across my chest to stop, "No!" he shouted. "Do not disturb it! Allow me, and hand me the necessary tools!" In my excited state, I rushed over to our backpacks which had the needed tools and instruments to examine the remains. I snagged them and set them next to Dr Gilders. I saw him go to work and eagerly studied how he proceeded. As the professor worked, he spoke, "The fact the skeleton is buried face down in the grave is consistent with somebody whose behaviour marked them out as odd or threatening within this community!" My eyes blurred from the wind and flashes of lightning. My ears picked up segments of Dr Gilders' voice from the sonorous thunder and flapping of the wind. With gloves, I observed Dr Gilders touching the skull to examine it closer with his instruments, "The corpse's tongue has been cut out and replaced with a flat stone!"

"Why was this done?" I cried while shielding my hand against my brow.

"I speculate perhaps a punishment for spreading malicious accusations. Or, perhaps the corpse was a scapegoat for severe weather. In other words, people disinterring a corpse in order to combat storms, frosts or drought... I need to prepare a sample of the bone to study if any bacteria can be found in the skeleton's bones, there could have been a contagious epidemic at work, for which the deceased had been blamed, leading to the stone being placed in its mouth as punishment!"

As Dr Gilders explained, I prepared a bone vessel for the sample and handed it to him. He collected a fragment of the skull and parts of the radius and ulna bone. Its hands were bound together as they fell. Dr Gilders handed me the vessel and I stored it in his satchel. Lightning struck slightly below the summit as we both jolted from its rupture. Dr Gilders roared and pressed his hand against his brow, "We will come back later to this site! We need to leave now, it's too dangerous to proceed!" I nodded my head as we gathered our equipment and exited the summit. We marched down the trail with intention. Within minutes, a thick mist dropped our visibility to ten feet and the trail transformed into a nightmare via ferrata. Sharp rocks towered with chains and cables bolted to their sheer walls, loomed and peered from the mist. Our progress down was slow, tremulous, and perilous. We moved up and over one gendarme after another. The granite was slippery and wet. The heavy chains dripped with icy water and had we not taken our time; I imagine it would have been impossible to cross down from these slick conditions. The time passed, which I did not know how long, but we made it back to our camp barely finding it in the fog.

I want to go home! I am beyond relief that Sasha was not with us. I don't... I can't bear the thought of what could have happened to her in these conditions. I could never forgive myself if she died, or if I lost her in this grotesque hell. Its deathly hollowed winds wail outside my tent as I am writing. We got what we came for, but I know we must wait until the weather subsides and collect more data. There is no chance right now of getting off this mountain, we must tough out these wretched conditions.

Nicholas Ainsworth

193

18 October 1939
Entry Thirty-Four

I have not seen the sun the past few days. It is difficult to breathe as the mist and fog suffocate my lungs. Ever since the discovery of the burial, I worry about Dr Gilders' condition. He's pale and jabbers constantly to himself as if in a trance. He reminds me of my father. The professor's hands shake and tremble. He isolates himself in his tent, scribbles, ponders, and fondles that pistol of his constantly. It terrifies me to approach him. He does not speak to me, but when he does, he has only asked me once to go to Brezoi for supplies, and shares about an artefact he discovered in the grave. The artefact is a seal, featuring lions with a sword and a bird with a cross. We cannot make out the rest of it as it is too weathered and faded. He never lets me touch anything from the grave or the site which strikes me as odd. He is self-absorbed, almost selfish for not sharing any knowledge, but he claims, "You as the student must observe as this is your first field assignment. Do not worry Mr Ainsworth, you shall excavate the site soon. We will eventually need to analyse the bone sample we've collected. The nearest university to study our sample is Bucharest. While I am away to Bucharest, I wish you to collect more data on the site." I must trust the professor, but there is something malevolent or odious. I cannot pinpoint this dread. Dr Gilders will not depart for Bucharest until he is satisfied with his notes and research. He does not sleep, he barely eats, and I observe the light from his lantern glowing in his tent all through the night. Honestly, his behaviour disturbs me.

Nicholas Ainsworth

20 October 1939
Entry Thirty-Five

Last night, I awoke to wolves or the wind howling all through the night. Footsteps echoed throughout the hollow ravine. These noises startled me. Through my tent, I caught the glimmer of a beaming light. I unzipped my tent, peeked, and saw this light floating amongst the darkness. I peered over to Dr Gilders' tent, but no light shone within. I strapped on my boots, lit my lantern, and exited my tent. The wind brushed against me algid and chilled. My breath was visible as I scuttled around. My heart raced, I bit my lips, and gazed upon the light. The light dipped, dropped, and dissipated as I got closer. My breath shallowed and my body jolted by a sudden shatter. Its sound reverberated across the ravine followed by a click, and I froze. My lantern swayed and, in its light, caught glimpses of a figure. My eyes strained and trembled between the light and darkness. I shuddered, "Ah, Dr Gilders... You gave me a fright." The figure before me was him as he wobbled over trembling. His boots crushed and crackled glass. I realised then, he dropped his lantern which radiated the light from earlier. He had dark red circles under his eyes, they flayed as he dangled the pistol by his side. "Strange cries of lost and despairing wanderers wallow across these alps," he muttered. My brows squinted as I rose my lantern higher above. Dr Gilders' eyes wandered like he didn't know I was in front of him. His mouth maundered, but in ravings I could not comprehend. This still bothers me... I had to take him back to his tent but in a fashion that was almost like I was herding cattle. He gnashed his teeth, his body felt cold, and his skin sweated. I believe we've been out here too long. Now, Dr Gilders is very ill. If he does not improve, I will take him back into the village.

Nicholas Ainsworth

22 October 1939
Entry Thirty-Six

Dr Gilders' health fluctuates but he still obsesses over the discovery of the burial. At times, his skin loses its natural colour, or he is too vibrant. He complains there is from time to time, a sudden surge of wind outside his tent. Though his tent is intact, I examined it for any holes. There is no way any wind can blow within. The tent is completely secured. "Are you sure you don't have chills from being sick?" I'd ask him. "Perhaps, you are right Mr Ainsworth, but there is an expanse at night with the wind... I feel it." Dr Gilders inspects the seal while alone in his tent. He is currently deciphering the inscriptions and tells me there are two phrases. He believes the language is not based on a Latin-Romanian alphabet. We will take the artefact and the bone samples to the University of Bucharest soon.

The Antiquarian

Nicholas Ainsworth

23 October 1939
Entry Thirty-Seven

Morning's light is shrouded by the eclipsing clouds. I did not get many hours of sleep. I dreamt of myself desperately fleeing from a black object within the abbey where I dreamt of the ghastly figure of Sasha. In my dream, I was in an extreme state of fear. In the distance, this pursing apparition moved in a strange manner and with incredible speed. Almost like the woman in the white dress. I repeatedly clambered over debris of the abbey's ruins before collapsing to the ground in sheer exhaustion. The bright moon shone its light illuminating the balcony entrance. The object chasing me revealed itself in the moonlight as a figure pale, fluttering in a white dressing gown. My dream abruptly ended, but each time I close my eyes, the scenario progresses, although the vision immediately vanishes when I open my eyes. For the remaining night, I have been reading and studying Romanian to distract my mind. As I was studying, I listened to the sound of scurrying outside in the direction away from my tent. I thought it was an animal of some kind prowling about. My lantern stayed lit the entire night and, in the dawn, as I am writing. I am afraid to close my eyes again and see this cadaverous figure. My neck tingles numb as if this spirit looms its icy breath upon me. The figure is white, faceless every time I shut my eyes.

Nicholas Ainsworth

26 October 1939
Entry Thirty-Eight

I wallow in gloom that I have had not the strength to write in my diary for the past few days. After some time in reflection of recent events, I have the will to write everything down and by doing so; I hope it will mend the wounds in my mind. A few moments after writing my previous entry, I hiked up the trail to the summit. I knew Dr Gilders would be there as he made it a daily routine to observe the burial site. A gunshot echoed throughout the mountain as a gap between the clouds peeked in the morning light. I rushed, fled, and heard the professor's shrieks. He was in pain, rabid barking reverberated followed by a set of gunfire. The light casted a shadow. Before me as I arrived, a white, large Eurasian wolf laid on top of Dr Gilders. The professor pushed with his might, but the corpse could not budge. I dashed to him, "No, stay away!" the professor commanded. I halted; blood mixed with white foam seeped out from the wolf's mouth. Terror gripped my heart, my eyes anchored frozen, and I saw blood dripping from Dr Gilders' right wrist. The wolf had left its bitten imprint on him. "Do not come near... me." He suspired breathlessly. The wolf tilted over, Dr Gilders crawled, and wobbled upon his feet. The light gleamed as he turned his head to me and spoke, "I am sorry Mr Ainsworth. I believe this is the end. We are too deep in these mountains, and there is no time. It appears I have been infected by this beast and I have very limited time before this brain of mine rots. You will find my notes in my tent, they have the information you will need, and please use them as you will but with caution." He limped over to his satchel, wrapped it around his body, and pressed on towards the edge of the cliff.

"No!" I ran but Dr Gilders cocked back the pistol. I stopped as he pointed it at me, "Do not come any closer Nicholas. It is better this way. These artefacts will die with me. Do not let my death be in vain. Promise me you will stay in Romania, go to Bucharest, and finish our work." I paused... Dr Gilders never once called me by my first name. It made me realise the severe gravity of the situation and the dire need to complete our research.

Saliva lodged in my throat as I swallowed it, my lips sunk, and I made my vow.

"I promise."

"Good, when a real man makes a promise, he keeps it. Every man knows that his word is as powerful as his actions. Farewell, Mr Ainsworth."

His body fell over the misty and rocky cliffs. I knelt down upon my knees, my eyes watered, and the sunlight blinded my vision. The corpse of the wolf laid before me, but it blurred from my distorted vision. I am alone. The days here are getting colder, and it was too inhospitable to stay in the Transylvanian Alps. I cannot not survive the upcoming climate changes there with the darker months approaching. I have what research is needed from Dr Gilders' journal and notes. I have settled in at an inn within Bucharest. I will read and study the professor's notes.

Mournfully,
Nicholas Ainsworth

30 October 1939
Entry Thirty-Nine

I am pleased to be writing this entry by the mantled fireplace on the ground floor of the inn. Its warmness and this breakfast comforts me as compared to my chilled and solitary quarters upstairs. This dish is just delightful! It is a traditional Romanian breakfast called "Omletă țărănească" or, "peasant omelette." It includes an omelette, fried eggs, boiled eggs, mixed with all sorts of vegetables and meat. The omelette is made with ham and tastes smoky. It's a bit heavy, but it will help to keep me going through the rest of the day.

Dr Gilders' notes are baffling and mysterious. He has many hunches which I believe will be answered through more extensive study at the University of Bucharest [Universitatea din Bucuresti.]. I don't have access to the university's resources considering Dr Gilders is now deceased... I must gain some sort of admissions to the university to access their archives and laboratories. I will investigate what requirements are needed for admission into the university. I'm relieved Dr Gilders advised me beforehand to bring my academic transcripts. In the meantime, what I find interesting about Dr Gilders' research are his depictions about the artefact seal he found in the grave. He writes:

"The seal comprises the coats of arms of Moldavia, Wallachia, and Transylvania: in the middle, on a shield the Moldavian urus, above the Wallachian eagle between the sun and moon holding a cross in its beak. Below the Transylvanian coat of arms, two meeting, standing lions supporting a sword, treading on seven mountains. The Moldavian shield is held by two crowned figures" (Gilders).

I know Dr Gilders told me about only some of the details on this artefact, but not all. He failed to mention the urus and the type of coat of arms the artefact derives from. Furthermore, he wrote down the two inscriptions from the seal:

"First, circular, in Slavonic using Romanian ~~Cyrillic~~ alphabet: 'IO MIHAILI UGROVLAHISCOI VOEVOD ARDEALSCOI MOLD ZEMLI, 'need to investigate translations through UB's archives... Second inscription placed along a circular arc separating the Wallachian coat from the rest of the heraldic composition, 'I ML BJE MLRDIE'" (Gilders).

It seems the language the seal depicts struck Dr Gilders. He scratched out the type of Romanian alphabet he might have believed it was in. I need to confirm if the language is Romanian Cyrillic, but I don't have the artefact with me! It's lost with Dr Gilders' corpse and the bone sample he had. The University of Bucharest [UB] must have something in their library archives about this language. I still don't know why Dr Gilders didn't let me keep the artefacts we found. It makes no sense... I'm still not through with reading and studying his journal and notes. I hope to find more answers than questions soon.

Yours Truly,
Nicholas Ainsworth

31 October 1939
Entry Forty

My fingers are chilled to the bone as I write. I can't stop shuddering and it's not just from the algid wind. Earlier today, I traversed to UB, but while on my way, I discovered a massive cemetery. It's called Bellu Cemetery as the gated sign read, "Șerban Vodă Cemetery." The cemetery is opened from 08:30 to 20:00. So, it wasn't like I was trespassing but ambling through this plot of land intrigued me. I imagine this graveyard covers roughly about fifty-four acres, but yet I believe it a most authentic cultural attraction in Bucharest. The clouds were grey, but the sunlight peeked through the sky and sometimes blinded me. While I was blinded by the sun's rays, I thought I saw someone by an isolated grave. I rubbed my eyes to combat against the light, but as I reopened my eyes, they became irritated by the friction of my hands. My vision waved and whoever was there was gone. It disturbed me because how can someone move that quick? I thought about the figures which haunted my dreams such as the young woman in the white dress or the apparition in the abbey ruins. This thought made me shudder as I scuttled to where I saw the figure. The grave itself wasn't as worn as some of the other graves and monument stones. Chiselled upon the tombstone read:

"Florina Dumitru

1911-1925"

This saddened me because of how young this person was. This person died at age fourteen and I'm eighteen going on nineteen in a few months. My sadden thought was disturbed by the sunlight shrouding behind the clouds. The light upon the grave dissipated and startled me. I panicked and studied my watch. My ears caught the sound of its ticking and my watch showed 13:15. I rushed out of the cemetery and eventually reached the university. I didn't realise how long it took me to arrive at the university. My feet were sore from all the walking as I glared at my watch and it was 14:03. It took me almost an hour, I was so drained from all the walking that I didn't pay attention to my surroundings. My mind only focused on getting to the admission's office. I needed to know what requirements and what paperwork to submit for my application. I asked one of the admission's clerk about admissions for the upcoming term. She seemed shocked about my English accent speaking the Romanian language, "Scuzati-mă," I said to her. She told me the deadline was fast approaching by mid-November. I also learned from her that as a foreigner, I am required to take the Romanian placement test. Dreadfully, today was the last day to take such a test as the last session was scheduled at 15:00. This aroused me and I hesitantly filled out all the necessary paperwork in great haste. By the time I finished, the admission's clerk placed me in the exam room to take my language placement test. I had no time to prepare and I was shaking like a tree in the winter wind, vulnerable, and afraid. This application wagers on everything I've worked for. It will take a few weeks to know my results. I will travel back to the university to check on the status of my application.

Dreadfully, Nicholas Ainsworth

10 November 1939
Entry Forty-One

I have been too anxious to write, but I can finally write from this feverish pen that I have been accepted into the University of Bucharest! I placed out of the second semester in my knowledge of Romanian. I am beyond proud of myself given the tragic and unfortunate circumstances. Oh, Sasha and Dr Gilders you would both be so proud! I miss them. I'm doing all in my strength to push my academic endeavours, but every time when I discover something or learn something new, my mind wanders to memories with them. I wonder how Sasha is doing. Throughout these past weeks, I have been tempted to send a letter to Sasha and write to her of the wretched news. Dr Gilders' death, the triumph in continuing his work, and our work. In my hopes to write to her, I withdraw because of the fear of her never responding. I do not know her thoughts.

This is the first in a while I have actually reflected on everything with Sasha. I still love her. She is the living light in my soul as when this is all over, I hope this light shall safeguard me and be the motivation for the journey home. I miss my country. I miss Yorkshire and London. I miss Uncle Henry and even my Aunt Helena. Sometimes, I wonder if all my strives in academics are worth the lost moments I could have had with them if I decided to stay. If I would have known the bitter isolation I would feel in this country, I don't think I would have gone. It is too late for me and I promised my dearest mentor Dr Gilders to finish what was started. I cannot break my solemn vow!

Nicholas Ainsworth

1 December 1939
Entry Forty-Two

It is wonderful now that I am a student at UB. The upcoming term starts in January, but I have decided to get a head start in Dr Gilders 'research. After spending hours at UB's archives, I discovered some valuable information about the language the artefact seal could be. I believe Dr Gilders 'hunch about the seal's inscriptions are correct! The Romanian Cyrillic alphabet was the alphabet that was used to write the Romanian language before the 1860s, when it was officially replaced by the Latin-based Romanian alphabet, however, Cyrillic remained in occasional use until the 20s, mostly in Russian-ruled Bessarabia. This is so exciting! The good thing is Romanian Cyrillic ceased only a little over ten years ago. I may be able to find other resources or speak to other faculty or staff about this language. I must gather more data first before inquiring to others about my research. I am weary of sharing such knowledge with others. This protectiveness of my work makes me chuckle. It reminds me of when I first met Sasha and how protective she was of her journal from me. She would love such knowledge especially with this language's relationship with Russian Bessarabia. Ugh, I cannot focus on this now... I must continue my work!

Passionately,
Nicholas Ainsworth

11 December 1939
Entry Forty-Three

This infernal language is driving me mad! Yes, mad! I spent all my past days between the inn and the UB library. Traveling back and forth between my solitary quarters and UB are taking its toll. All is shrouded with hard, white snow. The air is algid, but no wind sweeps. It's just desolated and cold. The warmth of the library revives me enough to continue my ambition. It is getting more difficult to write in this diary. It is the only solace I have in this place. I feel almost alienated from everyone. This, I feel, is mostly my doing. This academic endeavour is draining all the pleasures I once enjoyed. Pitiful enough, I cannot recall what it was I once enjoyed. The only thing that drives me is to see this study concluded because of my vow to Dr Gilders and the motivation of coming home. I recall what Sasha once said to me that "Home is where the heart is." My heart is with her and I feel empty, hollow, and bitter. The sooner I finish this task, the sooner I can come home to Sasha, work things out, and mend our bond. Today is her birthday... I am close... So close in deciphering the secrets this seal holds in its language. I shall write again if I discover more knowledge.

Effortlessly Yours,
Nicholas Ainsworth

30 December 1939
Entry Forty-Four

or, I've done it! I've bloody done it! These past two months were gruelling, but my efforts and labours have paid off! The seal! The first inscription in Slavonic uses the Romanian Cyrillic alphabet and translates as "IO Michael Wallachian Voivode of Transylvanian and Moldavian Lands." IO is the contraction of a title used mainly by the royalty (hospodars or voivodes) in Moldavia and Wallachia, preceding their names and the complete list of titles. The second inscription could be translated as, "Through the very Grace of God." Based on this evidence, the seal artefact must derive anywhere from the sixteenth and nineteenth centuries! I still need to narrow down this time gap... It's so infuriating! Just when I complete one piece of a complicated puzzle, something else takes its place. I also need to research this Michael Wallachian

Voivode. If I find more information on this royal, it can narrow down the time gap. It makes sense to find such an artefact in the Transylvanian Alps considering this royal was from Transylvania and the Moldavian lands. I've scoured Dr Gilders' journal and notes, but his last remaining entries are a bunch of scribbles. It's no worse than a doctor prescribing medication! I mean, Dr Gilders' handwriting is messy, but it's not as messy as the gibberish he wrote in his last entries. He was unwell and from observing him, he was not himself. I still don't know why he took the artefacts with him. Was he trying to protect me? If so, from what then? Too many questions that need answering!

Anxiously,
Nicholas Ainsworth

12 May 1940
Entry Forty-Five

Too many distractions and drained of energy. This semester was brutal and derailed me from writing in my diary and continuing my research on Michael Wallachian Voivode. Despite the setback, I am now an archaeologist and earned my degree in archaeology! With my credits earned from the University of London and at the University of Bucharest, I have done it! It's all a matter of the paperwork and for my transcripts to follow through with communication between both universities. My degree shall ship back to London and wait for me at home with Uncle Henry. I imagine Sasha has earned her degree this month too as I recall... We were to graduate together. I wish I could see the expression on my uncle's face once my degree arrives, but I must stay here and continue my research. My funds are slowly dwindling, but it can last for about one more year if I am cautious with spending. I hope my degree will not be delayed due to the impact of the war raging on. Romania has remained neutral, but I don't know how long this will last. The situation in Romania is rapidly changing throughout this year as well as domestic political upheaval may undermine this stance. Fascist political forces such as the Iron Guard have risen in popularity and power, urging an alliance with Nazi, Germany and its allies. Romania's two main guarantors of territorial integrity, France and Britain are crumbling. Newspapers from Romania's Epoca wrote that France may fall to Germany. I pray my countrymen and France will pull through for the hope that Romania may stay neutral.

Yours Hopefully,
Nicholas Ainsworth

25 May 1940
Entry Forty-Six

My research into Michael Wallachian Voivode is steady. He was known as "Mihai Viteazul," "Mihai Bravu," or, "Michael the Brave." He was the Prince of Wallachia as Michael II, Prince of Moldavia, and the true ruler of Transylvania. His reign over Transylvania was from October 1599 to September 1600. This narrows down the time gap of the seal artefact! The seal Dr Gilders and I discovered is a seal of Michael the Brave during his personal union of Wallachia, Moldavia and Transylvania. He is considered one of Romania's greatest national heroes and regarded by Romanian nationalists as a symbol of Romanian unity. His reign marked the first time all principalities inhabited by Romanians were under the same ruler. I will dive further into anything I can find about Michael the Brave. Bugger, I wish I could study the bone sample from the remains! I wonder what association the deviant burial discovered in the Transylvanian Alps has with Michael the Brave... I recall what Dr Gilders said when we discovered the burial, "I speculate perhaps a punishment for spreading malicious accusations. Or, perhaps the corpse was a scapegoat for severe weather." The first reason sounds most interesting, but I cannot make assumptions. I must find evidence and collect more data!

Yours Ecstatically,
Nicholas Ainsworth

8 June 1940
Entry Forty-Seven

This is frustrating!   My mind is scattered everywhere! It feels as if what I found here in the library archives is not as potent as before. There is nothing more about Michael the Brave that can help me discover the secret of the deviant burial found on Mt. Negoiu. I believe now is the time to prepare for another excursion to the Transylvanian Alps. The weather will certainly not be as treacherous as before with summer vastly approaching. I need to find Dr Gilders' satchel, collect the bone sample, and run tests on it at the university. This task will be much more difficult than before due to various reasons. One, I am alone. Dr Gilders is not here and two, tensions in Romania are high. There are rumours that the German assault on northwest Europe and the battle of France is ruthless. It has almost been a few weeks and there is no telling when it will end. The longer the battle rages on there, the more that fear consumes my mind. I am paranoid that the worst will happen if my countrymen and France do not come through with victory. I must utilise the time I have now, or otherwise, I may never have this chance again.

My progress with my research has not been as fruitful. Not only because of this war, my frustration with hitting the books, but also because of my mind. The more I push with my academics, the memories with those who are dear to me flood and haunt me. I can't get the horrid image out of Dr Gilders throwing himself off the summit. His sickly pale complexion fevers my mind and I am terrified about how our excursion affected his mind. I do not want the same fate for me when or if can I go back to Mt. Negoiu. He was as pale as a corpse. Flashes of the sunlight shining upon him right before he jumped festers my brain. I've never witnessed someone committing suicide. With this thought, I also think of my mum. I imagine her corpse hanging from a rope in my old home. The rope sways, her hair dangles and shrouds her face. The house is pitch black and I only see the mere shadow of her. I hear my watch as it ticks in time with her rope swaying. This happens when I sleep and scream from waking. All is silent except for my watch ticking.

Sometimes, I hide my watch in my desk drawer because I cannot bear its sound. It makes me think of the time that has passed. The other nightmares I've had with cadaverous figures, the ominous young woman in the white dress, and Sasha as the ghost who I sometimes see in the ruined abbey. Then, I think about Sasha and the memories I had with her. How Aunt Helena and Irene said, 'don't let her go.' Sasha has my heart, and I haven't let her go... She's still in my heart because I grieve. How this grief makes my life experiences and memories so much worse. Now, I really understand how Irene felt about me. Grief is this many – tentacled monster. I could be having a totally ordinary day on some pretty lake and all at once, it grabs me and tries to tug me under. Eventually, it tips me overboard less and less often but with no less force. I don't know if this thought makes anything I am going through or went through easier or better. I'm sure it doesn't, but it's worth writing because I find it worth writing myself. This diary is the one comfort I have and will only have. The kind of solace writing can bring to someone ties a special fellowship for me with this diary.

Sincerely Yours,

Nicholas Ainsworth

231

29 June 1940
Entry Forty-Eight

Romania grows despondent. Recently, diplomacy is resolving a series of territorial disputes in a manner unfavourable to Romania, resulting in the loss on most of the territory gained in the wake of the Great War. The popularity of Romania's government is plummeting, further reinforcing the fascist and military faction. The Germans have occupied France. This terrifies me not only for my safety, but my plans for my excursion back to the Transylvanian Alps. There is also the issue of the funds. Affording the equipment on my own is a challenge but I will persuade the university to grant funds for this expedition. With the funds, I can afford the supplies I need. I need to reach the summit and collect another bone sample from the burial site.

Nicholas Ainsworth

The Antiquarian

233

6 July 1940
Entry Forty-Nine

Receiving the funds needed is proving rather difficult! The board is not too keen on investing the money because of the tensions between the war and how it affects Romanian governmental affairs. I must keep trying... I have taken a position at UB's library. I now catalogue many of the manuscript libraries of the colleges at the university. This helps my finances, but very little... I'm getting too melancholy. In the newspapers, I've read that a Soviet ultimatum was given to Romania. Romania has agreed to give up Bessarabia and northern Bukovina. Two – thirds of Bessarabia are combined with a small part of the Soviet Union to form the Moldavian Soviet Socialist Republic. Fear grips and strangles me for what the results of such a loss to Romania will do. Knowing that many Romanian nationalists admire a hero such as Michael the Brave and how he unified Romania many centuries ago, will I think, cause a catalyst for Romania's entry into the war. Despite all this dread, I must stay committed to my work. With the time it will take to get the funds approved, travel on foot to the alps, and back to Bucharest... I hope the war does not come here.

Nicholas Ainsworth

20 July 1940
Entry Fifty

The university delays my progress! That is outrageous and unfair! They know nothing of what I sacrificed on a personal account of what I had to do to come here. I have been patient, reasonable, and understanding of their situation. This is similar to how Dr Gilders almost cancelled our expedition to this country when the war began. I must convince them... I've argued valid points on why this expedition to the alps would be beneficial to the university and to Romania herself. This is about the unity of Romania as my research entails about Michael the Brave who unified Romania. I argued this would raise Romanian morale considering how Romanian lands are stripped by the Soviets. These are turning into dark times and Romania needs a ray of light. Let the knowledge I gain from deviant burials be such a light just as the living light that burns within my heart for the one, I love. I must accomplish this for Sasha, Dr Gilders, my countrymen, and myself. My own personal money is running low... I am running out of time.

Nicholas Ainsworth

1 August 1940
Entry Fifty-One

Those snobby prunes officially denied me! They admired my ambition, dedication, and passion to the subject. They said it was even noble that a foreigner such as I strive for such knowledge and discovery on a mystery about Michael the Brave. They just cannot give the funds because of the war and tensions in Romania. Their denial of the expedition reminds me of Sasha turning away from the first expedition to the alps. No bloody war will stop me! Even as I am working at the university's libraries, I still do not have enough funds for a full-fledged expedition. I must acquire a basic pack of supplies. When I do, it shall be my burden. I need to reach the summit and collect another bone sample. I plan to leave Bucharest by the end of August or the beginning of September.

Ambitiously,

Nicholas Ainsworth

239

10 September 1940
Entry Fifty-Two

This will be the last time I will write from this cosy spot by the fireplace on the ground floor of the inn. I will miss the scrumptious delights of the traditional Romanian breakfast being served. I will depart just before dawn rises tomorrow. It will be quite a long journey on foot from here to the Transylvanian Alps, but I must admit that I do not have the enlightened spark that once shone when I entered the alps the first time. Swarths of emotions impale every inch of my being. I am despondent and numb. This morning, I picked up the newspaper from the city. I never pay attention to the paper when I traverse back to the inn because I like to sit and read when eating my breakfast. While eating my peasant omelette, my eyes glanced over, and randomly at the newspaper. I dropped my fork and it crashed against my plate. My hands convulsed in sheer terror while my breath shuddered. The headlines read clearly to me, "Londra bombardată de bombardiere Germane," or, "London blitzed by German bombers." I will copy and translate the article for my own therapeutic reason:

"The German air force has unleashed a wave of heavy bombing raids on London, killing hundreds of civilians and injuring many more. The Ministry of Home Security said the scale of the attacks was the largest the Germans had yet attempted. 'Our defences have actively engaged the enemy at all points, 'said a communique issued this evening. 'The civil defence services are responding admirably to all calls that are being made upon them. A five-storey building, housing civilians, had been hit and there were a number of civilians trapped beneath the debris.' The first raids came towards the end of the afternoon, and were concentrated on the densely populated East End, along the river by London's docks. About three-hundred bombers attacked the city for over an hour and a half. The entire docklands area seemed to be ablaze as hundreds of fires lit up the sky. Once darkness fell, the fires could be seen more than ten miles away, and it is believed that the light guided a second wave of German bombers which began coming over at about 20:30. The night bombing lasted over eight hours, shaking the city with the deafening noise of hundreds of bombs falling so close together there was hardly a pause between them. One bomb exploded on a crowded air raid shelter in an East London district. In what was described as 'a million to one chance, 'the bomb fell directly on the three-foot ventilation shaft – the only vulnerable place in a strongly – protected underground shelter which could accommodate over one – thousand people. About fourteen people are believed to have been killed and forty injured, including children."

There is more written in the paper about this, but I can't finish... As I recorded the contents of this article, horrid images filled my mind. London as a shambled ruin. Sasha, Uncle Henry, and Aunt Helena... Are they stranded, injured amongst all rubble? Or worse... Are they dead? The very nature of this gloom swallows me whole. I see it as truly malignant and makes me see it as less a part of me. It infects me like a disease which turns into this all – absorbing spectre of some kind. Here I am, writing about my own self-destruction as something supernatural. This is unlike me, it's important, but not easy. This is good that I'm writing about it. It's something I really don't think to express about aside from medical professionals. Though I've never been to one, but I would imagine such darkness is difficult to convey because of its euphemisms and vagaries when its essence is not acute. People can respond so strangely sometimes, and I feel this uncanniness inflicted upon me. But this is healthy and good to share, is it not?

Nicholas Ainsworth

11 September 1940
Entry Fifty-Three

There are delays while on my journey back to the Alps. Considering the uneasy turmoil of the Iron Guard, violent outbreaks are happening. The path that I took to arrive from the Alps to Bucharest about a year ago is blocked and not as safe. In the vast woods toward Gulia, a violent mob is outside. I cannot travel through Gulia without the likelihood of being caught in the middle of it. So, I decided to retrace my steps on a detour. I am somewhat lost as the sun is dying down. I've made a small camp in the middle of these woods. I believe I am somewhere just outside Bucharest. These woods are beautiful, serene, and dense. The tall, luscious trees bend and cave in. The dark green leaves and bushes surrounding them appear evergreen. The dirt pathways are shrouded with a mixture of broken twigs and green leaves. The slight breeze whispers to me as if

enchanting me under an intrinsic spell. What a wasted
day of travel.

Nicholas Ainsworth

12 September 1940
Entry Fifty-Four

Dawn rises as I write. It is the most delicate view I've seen in a while as the light dances upon the crowded trees. It's soothing but doesn't rid the torments on my mind. I must get a move on as I do not want to waste daylight, but my dream... I am afraid. I dreamt of the ballroom, my former home as a romantic ruin. The place where my love for Sasha fully bloomed was now a shadow of its former self. It makes me recall what I wrote earlier in one of my entries, "It was ethereal in the sense that it made me feel like I'm in an empty palace and there is a beautiful lady. One who keeps dreaming of a handsome man in beautiful places, but he turns out to be death." From a first-person point of view, I saw Sasha there as the moody, ambient melody we danced to echoed throughout the halls in my dream. She wore the same dress from the informal dance many years ago. While the melody played, we embraced each other. For a brief moment, all the life and blood within my body flowed vivaciously and brought me to life. An overwhelming thirst and passion filled me as my ears rang. The melody muffled as I closed my eyes. My point of view shifted to third and I saw her and me. My ears were consumed by the beatings of the heart; her heart. Sasha was a human shadow, but the pulse of her heart lit as bright as a fluorescent beacon. The red elixir circulated throughout her body. She is my defender of living light who breathes and radiates its warmth and vulnerability into my soul. Death cannot touch the love between us and our memory. As I gazed at us in an endless trance, the moonlight reflected against the giant mirror in the room. The same one where I wrote about catching a glimpse of Sasha and I dancing and how that moment is forever engraved into my mind. The moonbeams shone on the glass and reflected the ghosts of all who were in the ballroom around us. Somehow, this image transmits a sombre sensation that I've lost everything and everyone. Things my heart once knew and yearns to remember. Snowflakes fluttered from the gap above the ruined ceiling. The moonlight shone in through each and every window. Its light dwindled, I saw myself alone, and wallowed in the hollow, dead quiet halls.

I recall the lingering feeling after this moment as the dream faded. I still feel the marble stone floors of this ruin beneath me and they are colder than ice. It makes me tremble more than the small but mystical pond that lies before me. This tiny body of water is inconspicuous to me. It's thickly layered with green, gloating algae. I am drawn to it, but I don't know why. There's a mysterious, fluorescent, and unexplainable phenomenon around its vicinity. There are remnants of a fire nearby, perhaps for ritualistic purposes... There aren't any animals or wildlife that come around here. It makes me weary as I am tempted to touch its fluid surface. Something stops me as it feels like I'm being watched. This dread stops me from going closer to it, like it's something forbidden, but I'm curious...

In Dascălu... It's about fifteen to sixteen km from where that pond is... It's now the afternoon. I was interrupted by a whispered voice from trying to write this entry earlier. A woman's voice said, "Neprimită" like she was right next to me. When I heard it, the voice seemed so serious when she said this to me, but nobody was there. The word "neprimită" means "you are not welcomed here." I'm doubtful if that was the word I heard, or if it was the breeze shuddering my spine that made me think someone said this to me. I don't know, but glad to be away from that place. In all my time living in Bucharest, I never knew such a place existed like that pond. The forests here are eerie, strange, but beautiful and fascinating. It gives me chills ambling through them.

Yours Truly,
Nicholas Ainsworth

13 September, 1940
Entry Fifty-Five

It hasn't stopped raining... I'm in Snagov warming myself inside a small local tavern. I'm drenched and my teeth are clattering. I'm dry enough to write but still damp. My lungs feel heavy and snot dangles from my nose. I keep rubbing my fingers underneath my nose and wiping the snot against my trousers. Ugh, I'm fearful of the possibility of getting sick. I'm eating and sipping on some broth. It's a soup which the Romanians call, "Ciorba de Bureti." Or, translated as, "Mushrooms Soup." As a country pierced by the Carpathian Mountains and in many ways defined by the climate the mountains provide, and the dense forests from my experience, this soup is the best I've ever tasted. It is in places like these where some of the tastiest mushrooms in the world grow, I believe. My server said these mushrooms are, "Boletus, the rarest and most sought after species, also makes the best soup when cooked together with legumes and seasoned with parsley and sour cream. You will never find such mushrooms at a farm as they can only grow by themselves in the wild." Knowing this, simply adds to my delight and flavour for the dish.

As I am multitasking between writing and devouring this delicious soup, I hear gossip among the tavern's patrons. Many Romanians are upset about the divide of Transylvania. Apparently, Germany and Italy mediated a compromise between Romania and the Kingdom of Hungary. Hungary received a region referred to as 'Northern Transylvania, 'while 'Southern Transylvania ' remained part of Romania. I hear conversation snippets about the Treaty of Craiova, Southern Dobruja where Bulgaria had lost after the Romanian invasion during the Second Balkan War, was ceded to Bulgaria under pressure from Germany. Despite the recent acquisition of these territories, they were inhabited by a majority of Romanian, native speakers. So, naturally, many Romanians see them as historically belonging to Romania, and the fact that so much land is lost without a fight shatters many. This terrifies me because these series of territorial losses this year makes me ponder what side of the war Romania will choose... I pitched a room upstairs for tonight.

Your Weary Traveller,
Nicholas Ainsworth

The Antiquarian

255

8 October 1940
Entry Fifty-Six

I cannot help but quiver in fear of Nazi Germany taking over the country of Romania. It is too late for me to flee the country, for many of the soldiers have occupied too many cities. In Snagov, I was delayed because I became ill from the hours spent traveling amongst the downpour. The innkeeper took well care of me and nursed me back to health. By the time I departed, it was already October. I arrived in Ploesti when the Germans came. Countless German troops invaded Romania. They quickly seized Ploesti. During the occupation I got lost until I wandered here in Câmpina. I can still hear the engines of the German tiger tanks, as they shot many of the buildings. I can hear the roaring within my skull, the sound of planes as they soared above and dropped their bombs along with the foot soldiers as they stormed out of their grey trucks and shouted in their

German language. The screaming of the people being shot down still haunts me even after I was fortunate enough to escape.

I have found shelter in a folly house, and miraculously this house is in the form of a castle. When I came to this place I couldn't see much, it was already dark, but from what I have seen of the outside it has three towers made of stone. The main entrance is a huge door made of stone and has a fixed diamond bearing. On the outside of the door there is some kind of written sign that is engraved with an odd symbol however, I do not know of it. Strangely, this door also has two texts written upon it as well. The words are in Latin and say, "Pro fide et Patria" and "e pur si muove." These translations I believe are "for faith and country" (Pro fide et Patria) and the second text is "and yet it moves" (e pur si muove). The door swivelled around a central axis, allowing access, and above it, an "all – seeing eye" in a triangle, surrounded by rays. The main entrance to this castle was also guarded by two stone thrones, and symbols of divine nobility. Opening the stone door was eerily easy to open which made me feel sort of uneasy upon entering. It was dark as if no one had ever lived here in quite some time. I couldn't see a thing nor could I find a light switch anywhere. I spread my arms about to feel my way around, but within seconds I became alarmed because there was nothing around me to touch. I kept moving forward taking precious time to find my way.

I scuttled to my far left and suddenly bumped into a smooth wooden door. I felt around for the doorknob as I opened the door. As I proceeded inside, I continued to feel around the entrance of the room hoping there would be a light switch, but to no avail. I was more unnerved than ever, there was no sound of any kind except for my heavy breathing and my own heartbeat. Anxiety started to take control over me, I began to panic because of the absolute darkness with no light of any kind to guide my way into this strange place.

"Hello, hello..." I called out loudly.

My lips pressed together tightly, I proceeded to hum nervously as I was becoming afraid. As I was humming, I trudged further into the room where I suddenly slammed into something. It gave me such a fright that I yelped.

"Ah, what's that, what's that?"

Using my hands quickly, I patted down the object in front of me and chuckled.

"Ah, ha, ha, a desk, you silly goose..."

Feeling around the desk I found a candlestick and becoming excited, I rushed behind the desk hoping to find something to light it with. I felt about the top of the desk, but nothing felt like it could be used to light the candle. I put my hands where the drawers were and opened them hoping to find something.

"Ah-ha, there you are... You beastly devil you!" I said to myself. I discovered a box of matches inside the desk, opened the box, struck a match, and lit the candle. With that little bit of candlelight, I could finally see! I did not dare to venture throughout this place as I was too afraid. Instead, I looked around the room and found it was a study. The walls were of a scarlet red colour, the floor was made of hardwood, but most of it was covered by a rug that had many different designs on it fitting well with the hardwood floor and atmosphere of the room. There was a couch in front of a window but was covered with a long white sheet. I pulled the sheet away from the couch and dust accumulated onto my nose. I rubbed my nostrils and blew my nose because of all the dust. My eyes observed the couch. It was an elegant, bright red colour that matched with the walls and rug. Still holding the candlestick in my right hand, I turned towards the desk and saw on the wall a portrait of a young woman.

Her beauty grew apparent as I walked closer to the desk to get a better glance of the portrait.

The young woman was wearing a white dress with yellow gold designs running down from her collar, past her breasts and chest where her hips met. The bottom part of the dress was white, and, in the portrait, she was leaning against the side of a table with an open book in her right hand as she had her other hand placed upon her chest between the top of her breasts. She had long, dark brunette hair that was swept up and off the ears and her hair just touched her shoulders. She had a long slim neck and astounding facial features that would make any man fall in love with her. Her eyes were mysterious as if they could see through my soul and it looked as if she was staring right at me. After seeing the portrait, I looked around the study and it gave me a feeling of opulence, the room was just absolutely decorated beautifully and elegantly as if the royal family of Great Britain was living here. I feel myself becoming tired now as I feel I need to write at another time... It's just something about this place that makes me feel tired, drained, and yet sad...

Yours Truly,
Nicholas Ainsworth

The Antiquarian

9 October 1940
Entry Fifty-Seven

Ever had that feeling of being asleep and awake all at once where one can't tell if they were asleep or awake? Falling asleep on the elegant couch there was a point in time when I heard voices, but I am unsure if it was from my dream or not. I could clearly hear and understand the voice asking me, "Who are you? What are you doing here?" I kept hearing those two questions over and over again, in an echo of a whispered voice. I could, with my eyes closed, still half-asleep, have a sense of where I was, but I couldn't wake and open my eyes. Instead, I continued to hear those same two questions being spoken to me in a chilling whisper. Suddenly, I awoke in the study where I had fallen asleep on the couch and it was then that the voices stopped. It was daylight as the sun shone within the room, and all was quiet.

Now that it was daytime, I could clearly see everything as I began exploring this folly place. After leaving the study, I found myself inside of a strange room that looked as if it was a cathedral and I felt as if I were in a memorial shrine. I felt uneasy because I didn't quite understand why such a place would have a cathedral, or at least, a room structured like one. As I mooched further ahead, I saw an altar with a giant crucifix mounted high above the altar, and before it, to the right and left were thrones made of stone.

There were no pews or anything for the common people to sit, so it was rather strange just seeing an altar with stone thrones on the right and left. I creeped up to the altar, and behind it I discovered spiral staircases that took me to the second floor. My footsteps echoed while going up the spiral staircase and while going up each step I began to see a giant, long, and rectangular stained-glass window. It was delicately and flawlessly designed, just like any average Christian church, and the light from the day beautifully shone unique colours on the second floor. The hallway on the second floor was made of hardwood just like how the study was. The hallways were long and narrow, and it would give one a creepy chill, and I for one did not want to explore these halls, but all at once I was completely curious to explore them. I could only turn left or right after reaching the top of the spiral staircase. I kept looking left and right, not sure of which way to go. Eventually, I decided to go down the right side of the hallway.

Going down the hall, my footsteps caused the floorboards to creak very loudly as I ambled at an uneasy pace. The hair on the back of my neck began to rise due to random chills from the atmosphere. I turned to my left into the first room as the door was left ajar. Standing at the entrance of the room there was a writer's desk against the left side along with a wooden chair. Upon the desk, there was a girl's doll in a fancy bonnet and dress sitting up against the wall. It gave me an eerie feeling glancing at the doll, seeing its cloudy, marbled, eyes. Looking on the top of the desk, I found it was neatly organised with papers stacked upon it along with a fancy quill pen. I found handwritten musical manuscripts, along with poems, and even short stories.

Above the wall from the desk, I was intrigued to see the same portrait of the same young woman from the study. Observing the portrait again, I made the conclusion this woman had to be close to my age. I began to think that obviously this woman must live within the castle and probably still does, considering how neatly organised everything was in the room. I also drew conclusions that the room I was in was this young woman's bedroom due to the doll sitting on the top of the desk and all these papers neatly stacked and organised. Then, something caught my attention... A book entitled *Sic Cogito*. In English, *This is How I Think*. Upon opening it, I began reading a random passage of the volume:

"Six months have elapsed since my daughter's death. It was in March, winter had gone; spring had not arrived. On a wet and dull evening, I was sitting alone in the study, near my working desk. In front of me, as always, there was a packet of papers and some pencils. How? I do not know, I do not know, I do not know; but without understanding how, my hand took a pencil and put its point onto the paper. I began to feel a short and strong tapping in my left temple, as if there was a telegraph receiver inside my head. Suddenly, my hand began to move restlessly, for no longer than five seconds at a time. When my arm stopped moving, and the pencil fell from my fingers, I felt as if I had been awakened from a deep sleep, although I was sure I had not fallen asleep. I looked at the paper and I could read very clearly: 'Je suis heureuse; je t'aime; nous nous verrons; cela doit te suffire. Iulia Hasdeu. '('I am happy; I love you; we shall see each other again; this must be enough for you. Iulia Hasdeu.')"

I closed the volume placing it back in its place unable to speak. I glared up at the portrait of the young woman. Could this be her? Could this be Iulia? Everything went cold and it felt as if someone was watching me. I began to shake, my hands could not be still, and I heard the floorboards creak as if someone moved just an inch. I looked behind me and saw a small hole on the window. It was a round window, and I looked through it out of curiosity and, in a quick second, I saw a young woman staring at me through the window. I screamed, dashed, and ran out of the room, and then I came to a sudden stop because I began to hear a piano playing.

It was a haunting, but beautiful melody; full of the emotions of sadness, happiness, and love. I wasn't sure if I should follow the sound of the music, but I did. My heart was pounding as if it would beat out of my chest, and I was hyperventilating as I tried to compose myself while slowly coming down to the first floor. The music was becoming louder as I was getting closer to its source. I came into another room slowly pushing the door open. The door creaked like it hadn't been opened in centuries, and as I wandered into the room, the piano music stopped. I looked towards the piano, but no one was there, and as I walked closer someone asked…

"Who are you? What are you doing here?!"

The voice that spoke to me gave me a fright as I turned around to face a young woman. I had my hand over my heart, and I had begun to breathe heavily. I was shocked, almost speechless seeing that it was the young woman from the portrait.

"I'm sorry, I didn't know anyone lived here." I barely answered.

"Well, I live here, and you are intruding."

My lips smudged, "I apologise I don't mean to intrude; I just don't have anywhere else to go. I am a foreigner of this country hiding from the Germans. My name is Nicholas Ainsworth, and I'm an archaeologist from England and during the Nazi occupation… I randomly stumbled upon your home after escaping with my life."

I was terrified but at the same time my heart began to ache.

"I see…" she answered studying me.

There was a pause, "Why are you staring at me like that?" she added bitterly.

My eyebrows jumbled. I didn't realise how I was staring at her, but my heart was trembling with fear, and yet, another feeling grew that I did not understand in my heart and soul.

"I'm sorry... I... I didn't mean to you're just... Beautiful."

It was silent again as it became awkward.

She stuttered her words, "Well... Eh, thank you..."

The dreadful silence brewed my anxiety as I hastily spoke, "Well again, I am sorry for intruding into your home. Please forgive me... It's a beautiful home. Take care!"

I started in the direction of the exit, but I didn't get a chance to leave the room.

"Wait!" she called.

I didn't turn to face her.

"You may stay," she said.

I turned to face her, and she continued, "Just by judging what you said, I feel sending you back out there isn't the right thing to do."

My mouth parted, "I thank you, and sorry again for intruding into your home. I did not mean to..."

Her eyes rendered my soul, "It's fine. I forgive you, but there are some rules you must know when staying here." I nodded my head in understanding.

"Follow me," she sauntered toward the exit of the room.

I followed her into the cathedral room where the crucifix was mounted.

"As you can see, in this room the ceiling of the main tower is vaulted. A circular metallic parapet links the inferior plane of the material to the superior one – the eternal spirit world. Through this very symbol, the tower represents the union of matter and spirit, of heaven and earth."

She turned quickly and glared at me, "Whatever you do, please, do not laugh or make mockery of the statue of Jesus. Consider this as your warning."

"Understood," I answered firmly.

I didn't quite understand why anyone would make mockery of the statue of Jesus as there's nothing humorous about it.

She began to walk with me through the castle and said, "I'm sorry... I didn't introduce myself... I'm Iulia Hasdeu."

"It's good to meet you, and I have a question if you don't mind."

"Yes?"

I cleared my throat, "Was that you who played the piano earlier?"

Iulia smiled, "Yes, that was. I've been playing for seven years and graduated from St. Sava Gymnasium and the Conservatory of Music from Bucharest in piano and canto."

My eyes grew wide, "Wow, impressive your English is very good too, I might add."

Iulia was evidently flattered by my comments from how she puttered her words, "Oh, why thank you; you think so?"

"Yes, did you study English during your education?"

Iulia smirked, "No, I taught myself honestly and I know French and German as well."

After her words, Iulia escorted me to the second floor, and we took a right down the hallway. "I took Latin during my time at the University of London and learned some Romanian during a semester at the University of Bucharest." I added bluntly.

"The University of London is such a fascinating university I hear, and Bucharest is lovely, but as far as my education, I went to Paris."

I flickered my eyelids. I was about to say something until we stopped at the entrance of the room where I was. Iulia spoke, "This is my room, and please, I ask you kindly to respect the items, and possessions I have, and do not touch them. Everything has its place."

I nodded my head, "Of course..."

My teeth bit against my lip, it became quiet, and Iulia noticed how I was biting my lip. She tilted her head suspiciously and asked, "Is something wrong?"

"Well, um... I..."

"What?"

I groaned. I was afraid to tell her I went in her room before. I didn't tell her I touched a book in her room, but I told her that I looked in her room. I said I was intrigued by all the musical manuscripts and writings she had. Iulia wasn't mad. She told me from a very young age she had written poetry and prose in both Romanian and French. She also told me her father, Bogdan, had published a few of her works. Though she seemed not too thrilled about her publications. I don't know... I can't describe it. For my stay, I was allowed to sleep on the couch of the study. Iulia told me that the study is where her father usually works, but he would not mind me utilising the study as my living quarters. I don't know how to feel about all of this, I have many unanswered questions. For instance, why haven't I met Iulia's father yet and why didn't I meet Iulia the night I came into this place? Iulia is calling... Until next time.

Yours Truly,
Nicholas Ainsworth

273

12 October 1940
Entry Fifty-Eight

This armchair is stiff, firm, and squeaks as I'm writing. There is a clock next to me on my left as Iulia told me it belonged to her great-grandfather. The clock does not tick as it's stuck at 11:20. Odd. The walls are painted white with shades of light-green nearby where the ceiling and the walls meet. Across from me is a black piano. This room feels slightly claustrophobic, but the rays of the dying sun is a warm comfort. The room is decorated with what I assume to be family portraits of the Hasdeus and laurel leaves are imprinted within the shades of green. There is also a drawing room nearby, but I am too anxious to explore it. It's just... I have not seen Iulia all day. I can't seem to find her which is strange. This place seems uninhabited. I do not know what to make of it.

Yesterday, my mind was consumed by the book I discovered from Iulia's room, *This is How I Think.* I thought perhaps it could give me answers to the story and mystery of this castle. I prowled, exited the left tower, and into the centre temple. The great crucifix was erected in the middle of the dome. When I looked at it from the front or from behind, it had the shape of a cup. In the upper part of the cross, the statue of Christ stood. The statue was a painted, wooden sculpture of Him, and His hands were raised in blessing under the temple dome of the castle. Above Him, the ceiling was painted deep red. A gold labyrinth led to a flaming circle in the ceiling's centre. I extended my arm and hand to the statue but trembled. I withdrew my hand and toddled past it to reach the right tower. My footsteps crept at an uneasy pace, but I pushed open the door to Iulia's room. Everything was left as it was when I first entered. My nose whiffed the scent of calla lilies. I never noticed them before, but probably because of my nerves. I glared to the desk with her doll sitting up, it stared at me with its cloudy eyes... I saw the black book and knew that was the one. I reached but with the doll in my view, my eyes shifted between it and the book. It was like the doll was watching me as Iulia's words rang inside my skull,

"Everything has its place." Phrases of her warnings crawled and echoed in my head as my arm continued to stretch forward, "This is my room... Respect the items, and possessions... Do not touch them." As her words rang, they stopped, and my eyes caught a glimpse of another book next to the one I desired. It was a notebook with a red cover and appeared rather thick as if extensively written. I shuddered and closed my eyes. My eyelids squeezed and I snatched one of the books. I darted out of the room as I opened my eyes. I did not look at which book I snatched; I didn't want to look. I scuttled down the hall, past the centre temple, and returned into the study where I had been sleeping. I sat at the walnut desk, slapped the book in the centre, and observed it was the black book.

All that day I worked restlessly in deciphering its context with my Romanian materials from my satchel. I was lost in a trance as one of the clocks in the room chimed. It was 23:20... After the clock's chimes, all was silent. My wristwatch ticked as my breathing was steady. A voice softly lamented into a song. Was it Iulia? The voice echoed across all the vast rooms. I came into the centre temple, and down into the nave. The door to the first hall was unlatched. My shoes reverberated upon the marble floors. Upon opening the wooden door, through a passage, lined parallel mirrors arranged side by side. My mind became distracted by all the mirrors and observing my reflection in several different angles. Then, I heard the most beautiful and intrinsic voice singing. A mezzo soprano which harrowed a brooding lull.   I followed its melody; it raptured me to its source outside the main entrance.

The night sky filled itself with clouds, but the moon shone so bright and lit the entire courtyard. As I ambled down the stone stairs, I observed Iulia around the palace grounds. She appeared wearing her white dress and held a series of daisy flowers in her hands. She sang in Romanian. Her tone was cadaverous, sad, and full of gloom. One of the phrases I picked up was, "Nu mă împiedica a plânge..." [Don't stop me from crying...]. The moonlight waned its light upon Iulia. Her pale complexion glowed and ruptured my impervious heart.

"Nicholas, it's not polite to gawk..." she said.

Her words snapped me back into focus. "Oh, my apologies... Your voice is beautiful and what were you singing?" She smiled at my compliment, "It's a poem I wrote. Won't you come join me?" I forgot my gentlemanly manners, but like an innocent puppy, I obeyed. She held the daises in her hands as we strolled side by side. Our feet scuffled against the cobblestone pathways, "That was your poem? I would love to hear you read your poetry." I said breaking the silence. She gasped and chuckled, "I have fully revised several times all that I have written." I bit my lip as my eyes catch hers glaring upon the ground. I thought about giving her encouragement, "I beg to differ Miss Hasdeu; the poem sounded pleasing to my ears and enlightened my soul. You should consider publishing it." Her lips sunk into her mouth and she did not look at me, "Your words are charming Nicholas, but I am too young..."

My head wobbled and jolted as my eyes squinted, "What, too young to publish? Nonsense! You told me your father published a few of your works already." Iulia stopped, her eyes lifted upon mine, "Yes, he did... And 'too young to publish 'sounds like something my father would say." A cool breeze chilled me. Iulia's face moulded into a plain sombre as if my words triggered a stream of memories. Iulia swallowed, "In August..." She halted her words as her eyebrows quenched, "My father discovered a few of my poems. On his request, I agreed to read a few of them, but I refused to publish them. Father fought against my strong opposition and decided to publish four of my poems. He brought me the Romania's Star Newspaper. I saw the titles of my four poems: 'The Blue Stories,' 'Tears of a Child,' 'Disdain, ' and 'The Wish of an Ugly Girl.'" She groaned, "I recall one of the literary editors, August R. Clavel, making a beautiful review as it read, 'Miss Iulia Hasdeu, the Poetess.'"

The relationship between Iulia and her father intrigues me. I've been hiding the spiritualist volume in my satchel. There is much research, documents, and experiments in its content and context. B.P. Hasdeu established a vast, dense record of things I do not quite understand. For example, in the second chapter, Iulia's father writes, "To sleep means to dream," and he considered that the dream, "is already an impulse to the unlimited." He shows that in his attempt to demonstrate the independence of the soul towards space and time, as well as the possibility that souls communicate with each other. What is the role played by sleep for the human being? This is my question but it's also a question Iulia's father raises too. B.P. Hasdeu appeals to two situations when the so-called, "limitlessness" of the soul can be produced: dream and sleep walking. Why is Iulia's father so drawn to such rubbish? The "existence, occurrences and teachings of the spirits" is just absolute rubbish and has no place in science. Of course, that's what I thought when Sasha introduced me to deviant burials in regard to hoaxes about vampires. I shall decipher more of the volume's material and record my findings.

Nicholas Ainsworth

13 October 1940
Entry Fifty-Nine

A restless night of sleep. I slept but flashes and images raced through my mind. I couldn't tell if I was asleep or awake again. I felt as I did when I dreamt about the young woman in the white dress. As I had flashes of her, I thought about Iulia, and I bolted up from the elegant couch. I thought I saw a figure standing by the entrance of the study. A man by seeing the shadowy form of a thick, bushy beard. It moved too quick for me to completely observe it. I crept out the room, but nothing was there except the darkness. In the midst of this darkness, I heard voices. These voices echoed throughout the castle and I couldn't tell which direction they were coming from. These voices chanted, "Lili, my angel, Nicolae, my angel, my angels, when I call one of you, I never forget that you all are a whole to me, with my Lili as a centre and Christ as an accessible peak, the great meditator..." My feet shuffled along to the centre temple as this was said. The way this chant was said chilled my spine. Hearing a variation of my name called knotted my stomach. My eyes adjusted to the darkness as they lifted up towards the statue of Jesus. A figure sat and meditated on the circular balustrade that borders the vault, close to the "Heaven" depicted there. The figure lamented a woeful sorrow. It wept as if the celestial symbolism overflowed its benefice effects upon its soul. Like it was invaded by the burden of an eternal torment and grief.

"Dear angel...Admirable angel..." It whispered.

The folding stair, a point-levies, was lifted as the figure meditated in silence. Once I stepped farther inside the temple with its dome above, it revealed to me, and in the middle of the dome a Great Eye projecting downward by the reflection of a mirror. From downwards, two iron stairs emerged laterally; they intersected up, under the dome, and on the platform where the statue of Jesus at a large scale was blessing the temple. Right under the Great Eye, my eyes grew wide at a marble bust of Iulia. There, in the celestial sphere, the bust is covered with a thin, white veil. As I gazed at the bust, a woeful piano wailed and echoed. It startled me. I jolted and turned where the sound was coming from, however, I glared back to where the figure meditated, but it was gone.

The piano music played on and entranced me. I shambled into the room where I first met Iulia. The moonlight shone through the window against a black piano. I saw Iulia hypnotised by the melody she was playing. Her sallow skin was fluorescent and beautiful in the light. Candles were lit on candelabras around the room and tea-lit candle holders were placed upon various furniture. Such a setting lured me into a seduction and a tenderised feeling. I shuffled towards Iulia as this feeling grew, but I doused this feeling once my brain flashed back to Sasha. The memory of us dancing to Clare de Lune. When the memory ended, the piano music stopped, and Iulia stared at me.

"Nicholas, did I disturb you?"

Iulia sounded empty, but her eyes conveyed a sombre solace.

"No... I..." My words shallowed. I felt a looming despair I couldn't describe. I didn't know if it was the ambient moodiness this place gave me, or my heart grieved by thoughts of home and Sasha. Iulia studied my despondent frown, "E legea naturii ca orice om, orice fiinţă să sufere," As she said this to me, she rose from the piano bench, and walked towards me. Those words struck me deep within my core. She smiled at me and repeated what she said previously but in English, "It is the law of nature for every man, every being to suffer." I trembled hearing the words in English and sighed a shattered breath. My eyes caught her gaze at me. It's like she stared into my very soul like the night I first saw her portrait.

"Come." She commanded. She ambled away from me to follow her. "Would you mind grabbing one of the candles for candlelight?" This request made me uneasy. If I'm the one following her, why wouldn't she grab any of them near her? I mooched over as I grabbed a random tea-lit candle inside its holder.

"Nicholas. Trust me, please."

I scuttled behind her with the candle and followed her into the centre temple where the statue of Jesus was and where I saw the humanoid shadow above me. We faced the altar, "This altar is flanked on both sides by two libraries. On the altar are my cottage piano and my bust made from Carrara marble. The books, symbols of knowledge, and science drive away the darkness of ignorance! Through lateral doors, from the domed temple, visitors enter the dining room, sitting room and the parlour situated in the left wing of the castle. And, situated on the right wing are father's study and bedroom." As she was explaining more about the centre temple and the layout of the castle, I noticed streaks of moonlight seeping through the walls and illuminating the statue of Jesus.

"Iulia, is this castle falling apart?"

Iulia turned as I said this. Her smile talking about her home withered into a despondence. "Yes, it is… Wars, earthquakes, and human ignorance have affected the castle, turning it, some time ago, into a ruin; but the statue of Jesus from the castle's dome was never touched by such evil! A few years ago, in 1936, finding the impressive statue in the middle of these ruined walls you see, two young men had their photo taken together with Jesus. One of them had placed a peaked cap on the hand of the statue…"

She stopped. As she was telling this story, bitter resentment filled her words. Iulia balled her hand into a fist, and it trembled. This terrified me on how bitter and angry she was. I recalled her warning from earlier about not making a mockery of the statue of Jesus. My palms sweated as I clutched the tea-lit candle, my mouth dried, and my tongue licked against my dried lips. I desired to know what happened to these young men, but I stalled. Her anger terrified me. I tilted my head to the side and saw her eyes. They were crimson with hints of violet, but I squeezed my eyes shut and re-opened them. Iulia loosened her grip, she stared at her open palm, and groaned out a breath to ease herself. She turned her head to me and stared. Her eyes were brown. She said calmly, "This beautiful sculpture of Jesus by Rafelo Casciani is standing above today, as it did for one hundred years."

"Iulia, are you okay? I thought I saw your eyes change colour..."

She smiled, "Oh, really? Interesting... It must have been the complexion of the candlelight. I apologise if my anger startled you... It's just... My castle is a place of recollection, where the profane and the sacred unite in harmony. The strong belief in God and love defeats death and removes the barriers between the seen and unseen worlds. From within these limitations, we ask ourselves; 'Where do we come from? Who are we? Where are we going?'"

The candlelight hummed and flickered, "And what answers have you found? What are you trying to show me?" I asked this while feeling the heat of the flame tingling against my cheek.

"My father and I believe we found the answer to those questions. There is no youth, no old age; life and death are merely stages of the eternal line."

A shiver crawled down my spine as I slightly squeezed the candle holder and jolted. It terrified me to know what she meant about life and death as "stages of the eternal line." At the same time, I was curious to ask. I wallowed in a contemplation on whether to ask what she meant by this answer. Iulia spoke again, "Nicholas... I know you are haunted by a darkened gloom. I've seen you sleep as you toss and turn. If you wish for peace to come to you, if you wish to find tranquillity in a world too heavily overloaded by matter, then I'm glad you're here. In this castle, allow yourself to be charmed by the beautiful story of youth without old age and life without death. This place is full of symbols of the old beliefs, offering living water to the spirit of those who long for knowledge."

Sasha's words about knowledge clicked, "Knowledge is power."

Iulia raised her right eyebrow, "Wise words, and what would you do with such power?" Memories of the events that happened at the Transylvanian Alps flashed in my mind. The cold, the frost, and desolation. The deviant burial gravesite, the ghastly remains, and the artefact seal. Dr Gilders' deathly face flashed before me as he threw himself off the summit. I broke into a sob, wept, and plummeted onto the marble floor. The candle was still in my hand as I laid it next to me. Iulia knelt down upon her knees and was levelled with me. Her presence casted a chill upon me like I was back in those wretched alps, but as I stared at her, my heart warmed by her brown eyes. The candlelight illuminated them tenderly, "My mentor... He's dead. My heart is so grieved by his death that I do not know if I have the strength to carry on his promise. I promised him that I would continue our research for knowledge. Knowledge on deviant burials. I came close at times discovering the secrets of the gravesite we found on Mt. Negoiu. I tried to convince the University of Bucharest to support me, but they turned me down. It's my life's purpose to possess such knowledge." Tears streamed my cheeks as I gazed upon Iulia. She showed no facial emotion, but her eyes said otherwise by the tenderness I felt when staring at them.

"I see... I find your academic pursuits enticing... What grave do you speak of?"

Iulia's words ignited a spark and a light which I haven't felt in so long. Finally, someone who cared about my devotions to science, knowledge, and discovery. Hesitantly and eagerly, I spoke, "The remains I believe, are descended or related in some way to Michael the Brave. My mentor and I found his seal buried in the pit." Iulia's eyes sparkled and her demeanour changed like she was healthy and all smiley. She gasped, "Michael the Brave! You're quite the antiquarian. When I was the age of six, I wrote my study on the life and work of Michael the Brave!"

"At six?" I was dumbfounded and discombobulated that she studied such works at a very young age. Part of me didn't want to believe her, but all at once I was curious. I rose from the floor, squatted back down to grab the candle, and held it. Iulia gestured her hand to follow her further.

In one of the rooms on the second floor, is what was called the Darkroom. There were three chairs on the left. There was a special table, it was small, and above it was a small hole. The same hole where I first caught a glimpse of Iulia. A dark violet rug with etched gold designs covered the wooden floor. The room appeared darker, decorated with butterflies, the head of an angel and apparently other unidentified symbols. Against one of the walls in the room was a family portrait. The painting depicted an old man and an old woman. The woman was sitting down on the left and the man was sitting next to her on the right. Between them was a marble bust of Iulia. Iulia stood next to me, "Those are my parents. My father Bogdan Petriceicu Hasdeu and my mother whom I was named after." My eyes studied Iulia as she walked to one of the chairs. She sat and pointed to the chair next to her.

"Sit."

I didn't know what disturbed me more... The family portrait with the family and the fact that Iulia herself wasn't in the painting, and only a bust of her, or how she commanded me to sit next to her. I obeyed her and sat next to her. My leg thumped up and down nervously. I didn't know I was doing this until Iulia spoke.

"Why do you tremble?"

I gripped my leg, squeezed it as my fingernails dug into my trousers. The flashback of Sasha gripping my leg raced through my mind. I was tongue tied, "I... This room is overwhelming... I can't describe it." Iulia's lips sunk into her mouth, "The room does have impressive colours, the shape and their symbolism overwhelm even the initiated guest. Each room has their profane destination, if we may put it this way, the castle hosts this 'room with animals.'"

I stifled in my chair, "What?" I croaked.

Iulia chuckled under her breath, "Look over there." She pointed to the wall behind me. My chair squeaked as I turned my body. My eyes caught where she pointed to as she spoke, "It's not restored yet, but there are two small areas of old frescos which still exist on the walls. What you're looking at is my head, having a pair of indefinite wings, illustrating the impression of my seraphic appearance together with the Trinity's Triangle. Just below, there is a round niche, an energetic receiver transmitting symbols of harmony. The room's obscurity is important because only in the darkness the little light at the end of the tunnel can be seen!"

As I gazed at the image on the wall she described, my ears heard a huffing sound and my candle went out. I dropped the candle from the sudden light vanishing; surrounded by absolute darkness. I panicked, shuddered, and shallowed my breaths. My heart palpitated against my chest as I gritted my teeth.

"Don't be frightened..." whispered Iulia's voice. I couldn't tell which direction her voice came from, but I knew she was next to me as her breath tickled against my ears. As the words echoed and rang, my head turned in all directions to follow the sound. My eyes saw the light at the end of the tunnel she spoke of. The light illuminated the image she described upon the wall as the sound of her voice lulled me. "Who will reveal yourself to their eyes? Death." Goosebumps tingled and numbed every inch of my body. After her words, Iulia's breath soughed against the side of my throat. It made me shudder seductively in a trance as I tilted my head to the side. I glared and spaced out at the light that beautifully shone the image before me. My heart raged tenderly as its rhythm consumed my ears. My body felt heavy as I thought I was going to fall over, but the sudden whiplash of a shuttered window in the room jolted me out of my delicate state. Iulia was by the window as the moonlight gleamed upon her gloaming figure. There was a darkened allure to her as my eyes refocused. Iulia eyes fixated towards the window, "In the garden, there are three other towers. The third tower houses a private library, archives, and a reading room. You may use the third tower on the far right to your heart's delight."

"What about the other towers?" I muttered.

Iulia's face moulded into a cold, serious gaze, "Off limits. There are parts of the castle that lie in ruin and are not safe to dwell. Had it not been for Jesus's wonderful statue, the castle would have collapsed." Iulia turned her body and faced me. She warmly smiled, "When you are done with your studies after the day has passed, come to the parlour where the piano is."

My eyes wandered and my eyebrows rose, "Oh?"

"I noticed how my ability to play the piano lulls and comforts you. I would like to teach you the piano." Iulia padded over to me, bent down, and whispered in my ear, "Inimilor tinere le trebuie ceva spre a îmbrățișa cu fericire." My heart meandered to her words as they translated to me as, "Young hearts need something to embrace happily." Iulia desired to teach me piano because she wants to help me heal. The process of healing is difficult because there is no greater pain than a broken heart and even when it is made whole and "healed," the cracks will always remember such sorrow and despair.

Nicholas Ainsworth

14 October 1940
Entry Sixty

I've never seen so many books and papers! This is a literary paradise. So many things catch my attention, but all at once I can't help but feel uneasy. I haven't felt the same since what happened in the Darkroom with Iulia. I've never felt so vulnerable and powerless. It felt like there was a telegraph receiver inside my head... It's almost like the experience Bogdan had in which he first described in his book, *This is How I Think.* He claims his handwriting imitated his daughter Iulia's. I am terrified of Iulia. I don't know what her intentions are with me, but yet I can't help but feel a strange attraction for her. My heart yearns for a counterpart companion ever since time has elapsed after leaving England. I long for a shared intimacy which offers vulnerabilities, and envisions a deep physical, emotional, intellectual, creative, spiritual, and experiential connection. A bond of mindfulness and personal growth. I miss Sasha, but Iulia seems very intellectual and that in itself, is an endearment to my saturnine beating heart. Yet, at the same time, Sasha embellishes me with ardour. Every tender and sublime emotion radiates with every sentiment. She is my defender and I will come back home to the ruins of London. I will find Sasha and embrace her again! I must keep hope in the darkest of times and places.

Speaking of places, this library with the reading room is opulent. I hope this silent space will be a comfort. I'm surrounded by a diverse range of tomes, volumes, and books. Many of them are fully bound in genuine leather, twenty-two karat-gold, and deeply inlaid on the spine. Each page is superbly printed on acid-neutral paper that can last for generations. The pages themselves are sewn and not glued like ordinary books. Satin-ribbon page markers, gilded page ends, and bound in superb craftsmanship for a commitment on quality. The appearance of the room is similar to Bogdan's office and study where I have been staying in the castle. There is a fireplace... Perhaps I should request this room as my quarters. This way, I won't feel I am intruding in another man's personal space. I feel I am learning more about this man as I read his work. I've made more progress which I will record and share my own thoughts. There is a chapter I've translated called, "The Telegraphy of Love." The scholar identifies three types of love. He speaks of the "infinite," using the two concepts "delimitation" and "limitlessness." He writes about one love as "altruism." Altruism and delimitation, which characterises the human body or the sub-organism. This is sexual love, I believe... Then, there's nonsexual which entails altruism and limitlessness. This characterises the soul or the supra-organism and marriage in forms of sexual and nonsexual love. What intrigues me most about this volume is that it deals only with the nonsexual love, which Bogdan termed as, "The holy love through which the telegraph between the souls can occur, first between earth and above, and afterwards between above and above." This fascinates me... Especially how Bogdan phrased "the telegraph between the souls can occur." It makes me reflect that moment in the Darkroom. What kind of love, connection, and communication is Iulia attempting and for what purpose? I wonder if she too, desires the same intimacies and vulnerabilities as I do... I shall see her tonight.

Nicholas Ainsworth

15 October 1940
Entry Sixty-One

My first lessons with Iulia was almost as uptight as my waltzing lessons with Uncle Henry. I am up for the challenge though. There were times Iulia bit her lip at me, or her tone appeared agitated because of explaining music theory. It is something I've never learned or taken during my education. So, I learned about middle C, parts of composition, and their symbols. The basics like the staff, the clefs, and the notes. She even demonstrated hand motions on the piano to highlight some of the basics such as lines, spaces, and the represented notes ranging from A to G, and the note sequence moving up the staff. I have much to learn but it is a nice distraction from my own extensive research.

We engaged in academic discussion between the lesson. We talked about Michael the Brave which led into a wide range of conversations about Iulia. We spent our time next to each other on the piano bench. I asked her, "What's the coat of arms on the main entrance to the castle?" She smiled at me and her eyes gazed at me tenderly, "My father once wrote to me while I studied in Paris, 'You must study well, behave well, never forget your name is Hasdeu, and the slogan of our family is: country, honour, and science.' My family's coat of arms, which is the emblem on the main entrance has a party per pall reversed shield; dexter chief, purpure, charged with a flag and a cross. There is a sinister chief, blue, charged with the Moldavian urus, black, with a star between horns, with the sun and the moon above. The base is red, charged with a gold arrow and sword, crossed. The shield is surmounted by a helmet."

As Iulia described her family coat of arms, it made me compare it to Michael the Brave's seal. There were a few resemblances such as the symbols of a shield, the Moldavian urus, the sun and moon, a cross, and a sword.

"Is your family descended from Michael the Brave?"

Iulia chuckled at how random I blurted out this question.

"I can see how you can draw that connection because of the similar symbols on the seal of Michael the Brave, but my father attributed our coat of arms and considered us related to voivod Stephen Petriceicu, who ruled Moldavia three times between 1672 and 1684." I plopped my elbow and groaned. The low tone from the piano startled me but conveyed exactly how frustrated I was about the mystery behind the remains. As I lifted my arm from the piano quickly, I spoke, "Ah, this is frustrating! I need to know whose remains are in the burial site!" Iulia smudged her lips together as if in thought, "Well, those remains could be anyone's... If you're thinking that those bones are related to Michael the Brave, then the only information I have based on my studies, is there might be some descendants of the great ruler through his daughter, Florica. She died in 1678 and was followed by a niece, Alexandra, who married Commissar Udrea."

A quick spark lit in my eyes, "Could those be Florica's remains?"

"No, Florica's remains lie buried at the Mihai Voda Monastery in Bucharest."

I mumbled, "Bugger..." Silence filled for a moment as Iulia and I gazed at each other. I bluntly asked, "How do you know so much about Michael the Brave? Did you really write works about him at six?"

When I asked Iulia these questions, she opened up more about herself. She told me she was born on

November 14, 1922. When she was only two years and half, she was able to read and proved an astonishing memory, reciting long poems. When she was four, she knew how to write and at five she was composing poems. At the age of eight, she could speak fluently in French, German, and English. When she was eleven years old, she graduated from the gymnasium "St. Sava," with the first prize, and also brightly completed her musical training at the Conservatory. Due to Iulia's higher performance compared with her colleagues, she was allowed to give all primary school exams. Most of all, at only sixteen, she was accepted at Sorbonne, thus becoming the first woman from Romania who studied at the prestigious university. At the university, she managed to impress the teachers with her knowledge, intelligence, and creativity.

I was speechless as Iulia had told me all of this. Some of it, I even doubted as she seemed like a prodigy genius. Her eyes lingered at me, "What, you don't believe me?" I bit my lip as I pressed it into a thin line, "It's not that... It's just I don't know what to say. You have all these talents. You're like a genius. You have a beautiful dark disturbing mezzo soprano voice, seductive but delicate abilities on the piano, and a talent with writing. From what I've heard you sing a few nights ago, your poem has a special sensitivity which flows abundantly..." Iulia broke a smile, the first time I've seen a smile from her, cheek to cheek. As she smiled, her breaths soften and her deep, brown eyes gleamed. "Oh, Nicholas... I'm flattered by your compliments." After she said this, her behaviour changed. She seemed happy, bright, and full of life; not the same melancholy as I am used to. "The one who discovered my literary 'genius 'as you say, was my teacher from Sevigne College, Maurice Albert, the son of the famous Paul Albert. He taught me Greek free of charge! I've been told that my written works are very natural, but I published them posthumously. My first volume of poetry Bourgeons D'Avril appeared two years later with my poetry collection Oeuvres Posthumes. I use the pseudonym Camille Armand."

Every word she spoke, passion and delight filled her. It eventually made me smile warmly which I haven't smiled since making memories with Sasha. I chuckled, "Why the name Camille Armand and not your real name?" Iulia shrugged her shoulders, "It's something I longed to be known by the public. Maybe, it was because father published my works without my consent. I would follow my inspiring persona and think: 'Camille Armand writes with no effort; the pen slips on the paper. Her inspiration is alive and burning. She writes only when the inspiration comes to her, with the soul full of its subject, subdues to golds, as she would say; the pen seems to print in her hand with fire traits on the paper.'" Iulia's mindset on her inspiring persona enticed me. I squinted my eyebrows shortly and squirmed on the piano bench. It creaked as I asked her, "Speaking of inspiring personas, who inspires you?"

"Oh, there are three who I love! Napoleon I, Ferdinand de Lesseps, and Victor Hugo! While in Paris, I continued singing and did painting lessons. I studied everything I could about the French language and the culture while writing poems and prose in French!" I laughed at Iulia's enthusiasm and passion for the French. When I laughed in what I thought was a cheerful manner, Iulia turned her head towards the window where the night was pitch black.

"Iulia, I didn't mean my laugh to sound like..."

She interrupted me, "No, you're not being rude... I know you're happy to know my passions as it's wonderful to share them with someone... It's not you. We should talk again tomorrow night. I'm tired..." I nodded my head, got up from the bench, and exited the room.

I'm noticing a pattern with me... Every time I get to know someone, I have this urgency to swoon into something more with them. It happened with Sasha and now I'm repeating myself with Iulia. I've written many times how I find this diary a comfort in this time of solitude and isolation, but I am thankful for Iulia's company. This diary is helpful in teasing out my complicated habits with romance and love. I'm torn by two women again... Bloody hell, I'm awful. I feel guilty for having intimate feelings for two people at once. My watch reads 19:30... The sun is about to set. Another evening with Iulia comes!

Your Casanova,
Nicholas Ainsworth

307

16 October 1940
Entry Sixty-Two

Things have been rather interesting. I've translated another chapter of Bogan's volume. In the chapter "Hypnotism in Spiritualism," he refers to the two notions of "delimitation" and "limitlessness," suggesting that the "unconscious" occurs in states. First, delimited within the body, second, when only the "unconsciousness" works in the waking state delimited in the living body, but at the same time, unlimiting itself in order to occur. For example, in telepathy, the unbound from the dead body is transformed into the "spirit." [Rubbish!] Bogdan asserts that the "inspiration was the highest stage of the spiritualist communication," and his work being created was due to a "friend from another world." Who is this other friend he writes of? I don't know... So many secrets... Enough about my babbling, I should write about what has been going on between Iulia and me. Last night, we didn't spend a lot of time together.

As I ambled inside the centre temple yesterday evening, I observed my surroundings. The side bodies of the castle each have two halls, one bigger, and one smaller. In one of them sits another piano. In the other hall is Iulia's library and her portrait in a natural size. I imagined she would be in her library as I made my way there. The last of the dying sun shone a mixture of orange and pink colours. The sunlight gleamed through the library's windows. The library was a corner room. The ceiling and wood guarding above the wallpaper was pure-white. A silver chandelier with eight glass light fixtures dangled. Dark, green paisley wallpaper shrouded the library's walls. On my left upon entering, there were two black marbled standings. Each of them held a bronze bust. I thought maybe the busts were sculptures of past relatives. In between these marbled stands was an oblong table. It was black with outlines of gold colours. Upon the table was a clock in the centre. It ticked as a pendulum swung. Two vases were by the left and right side of the clock. A unique design of bronze with tints of blue shrouded them. Above the oblong table and mounted on the wall was a horizontal sketch portrait of a harbour with boats and buildings. A gold frame shined from the light fixtures gleaming upon it. Further on the left side of the room was a large brown cabinet. Inside the cabinet were various books stacked and preserved behind the glass. The floor was a light brown hardwood as its pattern was shaped like arrows pointing down towards me. A large, light grey rug covered the centre of the room. It illustrated various paisley designs and circles. Over to my right, was a window with yellow drapes. A bit farther by the window, was a small round table with a candle lit upon it. Two chairs were across opposite sides of the table. I caught Iulia's aura complexion. She sat in the chair on the right side of the round table. Her eyes did not seem to notice me. She was distracted by a piece of paper she was reading. The parchment seemed stiff, dry, and crinkled. Her eyes shifted back and forth, her lips folded inside her mouth, and she seemed sad. I stepped forward as one the floorboards creaked. It startled her as her breath shallowed and her eyes met mine.

"Iulia, are you alright?" I asked. I walked to the chair across from her and sat in it.

She gripped and squeezed the paper in her hand, "You startled me... I'm quite fine. I was just reflecting upon a private letter I wrote to my father." She slightly crumbled the paper and hovered it over the flame. The paper started to burn as she spoke, "My mother and I... We went on the old Eylau Street to Victor Hugo's house. There, I took my pen in order to write in an open notebook, 'Miss Hasdeu from the Romanian colony, to the greatest of the poets, to the greatest of the citizens.' I cannot describe the feeling when standing so close to that wall behind which I knew that he, Victor Hugo, was lying: my heart was beating, my hand was trembling, I was red, red, red..."

This sentiment of Victor Hugo struck me. I drummed my fingers against the table while Iulia's eyes fixated at the fire. She turned her head sideways as the paper still burned in her hand and she slowly dropped it on the table. The fire died as some of the paper survived but was black.

"Is that what's bothering you, Victor Hugo? He died during the last century..." Iulia's hand rested upon the table, it trembled as she dug her nails into the table. Her eyes flayed quickly between brown and hints of crimson as if she was trying to suppress her anger. She glared at me, but her eyes remained brown, "I know he died last century, Nicholas." she muttered. "Don't you have any authors or writers whom you admire that are long gone, but are still saddened by their death?"

A dreadful silence loomed the room, I bit my lip, and Iulia's eyes never moved. They stayed glued upon me. The clock and my watch ticked in unison, "I... I don't... I never got into romantic poets or writers. They're all rubbish as they deal with flights of fancy. These writers legitimise the individual imagination as a critical authority and revolt against the scientific rationalisation of nature. Victor Hugo is part of this category because he, like many of the romantics propose that true love must mean an end to all loneliness." Silence. Iulia inhaled, held her breath, and withdrew her fingers from the table. My eyes lowered at the scratch marks. They were slightly deep as my eyes wandered to her fingernails. Before I could see them, she withdrew her hand in her lap. She clinched her mouth, "Many of his works have inspired music, both during his lifetime and after his death. He inspires me in such ways. I imagine his death was terrible news! The news that overwhelmed the whole Paris, the whole France, the whole Europe and the entire world: 'Victor Hugo is dead!' It distresses, consternates me; imagine reading it on the first page of a newspaper, framed as for a funeral, in black, thick and sinister letters, those words: 'Victor Hugo is dead... A great light is dimming...' I felt a knife in my chest. Even now, when I'm speaking to you, Nicholas; my hand trembles on my lap, I feel oppressed and I'm striving not to cry. Oh! It's not allowed to cry on such pain!"

Iulia bolted up from the chair as it fell backwards and thudded violently against the hardwood floor. "Ah! What a glory! I could never see something beyond this man. His life impressed me as much as his work. And his works moved me and raised me. Why was he such a great man? Because he was also a great man. Last night when we spoke of passions, I started to cry like a madman, as I understood the gravity of his disease, and my mother, who was also sad, tried to comfort me telling me that he died old and full of glory. 'It doesn't matter, 'I answered, 'we must shed a tear for him who often made you cry for others. 'And mother had to let me cry."

As Iulia was telling me this, her voice was distraught. She paced back and forth as the floor creaked. There were moments where I couldn't keep up with her speaking because of how quickly she spoke them. I sat frozen hearing her words as she ranted further, "How I wished I could see him at least once! I would have kept his sacred image in my heart forever. But, because this supreme happiness was refused for me, I want, at least, that his memory would never leave me. I'd so much wish to send him a crown of flowers..." Iulia groaned and shielded her eyes against the palms of her hands. A single tear shredded upon her cheek as she dropped her hands and stared at me. She said, "Victor Hugo died! I can't come into my senses. I can't understand this death; no, I simply can't. Good evening, Nicholas, I'm not able to say anything else now..." No words came to me. I was gripped by the terror from how she reacted against my opinion about the romantics. Iulia lurched out of the room, my hand trembled, reached for the burnt paper, and I sat there in deafening, deathlike silence.

Even as I'm sitting here today where I've been studying, Iulia's reaction to Victor Hugo disturbs me. There were times when she spoke, it sounded as if she was there during the time he died, but I believe that's only because of how distraught she was. I've never seen that kind of reaction from her. I know nothing about Victor Hugo except that he was a man who lived a long time ago in France and wrote a famous work called *The Hunchback of Notre-Dame*. I have Irene to thank for me knowing this much about Victor Hugo. Iulia reminds me of her a bit. They are both passionate about their romantic writers... Ugh! Cor, I've never seen a reaction like what Iulia displayed. Even when I told Irene my views about such literature, she would never go mad. Sure, we disagreed, but never... There must be something more behind Iulia's reaction and feelings... I should give her some space. It gives me time to focus on my research.

Yours Truly,
Nicholas Ainsworth

17 October 1940
Entry Sixty-Three

It's roughly a little past 01:00... I'm drained, tired, and weary. I've strained myself over too much research. My mind is numb and weak. My candlelight still burns, but the candlestick itself has shortened since I last saw it. I'm not getting anywhere with my endeavours on Michael the Brave... These volumes of lore I have pondered and studied upon; I have found no connection to anything that leads to the deviant burial found in the Transylvanian Alps. I feel like I'm reaching a dead end. While frustrated over this, I resumed my work on deciphering Bogdan's *This is How I Think*. I am afraid that in my strenuous efforts upon my other research, I only managed to translate a single phrase. In the chapter, "Materialism in Spiritualism," Bogdan states, "In the phenomenon of the spiritualist photography, the sensitive plate doesn't transcribe a real shape, but only an idea that is occurring in a medium's brain in that moment." I don't know what this exactly means... Bogdan sounds like a madman talking about a "medium's brain." Sounds like ghostly rubbish, but it has to do with something about this castle considering all the odd symbols I've seen... Iulia's letter is too burnt to make out anything. The only things I can make out are part of the date, "22 May" and the few lines, "Victor Hugo died [...] at 13:30, at the age of eighty-three, three months and four days." I'm too tired... I must rest.

Nicholas Ainsworth

Entry Sixty-Four

For a while, I've been staring at this blank page of my diary trying to find the words. As I had fallen asleep, there was a point in time when I heard voices again. A woeful voice full of sorrow, grief, and despair lamented across the hollow halls of this tower. It called the name, "Lilicuta." Startled by this voice and the name, I stiffened in my chair. The candlelight next to me still burned, but I felt no warmth from the flame. My hot breath suspired out of my mouth and I saw it haze. It was cold... Too cold. I huddled my arms around my body as I shuffled toward the door. I opened it and nothing was there except the darkness. I knew I wasn't crazy... I heard a voice wallow throughout this tower. I darted to the candlestick, gripped it, and explored the tower. As my feet pounded against the corroded stairs, I froze... Farther down the stairs, the moon shined at the entrance of the tower. A dark figure stood, bathed in the moonlight like a silhouette. The figure was inexpressibly thin, with a dusty leaden coloured suit, but fashioned from an earlier century. It was enveloped with a long, thick, and bushy beard. Its thin lips crooked into a faint and dreadful frown. Its hand tightly pressed against its chest and over the heart.

As I gazed upon it, a distant inaudible moan parted from its lips and the arms shambled into a stir. It called the name, "Lilicuta" again. I threw the candle at it and fled in sheer terror. My heart palpitated against my chest, my feet trampled upon the steps going up, and I fell. As I fell, I caught myself by placing my hands in front of me. Pain slithered to my hands and I gazed at them. They trembled as blood trickled down my knuckles from the impact of the fall. I groaned but bolted. I raced back into the reading room, slammed the door, and locked it. As I did so, a rush of wind swept in from the window. The wind howled and fluttered all the pages of the books and loose-leaf papers. Everything scattered everywhere inside the room. The room was dark and there was no light. Flashes of the ghostly creature consumed my mind. In a panic, I ran to the stoned fireplace, adjusted the flue, and started making a fire. The small illumination from the moon crept into the room as my eyes caught glimpses of my hands dabbed in blood. The light from the moon made my blood gleam in its light. In a few moments, a fire grew inside, and light radiated inside the room. I frolicked my hands and waved them as I searched the room to find something to wrap my fingers with. I rummaged through but found nothing. I used the bottom part of my shirt and wiped all the blood from my fingers against the inside. After my hands were somewhat cleaned, I found my diary upon the floor. It wasn't damaged thank goodness, but the front and back covers stood it up. While I picked up my diary and wiped it clean, my eyes caught words on a loose-leaf of paper. It was an article entitled "The Daguerrotype." It was published by Edgar Allan Poe with the paper dated January 1840. I sat upon the cold cobblestoned floor and read it by the fire:

" This word is properly spelt Daguerreotype, and pronounced as if written Daguerréotype. The inventor's name is Daguerre, but the French usage requires an accent on the second e, in the formation of the compound term. The instrument itself must undoubtedly be regarded as the most important, and perhaps the most extraordinary triumph of modern science. We have not now space to touch upon the history of the invention, the earliest idea of which is derived from the camera obscura, and even the minute details of the process of photogeny (from Greek words signifying sun-painting) are too long for our present purpose. We may say in brief, however, that a plate of silver upon copper is prepared, presenting a surface for the action of the light, of the most delicate texture conceivable. A high polish being given this plate by means of steatitic calcareous stone (called Daguerreolite) and containing equal parts of steatite and carbonate of lime, the fine surface is then iodized by being place over a vessel containing iodine, util the whole assumes a tint of pale yellow. The plate is then deposited in a camera obscura, and the lens of this instrument directed to the object which required to paint. The action of the light does the rest. The length of time requisite for the operation varies according to the hour of the day, and the state of the weather – the general period being from ten to thirty minutes – experience alone suggesting the proper moment of removal. When taken out, the plate does not at first appear to have received a definite impression – some short processes, however, develop it in the most miraculous beauty."

There is more to this document, but the way Poe describes this invention and its process strikes me. The recent discovery I found earlier from Bogan's book and the single phrase which deciphered earlier, "In the phenomenon of the spiritualist photography, the sensitive plate doesn't transcribe a real shape, but only an idea that is occurring in a medium's brain in that moment," came to mind. The type of photography Bogdan describes with "the sensitive plate," resembles the process of the daguerreotype. According to Poe's explanation of the scientific process behind it, such a development of the daguerreotype portrait requires a plate treated with silver, nitric acid, and iodine exposed to sunlight; the image is then developed with heated mercury. The books in this room are printed on acid-neutral paper that can last for generations. I wonder if this acid is the same kind used for daguerreotype. If it is, there must be a supply of it somewhere in the castle. Bogdan refers to spiritual photography... Does he mean "spiritual" photography like the daguerreotype? I feel I am on the verge of a major breakthrough! There must be more secrets in this tower!

Nicholas Ainsworth

Entry Sixty-Five

have not gained any sleep, but I don't care! My watch ticks and reads, "10:00." This gives me more time to conduct more research before the sun sets down. I believe whatever this shadow is or was, it wanted to show me something, but what? Shadow... Cor, I am sounding illogical, that thing must have been a manifestation in my brain. Perhaps it's a mirror image of my passion for knowledge and discovery. I am close. I found a scribble upon Poe's article. The handwriting in it is feverish but resembles the handwriting in Bogdan's book. I am certain that it is an annotation of his. I've transcribed and translated the language. It reads, "Daguerreotype photography captures spectral photographs of loved ones which augments my reflections toward intimacy and death. It is like a spiritualist manuscript of ectoplasmic photos and piques my curiosity. My dear angel...Admirable angel... Lilicuta." This chills me...

Nicholas Ainsworth

Entry Sixty-Six

The rumble of tanks echo and thunder across the far distance. The skies are bleak and grey. It's a constant reminder of the fear and terror which surround me. My mind tingles numb from the strain of my work, but I cannot stop... For a moment, earlier, I ambled the courtyard. I paced back and forth in an obsessive manner. My shoes scraped against the dirt paths. My eyes caught glimpses of the towers. This place is ominous and desolate. The silence is deafening like I'm the only thing here. I haven't seen Iulia since that brief moment in her library. Where does she go? What does she do? Where is her father in all of this? Loneliness is this man's main feature. His book expresses a tragic, crepuscular vision. I have been introduced into a philosophical system dominated by his logic where the echo of old beliefs in divinity can be felt. His intellectual rigour and straightforwardness exclude a hypothesis of a mystification. His facts are strange and require more research.

I reflected the knowledge I've learned in my head and something stuck me. There was the question about what role sleep plays for human beings. In this section, Bogdan approaches, first of all, the matter of religion regarded as an embrace of three dogmas: God, Immortality, and Confession. What confuses me is free of any particularity, religion includes theology, according to Bogdan, thus being a science without ceasing to be faith, meaning that it, "permits the cold and weighing cogitation, at the same time deeply moving the most sensitive chords of the heart." This is the explanation of the form in which Bogdan regards as spiritualism. He calls it, "faith-science." How can faith and science be intertwined in such a way puzzles me. He defines God as the infinite with no borders of which all beings were created, the one which, having no boundary, includes everything in itself. He talks about immortality as all the spiritualists, in a philosophical – theological and occidental way of preserving human individuality. What drew this man and scholar to spiritualism weighs upon my mind. His assertion about his inspiration drives from, "the highest stage of the spiritualist communication." Such a claim implies his work was created from a "friend from another world." I need to step away for a bit, and perhaps focus on my piano lessons for Iulia. Such an instrument is like staring into a pair of beautiful eyes, it pours out to the suffering in its despair.

Nicholas Ainsworth

331

18 October 1940
Entry Sixty-Seven

Learning the piano brings me comfort, but it also makes me think of Iulia. Last night as the sun bled behind the horizon, I dawdled upon the piano's keys. I started from middle C and executed the C major scale. It's the simplest scale as my fingers danced up and down the scale. Cloths are still wrapped around my fingers from my accident and there are some dried bloodstains. While practicing this scale, I thought about Sasha, our moment dancing to Claire de Lune, and our first kiss. As I thought about these memories, my eyes caught Iulia next to me. I jolted as I saw her; I didn't see her come into the room.

"How long have you been standing there?"

"Not long, but it seems you've mastered the scale. It's time to learn others."

She sat next to me and her pale hand hovered over the keys. Her hand trembled and withdrew quickly as my eyes wandered to her. Iulia turned her face away from my gaze, "What is it?" I asked.

"Your hand..."

"Yes, I..."

"Blood."

Iulia's voiced shuddered when she said 'blood. 'She squeezed her hand into a fist and her breath shallowed. Her mannerism and reaction reminded me of Sasha's fear of basements. I reached my hand out to hers in hopes that my touch would clam the trembling in her hand, but before my fingertips touched her, she cloaked her hand with part of her dress.

"No, don't."

I remained silent until I blatantly asked, "Where is your father? I haven't met him."

Iulia stared at me, but her gaze was empty and hollow, "My father... He's quite the writer and philologist. He has a keen interest in science and is appointed as head of the State Archives in Bucharest. He regularly informs me about his academic work. He's doing all his best to finish as much as he can. His work keeps his mind busy day and night and thus he does not have time to think about...” As Iulia was saying this to me, her fingers tapped against the keys in playing a scale. Her hand is graceful and eloquent as the motion hypnotised me. I didn’t hear the rest of her words. The notes faded from my ears as her voice serenaded me.

“That was the A major scale... Understand?”

Her eyes hone onto me. They were a deep, darken brown with hints of violet crimson shrouding the outer layer of her eyes. My vision blurred as I nodded. My head ached in a frenzy, my breathing slowed, and the touch of Iulia’s breath numbed and gave vigorous sensations throughout my body. All my fingers tingled and the sensations around my neck chilled me. My heart pounded hard and rapid against my chest. Its sound consumed my ears as memories flashed simultaneously. Flashes of a letter which read these words:

“In Paris you’d have already heard the old saying: ‘noblesse oblige. ’I’m not talking about the nobility of blood, which is a very unimportant matter, but nature endowed you with the superior nobility of intelligence, nobility that obliges you to increase, every day, the reputation you had so rapidly made since you were in the cradle.”

As these words presented themselves to me, a voice said them and rang inside my head, but the voice was of a man. The same voice which I heard from the shadowy figure from my study tower wept and called out Lilicuta. Another memory appeared and showed me a hooded figure. It walked toward me with its hands clasped. At that moment my body felt ill, weak, and vulnerable. As if I was sick and dying. My eyes caught a glimpse of red stains against the pillow. A cough croaked as if it came from me. Whatever was coughed out smelled metallic and tasted coppery. Its redness was tinged pink, slick, and foamy. The hooded figure spoke, "Death comes as the sky turns red. Its attraction ensnares a world from beyond, where the defunct spirit, in the immense suffering of the survivor, continues to manifest itself materially through existence, occurrences and teachings of the spirits." Pain festered throughout every fibre of my being as a young woman's scream lamented inside my skull. The flashbacks ended and my surroundings wavered into focus. I'm lying on my side. I shifted my body and saw nobody sitting on the piano bench where I was before. I rose to my feet. The room is dark, but candles illuminated the entire room. There was a mirror mounted upon the wall. I scuttled to it and observed my reflection. The candlelight around me dimmed my appearance but there were no wounds of any kind on me except for a bump on my head. My fingertips graced the bump as I spaced out to think that I must have slammed my head pretty hard against the hardwood floors. After this thought, a face stared at me from behind and I felt its arms wrapping around me. I jolted from its appearance, its frigid touch, and turned my head around. Nobody was there. I thought of the face as I realised it was Iulia's.

"Iulia?" I called loudly.

My voice echoed inside the desolate and lonely castle walls. When I called for her, a pain strained sharply against the left side of my head. I squeezed my eyes shut, gritted my teeth together, and pressed my palm against my forehead. Hooves trotted and reverberated inside my head against cobblestone as I heard rotating wheels squeal. A dark, gloaming image of horses and a carriage flashed. The carriage stopped. I see a little girl jumping out of the carriage into the arms of her mother, a handsome lad walking out of a pub, a blossoming woman in her thirties yawning in a window; I saw blood. Pictures sequenced as flashes inside my brain: torn, nails driven into flesh, blood splashing on the ceiling, a tinted and shadowed face buried into the oozing, squishy depths smelling like a slaughterhouse... These thoughts invaded my head, but they aren't my own. They are so intense that they made me flee in terror.

As I fled, I thought about my dream when I was desperately fleeing from a black object within the abbey. I stormed out of the castle and ran through the courtyard. I had no conception of where I was running. I just needed to get out of the castle.

"Lilicuta" groaned a voice. I halted from hearing the name called. I froze and stood before one of the towers in which Iulia said was off limits. I reached out to the knob upon the weathered, wooden door. The voice which called the name came from behind this door. Before my hand touched it, a rush of wind swept me, and a loud crash disturbed me. The sound came from the other end of the courtyard. The wind died down, but it slightly howled and rattled my ears. Another slam wailed and creaked, but not as rough as before. I followed the sound and crept to its source.

It's the other tower that was off-limits. Its door was ajar... My feet shuffled against the dirt, I raised my hand, and the door fell into my palm. I gripped the door and peered inside. Sconces were lit and revealed the tower's steps. Each candle in the scones hissed and flickered flames. The stairs were long, narrow, thin, and looked unsafe. Cobwebs and debris covered the stairs as I glanced left and right. I didn't know whether to climb the tower or descend. Terror gripped my heart, it raced as I decided to descend the stairs. My footsteps reverberated as I ambled into darkness with the sconces as my only means to guide my way. As I reached the bottom there was another door. Two single candles were lit opposite from each other from where the door was. I squeezed the iron, rusted ring to open the door. As I pushed the door, the iron ring broke apart in my hand. I threw the iron ring onto the floor as it clanked. I thrashed my body onto the door. It budged but only little until I slammed into it with all my strength. The door whipped wide open as I tumbled inside. Dirt and dust covered my hands and knees and I pushed myself up to observe this chamber. A flamed chandelier dangled from the ceiling over the centre of the chamber. Various giant candelabras were tucked away throughout the corners of this chamber. Further inside, there was a daguerreotype kit including a tripod, a box for treatment with mercury vapour, boxes for fuming with iodine and bromine, a soft buckskin pad for buffing the plates and a box of unexposed silvered copper plates ready for use. Much of these materials and equipment were stored in tintypes with flaking emulsions. These tintypes were in good condition, stored in sturdy four-flap enclosures, cased, and wrapped in acid-free tissue while inside folding boxes to prevent breakage and abrasion.

A desk with a lantern upon it was on the right side. As I treaded toward the desk, my shoes cracked glass and shards. I glanced up to the lantern and noticed it was shattered. A flashback of Dr Gilders' lantern shattering in the Transylvanian Alps consumed my mind. There was another book on the desk with a piece of paper tucked and sticking out of the book. I slipped the paper out and read its context:

"*[Unknown date,] 1893*

Bogdan,

I am grieved for you and your wife. I've enjoyed our days spent this past summer in Câmpina. My house is and will always be open to you, my friend. I know how you admire the large park in the vicinity of my property, and I pray your purchase of it brings you great comfort and joy. It will be a grand estate dedicated to dear

Lilicuta. I hope these supplies for the daguerreotype kit will serve you well.

Yours Faithfully,
Dr Constantin Istrati"

The book felt delicate, feeble, and rotted. I opened its dark, brown coloured pages. The writing is faded and not in English... The spine is loose as I shut the book to preserve all the papers inside it. I know it must contain the secrets I desire and the knowledge of this uncanny place. There must be reasons why Iulia forbade me from this tower, and I must unravel answers such as the date addressed to Bogdan. I searched the drawers and my mouth dropped as I picked up a photo. The photo itself was not a daguerreotype, but a more modern picture of this century. The picture depicted the two men which Iulia spoke of whom took their photo with Jesus. This was the photo the men took! One of them, had placed a peaked cap on the hand of the statue, and acid burns singed the photo. Specifically, the man who stood nearby the cap, I could not see his face because of the acid burns... Something is not adding up... I shall now study this book while here in my study.

- Nicholas Ainsworth

341

342

23 October 1940

Sixty-Eight

It's been quite a few days... I've been dividing my time between my research and practicing the piano. First, I must jot down what I've discovered in the book from the tower. It's a recorded account of "sessions." Uncanny, vile sessions which a proclaimed man of science performs... I still don't quite understand why such a brilliant mind as Bogdan Hasdeu would perform these experiments, he calls psychic photography. With these experiments he conducted seances. This would explain his interest in Spiritualism according to his book, *This is How I Think*. There is a brief news parchment I discovered in his recordings in an article from the Two Worlds on July of 1891. It states that he had written to the Revue Spirite to introduce a young

Romanian medical student, "mechanical writing medium," and a member of the Spiritual Society of Bucharest. Bogdan Hasdeu was presumably also a member and arrived sometime in Paris. As I've studied before, Bogdan determined to put his investigations on a scientific basis and explored the possibilities of photography as a means of objectively recording psychic phenomena. He was holding seances twice weekly, the sitters were all professionals, and allegedly even the mediums had university degrees! This is absolute madness! Whatever the truth of the latter claim, Bogdan's social standing had certainly attracted a circle of intellectuals. The reports written refer to photographic experiments in similar terms, that in light concluding:

"Some spirit heads, more or less visible, have been obtained by photography in the most complete darkness, the photographic apparatus being hermetically closed and sealed. Hasdeu expects, in a new work which he is preparing, and which will be a sequel to his 'Sic Cogito, ' to include all the spirit photographs which he has obtained, and to give, at the same time, all the details of these curious and interesting experiments."

This recorded account is not in Bogdan's handwriting and it's not Dr Istrati's either. This writing about Bogdan is dated 1907 by The Annals of Psychical Science. Bogdan Hasdeu and Dr Istrati documented an experiment they did. Bogdan termed what is called "psychicone" and described as showing "the possibility of the creative spirit acting on a plate without the help of the hand." A patch in a photograph was said to represent Hasdeu's brother "Nicolae," who like Lilicuta had died at age eighteen, his image having been "modulated" in Bogdan's mind and then projected... This makes sense now from what Bogdan wrote when he said, "In the phenomenon of the spiritualist photography, the sensitive plate does not transcribe a real shape, but only an idea that is occurring in a medium's brain at that moment." The name I heard nights ago in the temple wasn't mine, but it was Bogdan's brother's. Bogdan provides a detailed account of his experiment with Dr Istrati. Dr Istrati was, according to Bogdan, about to travel to Câmpina, the location of both the doctor's home and the future location of Castle Hasdeu, and he agreed to try to project himself onto Hasdeu's plates at Bucharest. When Dr Istrati went to bed on the night of the 4th of August 1893, Bogdan placed a camera at Dr Istrati's head and another at his feet. This is what Bogdan writes:

"As Istrati fell asleep, he exerted his will to appear on my plates. When he awoke, he felt he had succeeded, as he dreamt, he had appeared to me. Upon the plaque, there were three attempts of which one was extremely successful. The doctor was seen looking attentively into the apparatus, the bronze extremity of which is illuminated by the light peculiar to his spirit. On my friend's return to Bucharest, Istrati was astonished at the resemblance to himself of the fluidic image." (Hasdeu).

Castle Hasdeu was intended both as a tribute to Lilicuta and as a way to maintain contact. The castle's elaborate structure, full of esoteric symbolism was built between 1894 and 1896 to Bogdan's own design in mediumistic consultation with Lilicuta, and seances were held there. Such sessions or seances were held for Bogdan to communicate with his father, grandfather, brother and wife whom Iulia told me she was named after. Now, the castle has fallen into neglect... Iulia must be the last surviving heir. This castle, and all the secrets it holds. She may still be able to tell me distant recollections of her ancestral home... A rumble of thunder or tanks? I cannot tell anymore... As I glare out the window of my study, the clouds are a dark grey. Rain is tapping against the glass on my window. I am afraid.

I don't know what Iulia's intentions are of me and why I'm seeing things. Memories or dreams? I don't know.... Ghostly apparitions are not real! I know I haven't been sleeping well and I've been slaving myself over my research. I must keep the light which breathes life, burning strong, even in darkness.

Nicholas Ainsworth

The Antiquarian

349

28 October 1940
Entry Sixty-Nine

I've been stalling… It's been on the tip of my tongue to ask Iulia about the history of this castle considering what I know. Though I haven't said anything because I am afraid, she will figure out that I've broken many rules while staying here. First, snatching her father's book from her room, entering one of the forbidden towers, and acquiring knowledge which its secrets are not mine to know. I can't help it… I must know! Ever since the strange formalities or events that have happened a year ago within the Transylvanian Alps, and the strangeness in this place, it must all be connected somehow. The deviant remains of the skeleton discovered in the alps must be associated with the mystery behind Castle Hasdeu. Michael the Brave's seal and the Hasdeu coat of arms are too similar. I know Iulia has denied any relation with Michael the Brave, but there must be something more. What is Iulia not telling me? She must know something and if I can coax it out of her in a manner that won't raise suspicion, I'll be in the clear. For the past few days, I've been pondering on what to do while practicing the piano. Iulia says I am getting better at the piano and she thinks maybe if I keep at the good pace I am going, her and I could do an improv for fun. I think I know what I will do... I'll ask Iulia to dine with me and work those gentleman charms Uncle Henry has taught me. Instead of alluring to Iulia's charms, she'll be entranced with mine. Sounds rash, but I have learned one thing about Iulia. The moment I saw her image in the mirror and her arms wrapped behind me, I knew then she has an endearment for me. But what kind of endearment? This question terrifies me...

Nicholas Ainsworth

29 October 1940
Entry Seventy

Iulia agreed to dinner... We were sitting upon the piano bench as she demonstrated the aeolian mode. After my first attempt and a few more, I said to her, "Iulia, I wanted to apologise on what I said about your idol, Victor Hugo. I understand much time has passed, but I've been too prideful in my opinions and most of the time, I hurt people this way. To make it up to you, may we have dinner together? Out all of my time spent here, not once did we ever share a meal together." She gave me a blank stare. The silence was dreading. Finally, she raised her eyebrow at me.

"You apologise now, after all this time?"

I lowered my eyes but lifted them to her, "Iulia, this place has been a great comfort and place of reflection."

Iulia smirked, "That makes me content that you have learned to be enlightened by this place. Very well. Over dinner, you can tell me about your academic pursuits. I'm wondering if you've made any progress on Michael the Brave considering all the time you spend in solitude."

My lips sunk in my mouth as I remarked, "Sounds lovely. I would be happy to hear more about Victor Hugo and why as a person he influences you so much."

Iulia gave a dry chuckle, "Are you charming me, Nicholas?"

I held my breath. Iulia's words were honeyed in such a way that I didn't know whether she was onto me or not.

"I'm opening my mind beyond my views of Romantics."

She smirked again and rose from the bench, "Good, dinner on the 31st, then?"

Saliva slithered down my throat. Why of all days on the 31st of October? I nodded my head, Iulia walked away, and I croaked, "Wait, I don't have proper attire for the dinner." She turned, "Not to worry. You will have proper attire soon." Iulia continued onward out the room with her hands clasped. I followed her out of the room, but she was nowhere to be found. Her words frighten me. I must go through with this if I ever wish to see my home and Sasha.

David Edgar Grinnell

Nicholas Ainsworth

The Antiquarian

355

31 October 1940
Entry Seventy-One

This was more than I bargained for... When I awoke sometime during the day, there was a suit picked and laid out for me upon the chair where I study. The suit seemed fashioned from the previous century, slightly worn, but still in good condition. The frock coat was jet black with silver buttons which were a paisley pattern. The vest was also black with the same design of the silver buttons with black wool trousers. A black bow tie sat upon my desk and on top of my diary. I'm horrified... What if Iulia went through my diary? She was in here. What if she knows what I know now? She didn't leave a note or anything about the outfit. I will spend this time gathering my thoughts and when the sun sets, I shall don this attire laid out for me.

Nervously,

The Antiquarian

Nicholas Ainsworth

1 November 1940
Entry Seventy-Two

I cannot tell if what I experienced was a dream or reality. It feels all unreal but poignant. I wandered aimlessly around the castle until I discovered the dining room. A large, walnut table was centre, a giant, delicate chandelier dangled above. Upon the ceilings were odd symbols which represented the holy love between where souls intertwine. This made me reflect upon the information from Bogdan's book on the chapter about "Telepathy of Love." Iulia must have chosen the room for the specific reason of establishing an intimate connection with me, but to what means remains a mystery. The table was already set for two. The main dish was some kind of roasted pork and served with potato dumplings. A candelabra was lit upon the centre of the table. It was crafted in a bronze, gold design and stacked with layers of filigree. I thought about Sasha's heart locket because of how similar the designs were. I stood there waiting for Iulia to arrive. My attire was loose, but not too loose. I could still get away with wearing it, but the clothing still felt tight around me. I knew it must have been my nerves.

Footsteps echoed from the other side of the room. Iulia was coming, her heels clicked upon the hardwood floors. Her brown, wavy hair was swept up, she was seductively pale, and wore a dark, blue dress. The dress was definitely fashioned from the 19th century. It was buttoned up, concealed her figure, but there were ruffled patterns that ran vertical along her shoulders, past her breasts, and all the way down to her waist. The same pattern of the ruffles cuffed around at the end of her sleeves.

"You look dashing, Nicholas."

Iulia curtsied and her eyes gleamed brown with a hint of violet crimson. A sharp pain festered quickly inside my head as the image of the pinkish, foamy liquid upon the pillow flashed. The hooded figure appeared in a memory. I smiled at Iulia to rid of the sharp pain and memory. I bowed to her, walked to her chair, and pulled it out. Iulia creased a smile, padded to the chair, and sat in it. She gestured her sallow hand to the chair across from her. I inhaled and exhaled a shallow breath. On my side of the table, there was a bottle of wine which read, "Recoltare de Sânge."

"Blood Harvest?"

Iulia chuckled as she heard me mumble the words under my breath.

"A creative name for a wine, don't you think?" I grabbed the corkscrew next to the bottle and dug it inside the cork. As I twisted the corkscrew further, I observed the two wine glasses nearby. The stems and bases were wrapped and layered with filigree silver. The bowls were of crimson, red, and crystal as the rims were a darker shade of red. The levers on the corkscrew lifted as I twisted and spoke, "Why specifically this wine?"

"Festive reasons. Around this time of year, legend has it that the veil between the earthly plane and the spiritual world is thin, meaning the two realms collide, and it is easier for spirits to cross over and walk among the living, and vice versa. This ethereal curtain is believed to thin just as the days begin to get shorter and the nights stretch longer, perfectly timed with the season."

The cork popped as the aroma of the wine engulfed my senses.

Iulia studied the look upon my face, "Smells wonderful doesn't it? A cabernet sauvignon that savours enticing aromas of blackberry, ripe plum and mocha that leads into flavours of rich, black currant, and ripe black cherry. The wine finishes with hints of cocoa and oak spice."

I smiled as I poured the wine into the glasses.

"Your dress looks lovely by the way. It's a fashion I've never seen before."

Iulia placed her hand upon her lap, "I'm glad you like it. Usually, I wear this dress with my hat which has a black ribbon and bow to the side."

I minced over to her with a glass and handed it to her.

"You can place it here, please."

Her eyes gravitated at the table. My lips sunk as I smudged them together. Why doesn't she take the glass from my hand? I set the wine glass where her eyes wandered and scuttled back to my seat. The chair squealed as I sat and took the other wine glass.

"The food looks delicious!" I squawked with a smirk.

"Ah, ciolan de porc la cuptor or, roasted pork knuckles. It's a traditional Romanian dish especially popular in Transylvania. The pork is infused with garlic and cumin. It's cooked within a slow fire in the oven until crisp. It's quite miraculous." I breathlessly laughed; the dying sun behind Iulia made her glow like a spectre's aura. The nightmare of the pale figure, fluttering in a white dressing gown flashed inside my brain. My neck tingled numb as if this spirit loomed its icy breath upon me. The figure was white, faceless every time I closed my eyes. I re-opened them as I saw Iulia's pale face glisten behind the blood, red and orange light.

"Do you like the outfit I picked out for you?" Iulia reached for her wine glass and held it by caressing the bowl and lodging the stem between two of her fingers.

I cleared my throat, adjusted my bow tie, and flashed a smile, "Yes, it suits me." Iulia swirled the red wine in her glass, "Good, it was my father's when he was in his youth." She whiffed the wine as she said this to me, and more images ravaged inside my skull. The shadowy figure which lamented the name "Lilicuta," the family portrait in the Darkroom, and the shape of the figure's beard crept into my mind. Iulia's words disturbed my thoughts, "A toast Nicholas! As my father would write, 'Have fun, my dearest, amuse yourself and laugh as much as you wish because only the stupid natures are dull and mean.'" I raised my glass along with hers as I thought about the words she spoke. Such words I didn't believe because of what I've studied about Iulia's father. I smacked my lips, tasting the wine. The fumes tranced me with its toxication.

"You say your father writes to you; don't you ever see him in person?"

Iulia wiped her lips from the wine, "Father, I would imagine, considered letters as a way of surviving after mother's temporary separation from him, going to Brasov, then to Paris, together with me." Iulia sipped from the glass.

"Separation?" I set my glass upon the table.

"Yes, mother wrote to him very rarely, still affected by an anonymous letter that she had received, informing her about father's infidelity..." Iulia froze, she bit her lip, and asked, "Nicholas, carve the meat, please, before it gets cold..." I bolted from my chair, ambled over, and grabbed both the giant knife and fork. "I still don't understand why your father would write something as what you toasted to. It doesn't sound like him as an academic..." I bit my lip after saying this, "Oh, and how are you familiar with my father as an academic, Nicholas?"

Wildly, I stabbed the pork and carved, I said too much I thought. As the meat fell upon the serving plate, I croaked out, "Ah, books... Lots of books... From the library I've been studying and spending time in."

Iulia placed her hand upon the table, drummed her fingers, and grabbed her plate.

"I see..." She said. Iulia lifted her plate nearby as I gave her a serving. "A few of his works are in the library such as the Great Etymological Dictionary."

"Yes..." I sliced more for my own serving.

"Thank you," Iulia said setting her plate in front of her. As I grabbed my own plate, Iulia continued to speak, "It's obvious that father's correspondence is different from what you know about him. The academic, severe spirit makes room for a human, common nature, in total agreement with himself and with the world around him. As I've said in my toast of father's words, such words are due to the fact that he wanted me to grow up in peace and harmony. Although his soul was devastated, he never let me feel his inner tensions. He did not want to upset the pure and noble soul of a child. He was always advising me to be optimistic in nature, to laugh and be happy with my life, mother, and the scenery in Paris."

With my plate, I grabbed a dumpling, and minced back to my chair. It squealed again." Your father must have wanted you to be proud." Iulia nodded her head, "Indeed, he wrote to me once, 'Show the French girls that a Romanian can be even better than them if she wants to.'"

The scent of the roasted pork delighted my senses as I grabbed my wine glass and sipped. "Enough, I've been dominating the conversation. Tell me, have you discovered anything on Michael the Brave?" As Iulia asked me this, my vision blurred. I didn't know if it was the wine, the lack of sleep, or the exhaustion. While in this state, I blurted out loud without thinking, "The remains, are they Lilicuta's?"

"What?"

Iulia's eyes glared, but I couldn't see her face. My vision wavered worse than before, my ears started ringing, and my entire body felt heavy. Before I lost consciousness, objects around the table and surrounding the area flew and scattered everywhere like a rapid hurricane. My vision faded into black and refocused where I briefly caught a glimpse of Iulia's figure in front of me. She was speaking, but I couldn't interpret her words and I collapsed onto the floor.

In the midst of my wretched condition, gentle arms carried me. My eyes caught glimpses of a young woman, I thought it was Sasha as I croaked, "Sash…" I uttered the word as if my entire essence poured upon it. My past memories with Sasha flashed as footsteps echoed throughout the castle's walls. There was a special sensitivity which flowed abundantly in them, these memories revived me of life, but the numbness of my body drained and reminded me of the darkness. My fragile body plodded upon the eloquent sofa in the study of Iulia's castle. A pale set of fingertips graced upon my forehead and hair, but I couldn't feel their touch because of my condition. I was in a stream of constant dreaming and waking. There was so much pain that I cannot describe it. I jolted from my slumber again as my eyes harrowed at the sudden sight of Iulia.

"Shh... It's quite alright." After Iulia's words, a brief vision flashed and seeped into my mind. It was once more a first-person view with me seeing the hooded figure and the pinkish, foamy liquid stained against a pillow. After the vision, Iulia grinned and smiled, "We aren't so different Nicholas."

"What's happening to me?" I chocked and mumbled.

"You simply fell and collapsed into a slumber..."

I shuddered, my mouth and eyes widened. My vision blurred once more as if in a drowsing trance. Iulia pressed her finger upon her lips, "Shh... There's no harm. In truth, your strength surprises me... Rest."

With all of my strength, I uttered, "Who's Lilicuta?"

At this point, I couldn't observe Iulia's reaction to my question. Her words echoed inside my head as she said, "Nicholas, some things are best left buried in the past. My inheritance is not without condition; however, should you wish to claim such knowledge, you must stay here in this castle, alone, where you shall remain locked inside from dusk until dawn. Only by facing your fears can you truly embrace that which dwells in darkness."

Iulia's words torment and haunt me. I am in my study tower now, more recovered than I was before. What knowledge is there about Lilicuta? I feel sick and weary, but I must stay here to find the answers. Lilicuta must be connected to the deviant burial and the mystery behind the seal of Michael the Brave. The way Iulia reacted as my vision faded at dinner and how she avoided answering who Lilicuta was, points in a possible direction. I cannot assume though as I must gather data. I don't understand why I keep having the same vision of the hooded figure and the liquid substance. What does it all mean? I shall conduct a close review of the data I have gathered.

Nicholas Ainsworth

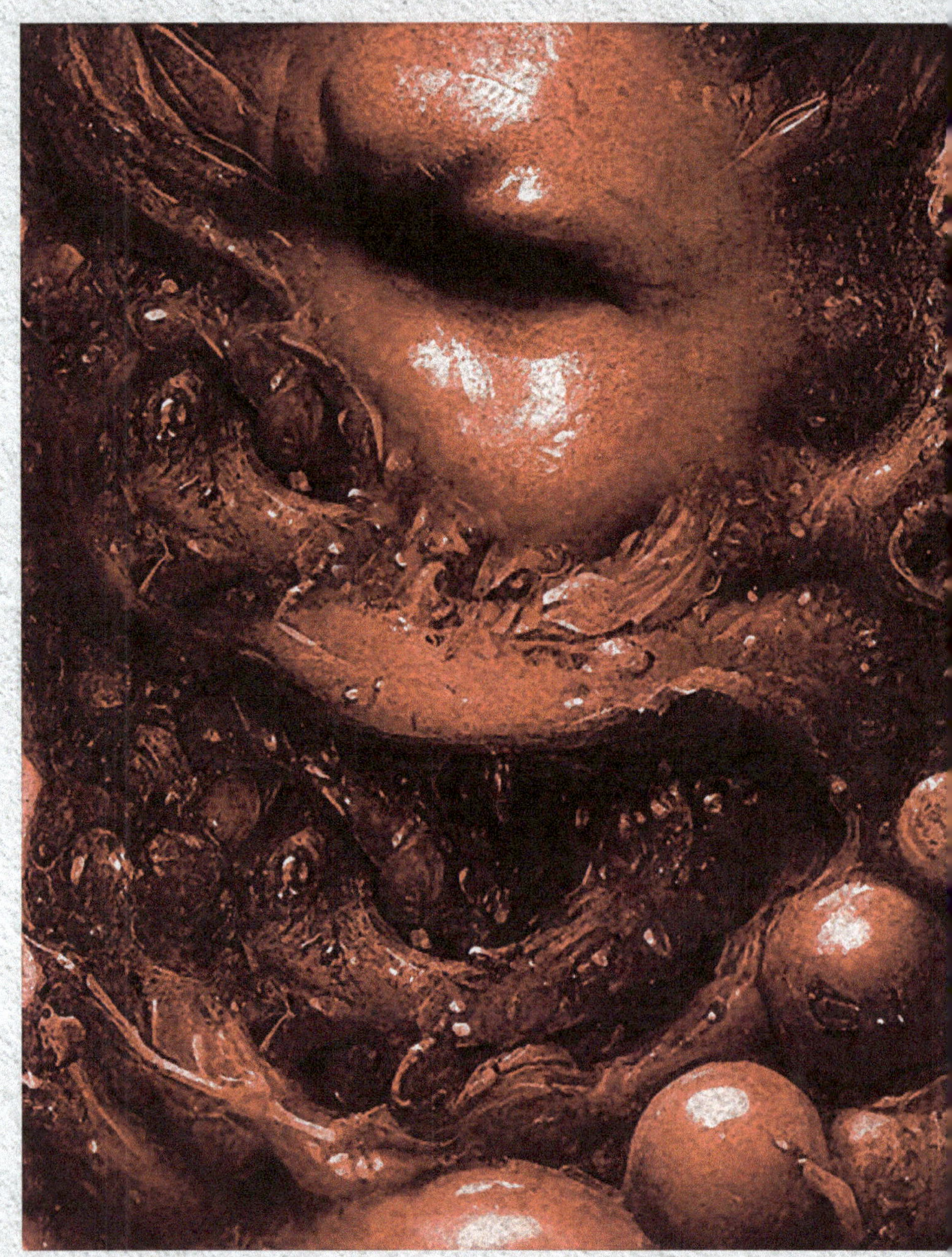

4 November 1940
Entry Seventy-Three

For the past few days, I've had no luck in reviewing the research I've obtained. It is obvious that Lilicuta was a daughter of Bogdan's just like Iulia. Though I imagine such a grief would turn Bogdan to other means to grieve the death of a young woman. Whatever spiritualism is, Bogdan focused all his energy and efforts into the practice to communicate with past relatives and even his Lilicuta. I don't think Bogdan discovered spiritualism on his own because he has references to a "spiritual friend." I still don't know who this friend is. If I can find out, I'm sure everything will be much clearer.

Iulia has been keeping a closer eye on me. She says that she is still worried about my condition and what happened during dinner. I feel she is always there next to me even when she's not in any of the rooms I wander aimlessly. I shiver constantly and paranoia creeps into my mind. A few times, she appears in mirrors next to me, but when I turn, she isn't there. Iulia's mezzo soprano voice croons and torments me. It disturbs me, but at the same time, it is a tender solace. The piano which only she specifically plays rings and echoes throughout the castle. Sometimes, I hear clapping after she plays, but when I arrive in the room where the piano is, no one is there. That's when I see Iulia next to me. Last night, that very same thing with Iulia playing and randomly appearing next to me happened. She asked me, "How are you feeling Nicholas?" I would lie of course, and respond, "I'm well... I was hoping to catch you playing the piano. Who was applauding your performance?"

The clouds parted through as the moonlight shone within the room through one of the windows. We were in the green floral room where various portraits of the Hasdeus were mounted upon the walls. Their ancestral clock which depicted the time 11:20 was still there as its face shined within the moonlight.

Iulia smiled, "It was father."

My eyes grew wide, "He's here?"

"He shows himself every now and then. Perhaps, you have seen him? He comes and goes at odd times because of his work."

"Odd... times?" As I muttered these words, I thought about the shadowy apparition which I've seen cry out Lilicuta and the figure's appearance with a long, busy beard. After this thought, Iulia spoke to me again, "As curious as it seems, father's work does not overwhelm him, as much as he works, because he feels alone and considers his studies a blessing on his soul. His work keeps his mind busy day and night. In fact, he reminds me of you, Nicholas." I grunted, closed my eyes and my head and neck wobbled. I gasped as the image of the hooded figure flashed before me. As I saw it, Iulia was already gone, and my nose bled slightly. My ears became plugged as I dabbed my finger against my nostril and saw red. A young woman's voice screamed and rang my ears. I pressed my palms against my ears to shut the noise. I shuffled my feet toward the other side where Bogdan's study was. As I made my way there, a voice inside my head said to me, "How could a child so divinely gifted not seek the problematic of existential, philosophical, theological and spiritual matters?"

I fell onto my knees, crouched, and gripped the sides of my head. I gripped my hair as I groaned hoping things would return to normal. A loud slam startled me as a rush of wind swept inside the room. I looked around as my mind subsided. I was in Bogdan's study as papers scattered everywhere from the wind. I bolted to the window and closed it. Bogdan's desk drawer was left open where I found the matches the first night I arrived here. I studied the floor as it was shrouded with random sheets of paper. I gathered them as one of them caught my attention.

"Spiritualism attracts me also, as it had attracted Sir Oliver Lodge, who had lost his son, Victor Hugo, whose daughter Léopoldine, had drowned in the Seine together with her fiancé, and others. From a sentimental point of view, it seems natural, the attraction of man towards a world from 'beyond, 'where the spirit, in the immense suffering, can manifest itself. A hooded man approached me. It was after my conference at the Romanian Academy. He gave me great comfort and I confessed to him information regarding the sacrifices that my wife made throughout our marriage, when she had to play various roles, such as those of nanny, teacher, study mate and, in the end, nurse, always awake, always admirable due to her energy and devotion. My wife's eyes were still looking for our daughter, she nobly carried the pain of Lilicuta's death. I told the stranger thus, 'When Lilicuta disappeared, and when we were left alone, without her, on earth, we only lived for each other and through one another, loved Lilicuta one in the other.' The stranger replied, 'I can ease thy pain. As a fellow Romanian, and seeker of knowledge, I hereby grant thee harmony and peace.' The hooded man flashed a weathered seal of Michael the Brave, 'My ancestors derive from the bloodline of Mihai Viteazul. The very same bloodline whose reign was marked as a symbol of Romanian unity. I will grant thee such unity of thy family. I am one of the collaborators of Allan Kardec. His books and the books of his collaborators such as I, entail subjects we magnetised, encircled in the process of vulgarising a movement initially started with the purpose to counterbalance the invasion of materialism. 'After these words, I was enthralled to gain such knowledge. Some of those who, as I, who had lost precious persons, accept the ideas of Kardec's works. I enjoy the satisfaction of the possible existence of the 'spirits 'and I am willing to experiment with this type of 'communication.'"

That is Bogdan's handwriting... The hooded figure I've seen... He must be the same one who enticed Bogdan with spiritualism. He is also descended from Michael the Brave and if those remains are his, then how is it possible he lived during Bogdan's time? It's impossible! For my research concludes that the seal is much older. The hooded man must have had the seal passed down to him and because of his beliefs with spiritualism, I'm sure the Transylvanian community condemned him to death because of his strange practices. It was Dr Gilders who said, "The fact the skeleton is buried face down in the grave is consistent with somebody whose behaviour marked them out as odd or threatening within this community!" Did Dr Gilders see the hooded man while we excavated the Transylvanian Alps? Is this why he went mad as I am now, seeing this figure? I need to escape this folly place, but I have nowhere else to go. The evil of the war and the Germans are outside these walls. There were seances held in this very castle... It speaks for the strange and abnormal occurrences that have happened to me during my stay, but this can't be real. This castle is alive and renders my mind slowly into madness. I am strong! Even Iulia said my strength surprises her. She knows more than what she lets on...

What kind of "communication," is she attempting with me? What is she? I cannot trust her, but at the same time, my heart allures to her grace and beauty. She has been a great comfort to me in my loneliness and despair.

Nicholas Ainsworth

14 November, 1940
Entry Seventy-Four

There's a difficult choice to be made... Earlier today for Iulia's birthday, we sat together on the piano bench. We played random notes together that turned into an improv song. After the song ended, I asked, "Would you ever teach other people music?" She just smiled and said, "Well, the closest thing to being a teacher was when I gave two lectures at Schools of Higher Studies in Paris."

"What did you lecture?" I asked.

"I lectured about the logic of hypothesis and the second book of Herodotus."

I gave her encouragement, "You should really consider undertaking teaching and education. You'd be really great at it!"

Iulia looked over at me as her lips sunk into her mouth, "I might consider it, but I can't really continue my education..."

"Why not?" I replied.

Iulia didn't know what to say to me and she looked rather sad and stared at the piano's ivory keys. Suddenly, it clicked within my mind.

"Oh, I'm sorry... I forgot about the war and the Nazis taking over Romania so how could you continue your education with the war going on?"

Iulia didn't say anything to me. She balled her hand into a fist, she still didn't look at me, and the room was filled with a dreadful silence. I tried to cheer her up, "Don't worry... It's going to be alright. Once the war is over, you can go back to school and get a doctorate or something!" Iulia grunted, her lips pressed tightly together, and she mumbled, "I was to prepare my doctoral thesis on "The Romanian Folk Philosophy: The Logic, the Psychology, the Metaphysics, the Ethics and the Theodicy..." As she had mumbled this, her words faded and fell silent. In moments, she started to cry. Tears streamed from her eyes and stained against the white keys.

"Iulia..." I answered. She turned her head, looked back, and up at me. I felt bad... All I wanted to do was to cheer her up and give her something to look forward to. I raised my hand to wipe the tears from her eyes. We stared into each other's eyes. It was like she could see through my soul and see the kind of person I was. My heart trembled and I just kissed her. I didn't know what came over me when her lips were against mine. I became frightened. Her lips were cold as ice. It was as if death had lips and infested my very soul.

"You're as cold as the snow..." I swallowed in fear.

"Nicholas..." she answered, "You need to go..."

At this moment, I was at a loss for words. I parted my lips, unable to speak. Finally, I croaked, "I didn't mean to offend you... Please, let me stay. I have nowhere else to go..."

Iulia screamed at me and it gave me chills down my spine.

"Leave!" She cried.

I bolted up from the bench and tripped over my feet. I staggered, wobbled, but caught my balance. I walked backwards and saw her bitter stare. Her eyes were crimson blended with tints of violet. I didn't quite understand what had just happened. I turned around and ran out of the castle. In the courtyard and gardens, I stopped. The hooded man's words rang in my skull, "How could a child so divinely gifted not seek the problematic of existential, philosophical, theological and spiritual matters?" I scuttled to one of the ruined towers that Iulia said was off limits. My hand reached for the wooden door before me, it's the same tower where I heard name "Lilicuta." I barged the door wide-open. Cool dry air swept against me as the door violently trashed. My eyes stared into absolute darkness. The light from the sky shone and revealed a narrow stairway. The stony stairs twirled downward into what looked like a bottomless pit. My feet scraped against the indolent and weathered stairs. My shoes reverberated upon each step. The farther I went; dread consumed every inch of my body. There was no light as my hands graced the stone walls. When I reached the end of the stairway, there was a glimmer of light in the far distance. I rushed towards the light; my feet pounded against the cobblestone within the darkness. The tunnel felt like it was eternal and gradually I slowed down. Eventually, I stopped. The light was still there, but it still seemed so far away. I lurched towards the light. With every step, memories flooded into my brain. Everyone I ever loved and cared for, but most of all Sasha. To me that light at the end of the tunnel was her, it was Sasha, my defender living in the light. When I reached the end of the tunnel, a set of stairs followed up. I plodded upon them and realised my surroundings. It was the Bellu Bucharest Cemetery. The afternoon light blinded me, and a layer of fog and mist covered the hallowed grounds of the cemetery. The light stung my eyes from the darkness...

Suddenly, someone grabbed my shoulder and I almost screamed, but the person quickly shrouded my mouth. It was an older lady, dressed in raggedy clothes, and she had an unusual stench about her. Her fingernails were black and dirty like they hadn't been cleaned in quite some time. With her other hand, she placed her index finger against her lips shushing me.

"Come with me. You don't want to end up like them, do you?" she said in a raspy voice. I trembled from her words and wondered what she meant by "them." She removed her hand from my mouth and signalled me to follow her. I followed her farther into the graveyard, "This way young man..." she said. We approached an isolated grave which I immediately remembered once I saw the grave. It was the grave I saw a year ago... It was the young girl, Florina Dumitru's grave. The old lady gave me a frown after I noticed the grave. She glared at me as if she saw something growing upon my face. Strangely enough she sniffed me. I leaned my body away from her, weirded out by her strange behaviour.

"Excuse me?" I squawked.

"You've been to Castle Hasdeu haven't you?"

"Eh, why yes I have... How did you know?"

The old woman gritted her teeth and flashed them. They were rotted, decayed, and black.

"I can smell it on you... I can smell her scent and sense the spiritual connection between you and Iulia. I haven't smelled that scent in quite some time."

I froze, not knowing what to say as the woman's breath wheezed upon my face. My stomach churned sour.

"I must warn you..." Her raspy voice shuddered my spine as she pointed her crooked finger at me.

"Warn me... Warn me from what?"

"The living and the dead aren't meant to mingle with each other and now Iulia has latched herself onto you."

Terror gripped my heart; every fibre of me trembled. My breaths shallowed, "What do you mean the dead? There's no such thing as the supernatural, ghosts, and the undead. Iulia is a live person just like me and you're a crazy old hag!"

"Silence!" she yowled at me.

Her darken eyes scowled at me, "You do not understand and so I shall show you."

We departed from Florina Dumitru's grave. Our feet crunched against the bright green grass and dead autumn leaves. "Why did you take me to Florina Dumitru's grave first?"

"In time young man... This way."

We floundered into a section of the cemetery I have not seen. The old hag stopped, and I discovered the most baffling, and shocking discovery of my entire life. There was a blue sign and it read:

Iulia Hasdeu
1869-1888

I froze in fear... Next to the sign were iron gates that surrounded a stone monument, and before the monument laid heavy iron doors to a tomb. As I observed the gravesite, the old hag spoke to me, "As you can see the tomb of Iulia Hasdeu; however, the grave is now closed. It seems to be abandoned, but it is a beautiful funeral monument to the young lady." My voice began to quiver as I replied, "What happened? Why is the grave closed?"

"Past those heavy iron doors are a few steps that lead down into the tomb. On the walls there are text written by Iulia from her childhood. They are mostly poems written in French, and into the chamber that is her tomb, there are placed pieces; remembrances of Iulia's life. The coffin is behind a crystal wall and it is protected by it..."

Anger brewed and seethed within me. I interrupted the hag, "How do you know this?"

She turned her head slowly towards me. The way her neck jilted gave me the shivers inside my bones.

"Many people made trips to Bellu Cemetery for fun, especially to Iulia's tomb but also to others who are laid to rest here. It was 1925 when a girl went down to Iulia's tomb to write down a few of the poetess 'poems from the walls. For a joke, a few children closed the very strong iron doors of the tomb and locked her there, wanting to make her afraid. The girl screamed, she was very afraid, but when the children went to open the doors... It stayed locked. They called for help and when the administrators of the cemetery arrived, the door could not be opened by them either. At that moment, the girl shrieked at the top of her lungs saying that someone came to her from the darkness of the tomb. Then the screaming stopped, and the door was able to easily open. They found the girl dead, strangled by the neck near the entrance of the tomb. Crime investigators and police presumed that the girl killed herself because she was afraid of the dark. So, several measures were taken to protect the entrance of the tomb from any future visitors."

All was then quiet. The only things I could feel was the slight breeze brushing against me and the beatings of my heart. The old woman continued, "The story goes that girl died because she was punished by Iulia for being in that special place. The girl's death is from a different cause than the one law enforcement decided upon."

The hag's story fuelled my anger. I didn't believe her. That couldn't have been the Iulia that I knew. After all, she forgave me for trespassing into her home and gave me shelter. She and I bonded for quite some time. We shared intimate things about each other, she was melancholy, strange, but kind... She gave me lessons in piano. Such time spent mended me. Iulia had my heart and I refused to believe some old, decrypted hag!

My anger exploded, "You're a liar! How do you know the story you told me is true?" I cried.

She gave me a blank stare. The hag showed no emotion to my anger and fury. She spoke in her raspy voice, "The story is true because the girl who died in

Iulia's tomb was my only daughter Florina. The children locked her in there as a joke because she was a witch like me. I miss her and visit my daughter's grave every day. Gone are the days when we'd make the pilgrimage to the Witches 'Pond and visit the pond on sacred celebration days. Law enforcement told me that my daughter strangled herself because she was afraid of the dark, but I know her better. She was never afraid to face any darkness whether it was physical or internal. As a medium, I could sense the strangle marks upon my daughter's neck were not her own because of that scent! I smelled Iulia's spiritual scent on my daughter's neck. It is the same scent I smell on you... All over you... And I must warn you to stay away from that castle-folly place before it's too late!"

The old woman ambled away from me and toward the direction of her daughter's grave. When I gazed upon her, I was reminded about my experience at a pond nearby the cemetery. The warning I received when hearing a young woman's voice say I was not welcomed here. I wondered if the voice I heard was Florina's.

A new thought crept into my mind as I thought about Florina and her death. What the old woman said about her daughter not being afraid of the darkness. I walked toward Iulia's monument and gazed upon it. My hands gripped the iron gates. I thought about the darkness of those whom I loved and cared for had to face. My father's darkest hours in the trenches of the Great War, my mother's loneliness, and isolation. Dr Gilders' brother, and the struggle of his internal demons. Dr Gilders grieving his brother's death... Irene grieving her love for me... Sasha's past with the darkness and death she faced. In their darkness, when it was just them and their thoughts, they let their true selves shine because in their darkest times is where they found the greatest strength. If darkness is in my nature, finding my way through it is part of the journey to discovering a truth of who I am.

This brings me now to make a difficult choice. I am afraid time is not on my side... The sun is dying down. I've been spending most of the day writing this entry by Iulia's grave. The wind howls and it rattles against the iron gates. I imagine her tomb is burdened by symbolism, evoking all signs of her traces on earth, her life, and not her death. It reminds me of the various symbols and objects throughout the castle. One of them I'm thinking about at this moment is the clock I saw a month ago halted at the time at the time of her death. The time when her father did not manage to part ways with her, the moment when his arms would stretch out to reach her forever, trying to pull Iulia back into his abandoned and clasped life. I cannot imagine the pain of his grief. On Iulia's funerary monument I can read the instruction to "sit a little longer." What happens if I linger at a gravesite? Is there something stirring whilst I wait? What moves around for me when I take the time to sit down and observe? Let alone write! Am I on the brink to leave, maybe out of fear, out of disheartenment, or maybe out of scepticism? Will I, the patient onlooker, be drawn into a father's occultism, spiritualism, desire and fantasy or into a deceased daughter's incapability to escape the earthly shackles demanding her to remain close by?

At the bottom of the monument is an unlatched-mouthed skull. In stone, it casts a text and reads, "Let the swallow build its nest." I believe this to be a juxtaposition that as I stare into the blackness of the dead, death and life are intertwined. That is, love and the afterlife, father and daughter, rebirth and invisibility, loss and regeneration. I shall write again after I open the tomb.

Nicholas Ainsworth

Iulia Hasdeu
1869-1888

own, in the sepulchre, the humidity and perhaps human unworthiness have destroyed the pieces of the broken marble partially preserving an old inscription. It reads, "And nevertheless, here she is! Iulia Hasdeu is among us!" No wonder the tomb is closed down. I imagine the tomb was visited by thousands of people and over time, it fell into desolation little by little. Now, the sphinxes and the earth globe are still in their place, as well as a throne still endures where there is a desk by it. The books on the desk are moulded and rotted. Nothing can be read on them. The flowers are wilted, the butterflies, the angels, and the portraits are decayed. Only the stars remain intact.

The stained-glass window to see Iulia through is weathering, almost faded. I see the corpse through the crystal window of the sarcophagus, but the glass is cracking. The earth preserves her immaculate body, even after death. Warmth has not wilted the lily. Through the magic glass of the mausoleum's window, I can only imagine how her father used to look every day at his embalmed daughter, sitting there for hours on end at this desk, surrounded by her dearest relics and talking to her in a language understood only by himself where Iulia can be seen, even now. As beautiful as she had been fifty-two years ago, she lies there, in her white, parchment like coffin. I still see her serene face and brown wavy hair, it rests under her pious hand that had caressed it for the last time, her small straight nose, her mouth in a final smile, overwhelmed by death on her snow-white face. Near her coffin is a huge altar with her relics in a white bag on top of it. There are still visible words carved in the marble:

"By the will of God, this spiritualist temple was accomplished, after the precise and detailed plan given by Iulia Hasdeu, the executor B.P. Hasdeu, on his demand working: Sculpture I. Georgescu; Marble and mosaic: Axerio brothers; Iron: A.O. Czipser; Stained Glass: Ziegler and Schmidt; Bronze: Ph. Sschwickert MDCCCXC by the will of God."

I'm not sure of everything and I don't know what to do. My mind keeps telling me no, but my heart answers, and it tells me yes to being here. I will search the tomb for evidence and find answers.

These walls are hollow and torment me. I'm inside the castle where Bogdan's study is. From the tomb, I discovered a secret passageway that connects to the castle. A catacomb where I would imagine Bogdan would go back and forth to visit Iulia's corpse. When I exited the passage, there was a section within the castle that was uncanny... The section was collapsed, the weather corroded the stones, and there are red shredded curtains as they fluttered from the hallow whispers of the wind. The sky is dusk... It's like my dream of Sasha's ghost or the various dreams I've had in the ruined abbey. I... I must write what I discovered in haste for I don't know if Iulia is around. I cannot be seen! I rushed into her room. Exhibited in her room with calla lilies, near Iulia's doll is the red notebook. I snatched it! I have gone through its contents and everything is as I fear, but do not believe. No logical mind will understand the secrets and the tragedy behind these ruined walls.

The notebook I speak of is Iulia's diary. It comprises of around fifty pages, full of various notes dating from the period 1881-1882. In the diary there are: the school timetable, homework, personal thoughts, literary attempts, drawings and... dreams. Iulia dreamt of becoming a famous playwright whose theatre plays would be staged at the theatres from Paris (the French Comedy and Odeon,) and the performances to be a huge success. Inside I have found various loose papers that are letters. Some of them are letters from Bogdan corresponding with Iulia's mother, and others are from Iulia, the daughter. The dates vary and do not go with the dates in Iulia's diary entries... I shall document these letters accordingly in order:

[Letter from Bogan to his wife Mrs Hasdeu.]
Bucharest, 4 June 1885

Still, I don t wish that Lilicuta wakes up at three in the morning, to damage her eyes and health, which will be so useful to her in the future. The study abuse is as dangerous, even more dangerous, than any other abuse.

B.P.H.

[Letter from Iulia, the daughter, to her father Bogan.]

Paris, 17 November 1887

So, I m eighteen years old, and I swear! I regret. I don t regret my seventeen years, but my sixteen! Ah! I will never be sixteen again! And I was sixteen for so little, only for twelve months. I've just tasted this and they have already flown away, that's why I'm so confused – and I m very bored of being eighteen. In spite of your insistence, in spite the wise advices of Doctor Percheron, in spite of mother s cries, I go to sleep at midnight and wake up at six o clock in the morning.

[Iulia]

[Letter from Bogdan to his wife Mrs Hasdeu.]

Bucharest, 31 December 1887

If Lilicuta loves me at least a bit, if she cares about my peace, if—finally—she doesn t want to bring you both back to Bucharest immediately, she must wear her sweater and she mustn t exaggerate with her work and wake too early in the morning. The age of eighteen and Paris are the most dangerous things when someone doesn t beware. Sweater and warm shoes are what I ask the most. And then, why don t you ask about the doctor? I m so worried, so torn, then I only with those words above, bitter and blunt words could I begin my answer to a long, delicate, full of happenings, and spiritual letter, which I had received after such a long wait. My hand is trembling as I write, as a drunkard s, and I must rest for a bit.

B.P.H.

[Letter from Iulia, the daughter to her father.]

Paris, 23 January 1888

Even if I hadn t exams to pass, I wouldn t work less.

[Iulia]

[Letter from Bogdan to his wife Mrs Hasedu.]

Bucharest, [unknown date; 1888]

Lilicuta is erudite enough, even too much. The best thing would be for you to come back to Romania, where the country air somewhere in the country, with no work or worries, would help her. One diploma more or less doesn t mean anything. I have no diploma.

B.P.H.

[Letter from Iulia, the daughter to her father.]

Paris, 22 March 1888

About giving up my studies and coming back to the country before graduation, no way. I won t do it, even if I have to die, and no human power can force me. I haven t worked all my childhood and youth to stop right when I m close to the harbour. I don t want such a life; not because I care about the diplomas, I m not such a person and you know that. But once in the battle, I won t retreat in the middle of the fight; also, I like this kind of work and I will never give up, for anything in the world.

[Iulia]

[Letter from Iulia, the daughter to her father.]

Paris, April 1888

I m still alive and I will never give up this work, as long as blood is still flowing through my veins and life is still breathing in my chest.

[Iulia]

That is the end of the letters I have found. Iulia was dying and not even death would stop her from achieving her dream. Iulia was a genius, an enlightened spirit, but with a destiny prematurely broken. Among the writings, they are scattered through several pages which forms an unusual diary. Even on her deathbed Iulia continued to write. In her last note on September 1888, Iulia addressed to her mother and predicted her own death:

"Mother, I leave you forever. I will not see you again. I will acquire my existence under an unknown name. I'll rich without help from anyone, on my own, the glory which I dreamed."

There's a compulsion which tempers the need for caution; an insatiable craving which possesses me. What is real, deception, and illusion? Knowledge is power but be wise in how to utilise such knowledge. Such happier recollections before the war, this castle, and my selfish endeavours. These impulsive random scribbles scorch my skull, they are so intense, and they make me flee in terror.

~~Nicholas Ainsworth~~

I must have blacked out... My watch stopped ticking and I just noticed it cracked. My vision blurs in and out of focus even as I'm writing. There are these visions, dreams, or even memories. These sequences are scattered everywhere in my brain... I can't tell if they real visions or just random images that don't have any real meaning. Maybe it isn't a dream; it feels so surreal and vivid. I feel cold and drained, but in this vision, Iulia calls for me in a gentle whisper. Her beautiful face flashes as I hear her laughing. It renders me eerie and strange, but her laugh is soothing to hear. Her eyes stare at me through my soul. We dance in the room of her castle where under the tall dome of the central donjon, in the middle of the circular hall, there is a pillar of rose marble, upon which two iron staircases rest, as they climb towards the belt of the donjon. Above the pillar supports the staircases with the podium bearing the status of Jesus in its colourful wood craftsmanship. The dome lights shine through three doors with stained glass. At the base of the marble pillar, there is Iulia's daguerreotype portrait from her funeral day.

The moonlight shines within as we dance and twirl round, and round. My ears listen to a delicate, soft, and soothing piano melody. It's the piano Iulia says she exclusively plays. As we are dancing, I see quick flashes of the piano playing on its own. I'm in a trance... I've never been so in love with someone as I observe Iulia wearing her white dress with the gold designs. I feel her body against mine. I can love someone who is in despair without falling into their darkness. Such darkness is like a window to the unknown, or at least what is not known to me.

"Come back to me Nicholas..." Iulia whispers in my ear.

Her breath chills me, my heart trembles as we kiss and embrace. During our kiss everything begins to fade. My body shudders with her algid lips against mine. Finally, the last words I hear ring inside my head...

"I love you."

When this sequence ends, I bolt up from the marble stoned floor with more flashes and visions. I still feel cold, and sense Iulia glaring into my soul. Her image flashes inside my head. I'm losing my mind, and a feeling of love and desire brews within my heart. It's the best, most overwhelming feeling imaginable... The moonlight shines upon the floor where I lie. When I rise from the floor, pain festers, and my hair is soaked. I stare where my head had rested and see the marble is stained. My breaths are shallow as I think I see a human shadow appear. With the shadow in the distance, I slowly creep up, stand, and I bleed. Drops of blood drip and echo throughout the cathedral walls. My eyes catch glimpses of red soaking the ground. I stagger and trudge toward the shadow. I enter into the first hall, through the passage, and lined by parallel mirrors. I stop and can't move because I'm staring at a ghost. The ghost has holes in its throat, and it becomes clear that the ghost is actually me...

Farewell,
Nicholas Ainsworth

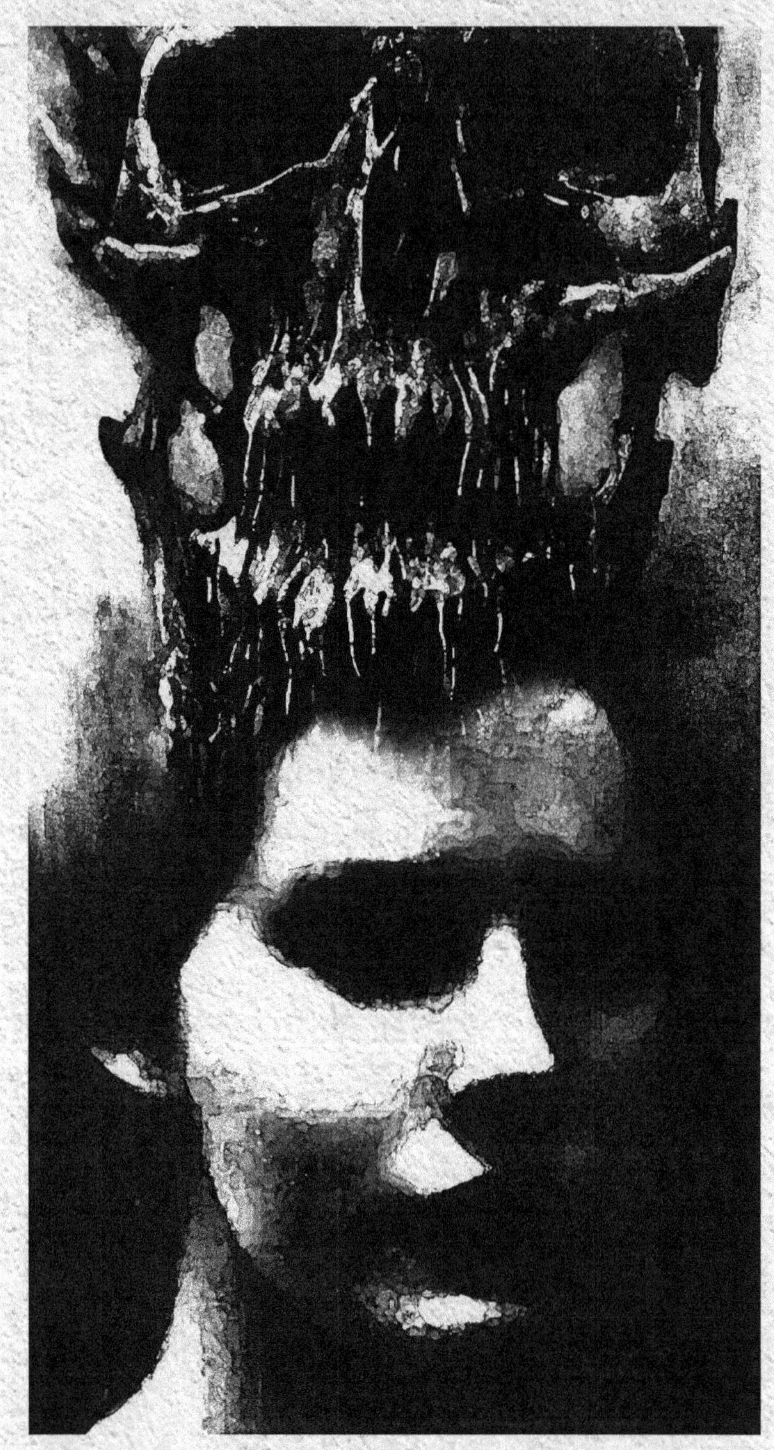

Works Cited

Beresford, Matthew. *From Demons to Dracula: The Creation of the Modern Vampire Myth*. London, GBR: Reaktion Books, 2008.

Beresford, Matthew. *The White Devil: The Werewolf in European Culture*. N.P: Reaktion Books, 2013.

Collins, Paul. "The Real Vampire Hunters." New Scientist (2011): Lexis Nexis Academic. Web. 23 Nov. 2015.

Hambly, Gavin R.G. "Elizabeth Bathory." Salem Press Biographical Encyclopedia (2015): Research Starters. Web. 23 Nov. 2015.

About the Author

David Grinnell who also goes by the pen name David Edgar Grinnell is a poet, author, and literary scholar from Cleveland, Ohio. He was born 1992 in Norfolk, Virginia, but grew up in the suburb of Bedford. In 2014 he attended Cleveland State University and graduated with his bachelors in English. Grinnell specializes in

Romanticism, the Gothic, and draws inspiration from vulnerability. He reflects and portrays love alongside hope, melancholy, and even occasional despair. Currently, he is a funeral director apprentice at St. John Funeral Home.

Other Titles by David Edgar Grinnell

Ashes - Alice Reaper departs from her hometown Boydton, Virginia after her father's tragic death. She begins anew in the small town of Bedford, Ohio as nightmares and the memories of the past haunt her. Longing for inner peace, she struggles against her own darkness, demons, and the ashes of a life she once lived.

Moonglade - Love, longing, heartache, and loneliness are illuminated in this heartfelt collection from David Edgar Grinnell.   Building on themes of budding relationships, misunderstood feelings, and innocent first loves, *Moonglade* creates a narrative that is relatable to everyone looking for love and companionship. Immerse yourself in a world of gothic romantic poetry that shines a soft light on finding and losing love in the twenty-first century.

Lightwaves - Charlie Parker Campel, is a man who fails at most things he attempts to do, and might have the worst luck on the entire planet. He believes he is like a scrawny, helpless squirrel searching for nuts in the frigid winter.   Losing his job at a history museum in

Washington, D.C. shortly after moving there from Kentucky, he must pull all the stops to find a new job. While on a job search, he randomly stumbles into the Holocaust Museum. During a self-guided tour, things get interesting when he finds a mysterious gold ring belonging to Michael Luke Adelman. He does all he can to find the owner during his visit to the museum, but to no avail. Deciding to keep the ring, he is determined to find the owner, but the question is... What is the story behind this mysterious ring, and who is Michael Adelman? Will Charlie find the owner, and what else or who else will he encounter on this journey? Does Campel finally catch a break, and will this mysterious ring send him on an adventure full of luck, introspective fortune, and love? Or will it send his entire life into a tailspin?

Acknowledgements

Thank you to all who have helped in the creation of this novel. This story has taken me seven years to write and a year to complete by the talents, dedication, and hard work from those involved in this book's production. A huge thank you to Ravven White for her empathy, determination, and support for taking on such a project. Thank you to other Curious Corvids such as Stephanie Kemler and Grace R. Reynolds for our deep intellectual conversations on gothic literature and to Gabriella who has invested her time in editing this work. I'm ever thankful to all of our corvids, the writing, and reading communities. Thank you, Star Sirius, for your persistence and patience in formatting this book. A special thanks to Mitch Green who labored and illustrated such beautiful illustrations for this work including the title page and the book cover.

Firstly, to my dear friend Tsezariy Patrick Iablonki where we spent countless hours together talking about our written works in progress. Our conversations and insights always inspire me, my friend. Thank you to my family of friends and those associated with BC's Bar. I love you all. An extended thank you to my biological family for their love and support. Thank you mom and dad; I hope you both are resting peacefully. To Amber Taliancich and her Fiction Workshop at Cleveland State University from the spring semester of 2019. All of you read the earlier draft of the novel when it was a short story and gave some key pieces of advice and encouragement. Keep inspiring creative writing students Amber! A thank you to all of the staff and professors at Cleveland State University who have supported me and pushed me to excel.

An everlasting thank you to anyone who has read, invested, and supported this story at any stage of its production.